DIMENSIONAL
OBSERVER

MICHAEL RETSINA

authorHOUSE®

AuthorHouse™ UK
1663 Liberty Drive
Bloomington, IN 47403 USA
www.authorhouse.co.uk
Phone: 0800.197.4150

Published by AuthorHouse 12/29/2018

ISBN: 978-1-7283-8217-3 (sc)
ISBN: 978-1-7283-8216-6 (e)

Contents

1

DISCOVERING THE
GAME FUNCTIONS

Michael Morrow logged onto his laptop at work to process the monthly salaries. He was thin, five foot seven, and almost thirty years old. He had dark-brown hair, and his eyes were hazel blue-green behind his glasses. He wore a plain, long-sleeved, blue shirt; maroon patterned tie; dark-grey trousers; and black shoes. After submitting the salaries to HM Revenue and Customs, he did some internet shopping to buy company office supplies. And whilst he was doing that, a pop-up suddenly appeared on his laptop screen, offering him a free download—software called Dimensional Observer. At first, he was naturally sceptical because of the many other pop-ups he encountered, such as sponsored ads and programs that redirected him to somewhere he didn't want to be when he was in the middle of doing something else. So he closed the tab, not really thinking too much about it. He just wanted to finish his shopping. After that, he switched off the broadband and logged off the internet to do more routine daily bookkeeping work.

Just then, he heard Melanie Ward ask Sarah Morrison a few questions in the room next door to his. She was having a problem with her computer, and Sarah, who was quite knowledgeable and had the deeper voice, helped her out. He knew them only by sight since they worked in different departments. Melanie, who was quite thin and about his height, had dark-brown hair, turquoise-hazel eyes, and wore a bit of make-up. She had only just started work yesterday. Sarah, who had been there only for a week, was about five foot five, thin, and quite busty, with ginger hair and brown eyes. For his taste, though, she wore too much dark-blue eyeshadow and red lipstick. When he saw them, they were both dressed in the standard women's work uniform: plain, long-sleeve white blouse with dark-blue trousers and black shoes.

Later that day, he thought back to that game pop-up, especially to the word *dimension* in its title. He'd thought a lot about the possibilities of alternative universes alongside our own, and that made him wonder what sort of game it might be. Would it be another virtual reality game based on the film *The Matrix* or something similar? He thought of other films he'd seen, such as *Journey to the Far Side of the Sun*. That one was about a laterally-inverted world or mirror-image version of our world. Then Michael remembered an episode of *Star Trek* in which time moved at a different rate. He thought that all these conditions were hypothetically possible in a different kind of universe.

That evening at his flat, he logged on to his laptop with the broadband turned off for security reasons. He saw the Dimensional Observer—DO—icon on his main screen, and he wondered how it had suddenly got there. It was delta shaped—a triangle. There was a white circle in the middle filled with the three primary colours—blue at the top, red on the bottom left, and green on the bottom right. The words, *Dimensional Observer* were written underneath the circle. This made him feel sceptical again. *Why is it there? Is it some sort of computer adware or spyware security threat?* He then decided, *Oh, it can't be. It's just a new game release. They're constantly offering new and up-and-coming computer games. I'm not online now, so I'll open it and see how good it looks.* When he did, all it said was, "This is a safe program available for download on your computer. Please at least try it out." Right out loud, he said, "Not on your nelly! What is this other than an unknown program? It could be a Trojan or something." So he closed the tab, put aside his computer, and did some reading.

After a while, though, he just couldn't stop thinking about this game. Michael decided to sleep on it at least.

The following evening, Michael logged on and downloaded the game from the internet, which took just over five minutes. He noticed a list of options but couldn't understand how they could relate to a game. They were: Random, Origin, Inverse, and Time Speed. He decided to select Random to see what sort of game it would be. After a couple of minutes of loading time, a picture of what appeared to be a scene in the middle of outer space came on the screen. A list of certain facts was on the left side of the picture, which stated that the direction he was looking in was 121 degrees, and the temperature was very cold at -271 degrees Celsius, just two degrees over absolute zero. He thought, *This is a very funny game. There are no directions on how to play it. What am I supposed to do next? What keys am I supposed to use, when a load of spaceships suddenly turn up that I have to destroy? How can I progress to the next level?*

He watched and waited for well over five minutes, wondering whether it was one of those games in which the start was purposely delayed so the player would be caught off guard and defeated. Stars were the only things on the screen; it looked just like a night sky except the stars were a lot brighter. It was as if he was actually seeing them in space without any background sound or light. *No, this can't be real. I can't possibly be seeing an actual scene in the middle of outer space. No, it has to be a very realistic virtual reality of some kind, especially since the temperature looks reasonable because there is no sign of a sun anywhere.*

Michael touched the pad on his computer to see what would happen. Nothing. He moved his computer slightly in a clockwise direction, and the picture moved likewise. More stars to the right of the screen suddenly came into view, and the ones on the left disappeared off the screen. He looked at the angle, which now read 129 degrees. *Now this is getting really interesting.* He was able to realistically alter the angle for just a game. He then thought about the direction his computer was facing and worked out that he was facing roughly north-west, so that meant the webcam was facing about south-east, making the 129 degrees just about correct for where it was filming. *What is all this? It seems to have a realistic built-in compass and could even be giving an accurate temperature reading.*

He slowly continued to move the picture to the right and saw constellations he'd never seen before. He moved it around until he went through a complete revolution. Michael wondered what was above and below him, so he tilted his computer slightly away from him, and the picture moved upwards. He moved his computer so his webcam could appear to show the sky above and then below, which it seemed to do. There was no sign of any sun, planets, moons, or anything else floating around, except for distant stars. *What sort of game is this? It can't really be an alternative dimension or universe, unless I'm dreaming. This has to be nothing more than just a well-designed, realistic, and elaborate con.*

Michael selected another random dimension, and after it downloaded in a couple of minutes, a similar picture appeared on his screen. He looked all around the scene again. He noticed that the constellations were different this time, but still stars he'd never seen before. Again, there was no sound, which was at least consistent with space as a vacuum. He thought, *Well, I'm getting nowhere with this. I wonder whether this download and everything could adversely affect my computer. Perhaps that's why this game, assuming it is one, is not working properly.* So he closed the program and checked to see if any of his files or documents had been compromised. There was no sign of anything wrong, so he logged off to give himself time to think about things before trying the game again.

Two days later, after he'd given it some thought, Michael went into the game again. This time, he was curious about the Inverse option, so he selected it. It took two minutes to download, as before, and another picture appeared on his screen. This one was similar to what he'd previously seen. The temperature was -250 degrees Celsius now, and the angle was 239 degrees. He thought, *Well, hey, that is the opposite angle on the other side of south. The webcam is facing more or less south-west there in relation to south-east here. That appears to be a mirror image based on the north-south alignment. How interesting this is!* He moved his computer slightly clockwise, and the stars again moved in from the right. The angle now read 232 degrees as if, mathematically, it had moved anticlockwise instead. *This game seems to have created a laterally inverted image. But what does a reversing compass prove? Nothing! But it certainly looks good. What a clever and well-worked-out program this is. It's trying to make me believe I'm effectively in a negative universe. It'd certainly be interesting if I could see the mirror writing, as in* Journey to the Far Side of the Sun. *This is interesting, though.* He chuckled.

He looked at the picture whilst continuing to move his computer clockwise. Then he noticed a sun that looked to be far away. He thought, *Oh, that's why the temperature is a bit higher this time because there is a sun nearby.* He saw, though, that there were no near planets or anything around him as he looked up and down and all around. He looked longer this time, studying the colours of some of the stars, wishing that the program had a built-in telescope through which he could maybe spot any distant planets orbiting the sun. He noticed a red star and a blue star that were more or less in line with the sun, and he thought that they could be a distant Mars or Earth. He then looked for Saturn and Jupiter, wondering whether his position may be in their vicinity due to the very low temperature reading, but he couldn't see any sign of any planets. He looked and looked, but as before, he just saw constellations that he, again, couldn't recognize. *Yes, there is a sun similar to our own, but no evidence of a solar system like ours, even if it is laterally inverted in these circumstances,* he thought. *No. Those two stars must be other distant suns, most likely red giants or very hot blue suns ... oh, what am I thinking of. I'm actually so stupidly, beginning to take this thing seriously. Come on, Michael, wise up. This is only a program from somebody's over-active imagination—someone who has been watching too many Hollywood sci-fi movies ...* The thing was, whoever had done this had done it so well and had made it believable and very interesting at the same time. *I'll go and watch* Avatar *or something like that. Maybe that'll bring me back down to Earth. At least something like that would be more feasible than what I could be imagining here, especially about reverse universes, or any dimensions at all for that matter.* He then closed the tab, again wondering whether his documents or files had been affected in any way. When he checked them, everything seemed OK, just as before. He then logged off, but he just couldn't stop thinking about what he'd seen, making him wonder what other variations were available to him in that game program.

Being too busy over the next few days and wondering about how far to go with this game, he didn't try it again. But he entered the game five days after his first visit.

This time he selected Time Speed. It asked him for the scale, giving him a guide: "1 is for the standard rate of time in your universe; 2 is for a universe moving at two seconds per one second of yours." He decided to try -1 out of curiosity, wondering what that might look like as he selected Random again. It took four minutes this time for the game to download before he saw the picture. He anticipated that it would look something like a negative photograph, after having thought about it on and off over the last few days, especially after what he'd seen so far when applying his knowledge of physics to the program. The picture came on, and that was just what he did see—loads of black dots on a white background, along with a few red ones and the odd blue one. Applying his knowledge, he figured the red ones would be normal blue stars and the blue one would be a red star or planet. He moved his computer clockwise.

The compass moved higher in degrees this time, it being a positive universe. As he'd predicted, he saw a large, dark-blue-green object that he deduced was a yellow sun. As before, though, he couldn't see any large planets nearby. He exited that scene, thinking, *By! The person who has created this program knows his physics well because even I anticipated the negatives of a photograph.* He then selected 0.5 time speed at random to see if the creator anticipated half-speed light intensity and the effect of it on certain colours. This time the program took only three minutes to download, which made him think, *Well it's not so complicated. Now it's a positive figure of moving forward.* The picture came on, and the light was much dimmer. The stars were still white, and he recognized some familiar constellations this time. He then had a shock when he noticed Earth's almost-full moon by its familiar landscapes, even though it looked a little reddish due to the effect of the time speed on its colour.

Michael moved the computer clockwise to see if he could see Earth. It appeared 172 degrees from the moon. Its colour was mostly greenish, representing the oceans. The red areas were land. He moved the computer webcam to a 358-degree angle since it was nearly midnight GMT. He knew that was the angle where the sun would be at well below the horizon this time of year. He then tilted his computer a lot so the webcam would focus well below that horizon. He saw that the sun was still a very bright but orangey red colour. He looked at the temperature reading which showed 10 degrees Celsius, and he realized that that was too cool for where he was in space. He then remembered logically that it had to be half the normal temperature for this position in space because this universe was only moving at half the normal speed through time.

He thought, *Well what do you know—I've just come across our solar system at last. By all accounts, it is not that remote after all, although the Earth for some reason is quite far away. I'm still not so sure, though, that this isn't just a logically based games program derived from the laws of physics. That has to be the most likely thing—to thrill us all who like science.*

He then became a little more curious and selected a time speed of 1.5. He selected Random again, knowing that anything more than that would have too much light intensity. After the two minutes it took to download and appear on the screen, he saw that the light intensity was high, but he was back to seeing no more than he'd seen the first time. It was just another one of those unfamiliar stars and constellations from another universe. The colours were logically correct according to the speed through time because there were a lot more blue stars and certainly no red ones because of the relative high frequency. There was the odd yellow one though, which would have probably been red at normal speed. The temperature was showing -268 degrees Celsius, presumably half again as warm as normal by the fact that there was no nearby sun again. He then decided to see what a -2 would be like, so he selected that at Random. Not unexpectedly, the program took five minutes to download, and he saw that it was only half as bright as compared with a -1 because it was twice as dark in reverse compared to twice as bright at 2. He saw the white background with very dark black dots, which were the white stars. When he looked closer, he just saw a few dim blueish spots amongst them, which he thought would more than likely be blue stars anyway, by logically thinking that they would be red at normal speed backwards, indicating blue at the standard speed forward. He thought, *Wow! Another bit of double-negative type thought*, whilst he noticed again that there was were no nearby suns or familiar constellations, or any known planets from our solar system. After that he closed the tabs and, as before, he checked to make sure everything was OK with his computer after playing the game again. After seeing it was, he logged off to give himself some more time to think about it.

Just over a week later, at the beginning of December

when he was doing some Christmas shopping on a Saturday afternoon, he saw a girl of about his own age who looked very much like him, except that she must have been only about five foot five. Naturally, he thought she was very attractive because of their similarity and because she was very thin with a lovely curvaceous figure. She was wearing a woollen hat and a short white raincoat with blue trousers and black shoes. He thought back to a few years ago when he remembered seeing a girl who looked so similar to Andrew, a friend of his brother. He then thought that the girl he had just seen here looked very similar to Melanie at the office—without all the make-up. He thought that certainly couldn't be her without any make-up on. When he curiously looked again, she had gone, and he was sure that she hadn't noticed him. He thought, *Oh well, never mind. I wouldn't have known what to say to her anyway, even if I'd had the courage to introduce myself. If I had done, that would have probably freaked her out anyway and made me look a bit desperate, because meeting a girl for the first time in a shopping centre isn't the best of ways.* He thought about his inhibitions, which limited him to just wanting to give girls a good impression by only talking about the best things, possibly because he'd never met the right girl—one who could make him feel he could share everything with her.

Later that evening he logged onto his computer, deciding to try the Origin function of the software. When he selected it, the software asked him to for a date, so he chose the afternoon of the previous day. After a two-minute download, a picture of himself appeared on the screen. He was dressed exactly the same as he was now, and he was sitting in front of his computer looking seriously at the screen. Everything in the background was the same as it was here. He thought, *Oh that's it—it's a selfie!* So he curiously said, "Hello, Michael," just to prove it. He heard his own words, and his voice sounded like exactly the same—a fairly deep voice that he'd heard when he'd rung himself up on his landline using his mobile, which he'd done occasionally to maintain his pay-as-you-go subscription. He did that because he very rarely used the mobile except for emergencies such as a possible car breakdown or something else. He said, "Hello, how are? Is that you I see?" He heard himself say the same thing. He made a quick wave and likewise saw himself do that. He forced a smile before closing the tab because he never liked hearing himself on the phone, and he'd felt quite foolish when he'd occasionally talked to himself in the mirror. He laughed at himself, thinking, *I'll be giving myself a green ticket next by possibly being a candidate for the looney bin.*

He then chose another date in December exactly a year ago. In three minutes, he saw the picture—the same room, but he was not there now. He looked at the surroundings; they were the same except for his old radio and CD midi-system. That made him remember when he'd changed it last summer after having made a good profit on the sale of some shares in the stock market. He thought, *Well, what do you know? Buying that new hi-fi system was only a split decision after all. Maybe there could be something in this. That may not have been a computer selfie like it appeared to be. Maybe I was just too close to me then and the differences between us hadn't diverged enough. It seems that here, though, there are just a few more differences. It seems that date of origin is true, when everything prior to that date was no different to the way it was before. That would explain how, if you could travel forward in time, those things you see that had happened but were still ahead of you, may not necessarily have to happen. It's like going along a branch in a possible direction but then being able to trace your way back along that same branch to where you'd started from—so being able to live it differently, a bit like the way things worked in the movie* Back to the Future. *Of course, when you've lived it properly, there is no way of going back in this universe. These alterative universes, though, seem to be the other possibilities that could have happened. In these, the history books could have been totally different. This dimensional program, if real, is therefore showing me the result after other possible outcomes, depending on the alternative routes I could have chosen after this date of origin. This almost seems the logical thing after what I've seen so far.*

He was trembling a little with excitement because of the logic of his thoughts and of what he was seeing in this program. He moved his computer around to look at the whole room, and he saw a few other minor differences, such as different clothes and fewer CDs in his collection, obviously due to the fact that he wouldn't have been as enthusiastic about buying more CDs if he'd still had that original player.

Curious, he then entered settings to go back ten years, and this time he saw that the furniture and surroundings were completely different. There was no patterned wallpaper or red patterned carpet this time. It was just a storeroom now, with wooden floors and a plain, white-patterned wallpaper and no bed. He thought, *Well, somethings happened in the last ten years. I must have taken a different walk in life or something. Who knows? I may have a better job and even be married, living somewhere else. Who can speculate?*

After that he chose an origin date of 1 November which was just over a month ago. After a couple of minutes, he saw the picture of his room appear on the screen again, where he saw himself doing some overtime book-keeping. He was dressed in a blue long-sleeved shirt instead of the white one he was wearing now. He remembered the girl he'd seen who wore a white raincoat! He suddenly remembered that the work he saw himself doing on the screen was the work he had planned to do himself tonight. Normally he would have been doing that work right now, so why wasn't he? What had changed? Maybe the "self" he was seeing on the screen wasn't in his current predicament. Maybe that self hadn't got wind of this DO program. Maybe all this was just a silly dream. He called out "Hi, Michael" just in case he might be able to hear himself on his computer in that version of the universe, but there was no reply, of course, because he didn't have his computer switched on there. He was just continuing as normal, making entries in the books, which gave him a funny feeling. Why wasn't he doing that himself right now, as he would normally have done? Perhaps he was supposed to, if all things were usual and he wasn't so taken up with the intrigue of this program.

He closed the tab and again checked to make sure his computer was OK. It was, so he logged off to do that same work that he had just been reminded of, whilst thinking now he was maybe in an isolated situation, in which what he saw on the computer was what he would be doing normally without ever seeing this program. He thought, *No. Maybe it was just a random alternative universe without it.*

2

CONTACTING HIMSELF

A few days later, after ten o'clock in the evening, he selected 1 November again. This time he saw himself on the computer as he had been before when he had tried that origin date earlier last Saturday. He noticed he was wearing the same clothes this time too, and he quickly said, "Hi, Michael. Is that you?"

The Michael on the screen replied with a surprised look on his face, saying, "Yes. This is the first time I've been able to speak to you properly—because you had the first word." He chuckled.

Michael said, "Me too. Our universes must have diverged enough for us to be able to be at a slightly different wavelengths and not be clashing all the time."

DO Michael said, "That's what I was just thinking and what I was about to say."

Michael laughed and said, "Well, at least I can share

about half of it whilst thinking about the other half when you're saying it."

DO Michael laughed and said, "Yes, me likewise, Michael. Well put. Anyway, what other things have you seen regarding this program?"

Michael answered, "Well all sorts, except Bertie Bassett." That comment came instinctively, and then he quickly continued, saying, "Yes. I started by seeing a lot in space—such things as unknown constellations, different movements in the time speed of some universes, and one in which I was sort of between the Earth and the Moon."

DO Michael quickly responded, "I saw similar things. I also saw a few mirror-image ones. Did you view any of them?"

Michael answered, "Just one. It was in space again. At least I think it could be a reverse one, when I saw a compass move backwards in degrees as I rotated my laptop clockwise."

DO Michael said, "Well, I saw that too, and after seeing a girl who looked so much like me and whom I saw was left handed as she paid for some things she was buying, I let my imagination run riot on the inverse functions of that program. Have you noticed a girl who is similar to yourself?"

Michael answered, "Well, I did see a similar girl, but only for a short moment. When I looked again, she had gone. How did you happen to notice somebody more than I did? And when and where was it?" He was curious as to whether she could be the same girl.

DO Michael answered, "I must have been in a

slightly different situation to yours at that point. I don't know why, but it was probably due to randomness at the time. Anyway, I saw her last Saturday afternoon around the markets. When I first saw her, she was looking at me, and then she immediately looked away and walked ahead of me. I was interested because she looked at me and she looked so similar, so I followed her to where she'd bought the items. Like I said, the fact that she'd opened her bag and was using her left hand got me into thinking about those reverse universes. I was too far away from her to see anything more. Besides it wasn't a good place to pick up anybody." Michael noticed him blush, then DO Michael said, "Excuse me for that. Anyway, when did you see the girl that you were talking about and what was she wearing?"

Michael, realizing that he'd forgotten to ask that extra-simple question about her attire, answered, "Well, it was last Saturday too but at MVS, and she was wearing a woollen hat with a short, white raincoat as I remember. We might have seen the same girl, but it doesn't mean that they're connected to any of this."

DO Michael said, "Well, the girl that I saw was wearing the same thing, so I must have seen the same girl. It's just that she looked so much like me—even more so the longer I looked at her. I had more time to look at her than you say you did, and that's why, perhaps, I've dwelled on this lateral thing too much, with the left handed business. The things I've thought about could be silly, but whenever I look in the mirror, I always think of her because she looks so similar. Besides that, she has a small blemish on her right cheek, and I have one on my left in the same place, so my face in the mirror is virtually the same as hers."

That made the hairs on Michael's neck stand up on end because he knew that his was on his left cheek too. He then looked at the surroundings in the picture on the screen to see if that was a mirror image, but it wasn't. Everything was the same, and he could even read the writing properly on his newish stereo system.

DO Michael then said, "I get what you've just done by checking to see if I'm inverse too. I'm not, of course, and you aren't to me."

Michael smiled and said, "Oh, excuse me. I was just checking." And he then thought about what his other self had just said. He responded, "You're surely not thinking that she is the reverse female version of us are you? That's a very tall order."

DO Michael answered, "Well, I have done, because of what I've seen."

Michael thought about the fact that she didn't wear glasses, but then realized that a lot of girls prefer contact lenses. He said, "You're imagining too much. It's just nothing more than a coincidence. I remember seeing a girl who looked so similar to a friend of my brother's. And anybody could be naturally left handed."

DO Michael responded, "Well, if you'd seen her as I did, I'm sure you would have thought about it too. And, yes, I too remember seeing that girl who was very much like Andrew. In that case, she could have been a cousin of his or something."

Michael said, "Yes, or coincidence, unless it happened then too." He laughed.

DO Michael laughed too and said, "Yes, I get you. Just imagine it, though, assuming that it could happen. How on earth did she manage to get here, let alone from a reverse universe? I've been thinking about that, too, of course, and I've had plenty of time to because of the way I've seen her. I mean, she could have brought all sorts of different cold or flu viruses along because her DNA, and all that would be reversed, and those germs could infect us. Ours could infect her too. Only a doctor or maybe a nurse would know something about that."

Michael got to thinking then. He got enthusiastically carried away and wanted to say his bit, although he was still very sceptical about it. "I've also just remembered about something I heard a while ago, about certain fruits tasting different due to reverse molecular structures of acids or DNA types. Well, certain DNA in oranges is the reverse of the DNA of lemons."

DO Michael quickly chimed in saying, "I've had the same thoughts. No doubt we heard that at exactly the same time, because our point of origin was well after that. Anyway, if she is who we think she is, she'll probably have realized that when she drank some orange juice. It would probably have caused her to gulp unexpectedly because lemon is very bitter and much more acidic than orange."

Michael smiled and said, "Yes, she wouldn't know the difference, though, if she'd tried it as a Saint Clements cocktail or something."

DO Michael laughed and said, "At least that would have been nicer and no different. What I do wonder now, though, is why she'd ever want to come into a reverse dimension. I mean, money, credit cards and everything—how could she live and even work properly in an environment that's back to front? It would be terrible, I should imagine. Besides, what about those bugs she might have brought with her as I said earlier?"

Michael said, "Maybe she came unexpectedly or something. That would have been even worse if she wasn't prepared for it. She would have been terribly alone."

DO Michael said, "Haven't you thought that that might be why we seem to be the only ones who have this program? It's for some form of contact for her? Who else could she talk to and confide in better than herself or an effective brother? Nobody else would believe her if she told them. What she has to say could make her a candidate for the funny farm."

Michael thought for a bit and said, "And bear in mind the fact that her heart would be on her right side, and even her other organs could look different, which could make her a subject for medical research. If we can think of all this, she would have thought of it also, especially because she is us, if our over-active imaginations are correct and all this is real. She'll think like us too, and that alone makes it more feasible. Goodness me, we could believe anything here. This is too silly for words now. This is what too much sci-fi can do to you. I think it's best to stop thinking and come back down to Earth now from these ridiculously high skies."

DO Michael said, "And it can't be right because there haven't been any outbreaks of anything, and if she is here now, she would have been here for a long time, especially after sending us that program such a long while ago. Now, I'm continuing with this unbelievable nonsense. Stop it, Michael! (Not you, me!)"

Michael then thought about what her name could be. *Susan Morrow, of course, if she hasn't already married. Susan would have been my name if I'd been born a girl.* He said. "I think I know what you're thinking, and I've thought that for a while. It's about Susan, isn't it?" Michael chuckled and said, "Yes. We can certainly read each other's minds, can't we?"

DO Michael replied, "Yes, but because I have more time to dwell on this, I have thought about how we could find a possible Susan in our place so we could know about her, if she at all exists."

Michael asked, "What have you thought then?"

DO Michael answered, "Well, the only way to do it is to pick a date of origin before we were born. Even then, it will still be random as to whether we'll still be here instead."

Michael thought logically about it and said, "Yes. It's one of these things that'll have to be done by chance."

DO Michael said, "Yes, I'll think about it. One other thing that's just come to mind is the divergence of the universes the further back the origin date is. We're just over a month different."

Michael had an idea of what DO Michael was implying. He said, "I can guess what you're thinking. I'll just get todays newspaper and look at the sports page. Oh, it's nearly half past ten for you on 8 December isn't it?" He quickly picked up the paper. With great excitement, he turned to the horse racing pages and saw that DO Michael was doing the same on the screen.

DO Michael replied, "Yes, it is. That's one of the first things I'd intended to ask you, to see if we were synchronized at the same point in time. At least that confirms one of the logical things I've thought about regarding this program." Michael was sure about that too, as DO Michael continued saying, "I think that, if anything differs, it will be on the very closely won races such as a photo finish or something."

Michael thought about that and picked a race result that looked as if it had been won by a narrow margin. They both read out the same winner. They then looked at the greyhound races and saw a photo finish, and when they compared those, the dog listed as runner-up in Michael's paper was listed the winner in DO Michael's paper, which he held up to the screen. Michael said, "I thought a very narrow result like that could prove that we are very slightly different. It also proves that, if you could travel back in time and put a bet on a declared winner, that contestant may not necessarily win anyway because you could be moving along an alternate path from where you came from. You couldn't therefore get rich after all by thinking you were gambling on a certainty, because you'd move into a different future that can change. There must therefore be an infinite number of possibilities you can go through, even from the past if you could go back in time."

DO Michael said, "Yes, it certainly makes one think. Anyway, I'm beginning to feel tired now after all this. It'd be great if we could talk again, if we could ever locate our same selves again."

Michael said, "Same here, and me too. I wonder how we could do that?"

DO Michael answered, "Well, I noticed a storage system when I went into inverse universes a few times. You could use that. And I will do so as well, now that I've spoken to you for the first time. I don't know if you're thinking about that?"

Michael answered, "Well, I'll try, since I haven't seen anything like that. Anyway, what sort of things did you see there?"

DO Michael answered, "They're no different to this, except in reverse. I've been in only a few, and briefly, based on this origin and one a year ago and ten years ago. That's all."

Michael said, "Yes, those were the parameters I chose in our normal universe."

DO Michael said, "Well, I'll get to talking to you again. I think you'll find your away around it by saving this origin. All being well, I'll see you again, Michael."

Michael said, "Yes, see you—hopefully—Michael." And then the screen went blank before it switched back to the program options. Michael clicked a save option, and the software confirmed 1 November at 12:00. He pressed save. The software told him "Date saved," so he closed the tab, just hoping he had done it right. He then checked his computer. Finding nothing wrong, he logged off, thinking, *There could be other possibilities, of course, if someone is trying to contact us through this. It could be like he says, an alternative self, but a proper one of her. Or it could be some other girl seeking me out who knows me from another universe. I could think of many different possibilities here.*

The following Saturday at about midday, Michael curiously tried out the program with an origin date of 1 July 1925. It took five minutes before the picture came onto the screen, and he found he was in a completely larger room about half a foot above the floor, near to a wall. There were two front windows instead of one, and it was a nicely furnished bedroom with flowery patterned wallpaper and a plain, dark-blue carpet. He thought, *I must be slightly above floor level because the height of the ground floor is lower or something, since I'm exactly in the same space that I occupy in this universe.*

He then curiously moved the computer to the near wall, since that was still in the middle of his own bedroom. He saw nothing more than a black screen because there was no light in the middle of a wall to illuminate anything. Another logical step for this program. He then looked to see if there might be a newspaper to tell him anything about this alternative time on 12 December. He saw one on a chair. The front-page news was still about the same, there being really no change about the European Union. He could do nothing more than see what was around him, and he thought, *I wonder if there have been any other historical differences over the last ninety years or so.*

He selected the Inverse option and chose 31 March 1980 as the date of origin. This was over five years before he was born. After four minutes, a picture appeared on the screen. He was in his room again. He reminded himself that the building would have been there then, as it was built in the mid 1970s. As he expected, he saw it was laterally inverted with his front window nearer to the left side than the right, and the walls were painted in a white emulsion while the carpet was grey. He looked at a clock which was in reverse, as the second hand moved anticlockwise. This made his hair stand on end a little, even though he'd half expected it. He saw his mirror on the opposite wall and looked at the picture on his computer through it. Seeing things properly gave him some relief. The room then looked like his except for the furniture, which he didn't recognize. A moment later, when he heard somebody enter, he turned away from looking at his laptop in the mirror. He then saw a tall, familiar-looking elderly man of about seventy come in to rest on the unfamiliar single bed. Michael suddenly remembered him as John Mitchell, who was another resident of the flats. Michael knew that John had always wanted the particular flat that Michael owned. Michael had, of course, been given first choice because his father was the original owner of all the flats.

John wore a brown jacket with the top pocket on his right, and he wore light-grey trousers and brown shoes. His watch was in reverse on his right wrist. This looked very peculiar, and Michael thought, *Well, at least I've seen it now. It's just like that film,* Journey to the Far Side of the Sun. *I think I'll just stick to regular universes instead, where I can read and recognize things properly.*

He then selected 31 March 1980 the proper way and saw his room, this time with a flowery patterned wallpaper and a dark-blue carpet. The furniture was more modern than what he'd seen in John's room earlier. After looking around for a bit, he saw a girl walk in who was very much like himself. She had straight, dark-brown hair, and she wore glasses that suited her. Her eyes were the same pattern and colour as his, but her face was slightly smaller because she was a girl. And her eyes looked larger than his. She also had the same slight blemish on her left cheek, proving that she was the right way round. She wore a long-sleeved white blouse with charcoal grey trousers and black shoes. He noticed that she was quite well endowed, which made her very shapely and even more stunning. He thought, *Well, if she's here now and she is me, she's at least still in her own universe. And, wow! She looks lovely. I know that I've hardly attracted any girl, but by! For me, she's beautiful in every way. There's no way she'll have any problems attracting a lad, and she looks just like that girl I saw last Saturday afternoon at MVS, except that she didn't wear glasses. It's just a pity that I can't talk with her. By the looks of things here, she probably doesn't have the DO program. Things, therefore, at least seem to be normal for her here.*

He watched her wash her face and then put on a little red lipstick before leaving the room. He noticed the same newspaper that he had ordered on a chair. He saw that it had today's date on it, and the headlines were not much different, except there was more snow forecast for today. After that, he saved the location and then logged off the program whilst thinking about this evening when he would be attending the office Christmas party.

3

OFFICE CHRISTMAS DINNER

That evening, Michael arrived at the restaurant where the party was being held. He wore a plain, long-sleeved, white shirt with a blue-patterned tie and charcoal-grey trousers and black shoes. As he was buying a drink, Paul Johnson came over to chat with him. Paul was fairly tall at six foot one. He had black hair and occasionally worked with Michael in accounts. He was wearing a short-sleeved blue shirt and light-grey trousers with dark brown shoes. He said, "Hi. How are you Michael?"

Michael said, "I'm fine. How are you? How did it go when you submitted those figures this afternoon?"

"Yes, thanks," said Paul. "I'm OK, and they went through all right as usual. There were none of those occasional hiccups this time. Anyway, Michael, aside from talking shop, it'll be nice to let our hair down tonight.

Hope you don't mind me saying this, but those two new starters are rather fit, aren't they, don't you think?"

Michael quickly glanced to his right and saw them both, noticing that Sarah was looking their way whilst Melanie was talking to Sarah. He thought Sarah was looking at Paul. He knew by now that Paul wasn't the sort of lad to mince his words too much, especially when he'd seen one beautiful girl, let alone two at the same time. Michael reservedly answered, "Yes, they are." He knew that, if he commented on Melanie being the one he was most interested in because she reminded him of the girl in the DO program, he'd anticipate Paul immediately saying, "Get in there mate. What you waiting for? The grass will be twelve feet higher in half an hour's time." Michael had heard him say that a few times before to some other work colleagues to goad them on.

It was worse for Colin Smith, who was in his early thirties, when at last year's office Christmas party, he had tried his luck by chatting up Stacey Dawson, a twenty-eight-year-old pretty blonde girl, who was abroad on holiday at the moment. He had had too much to drink, and that had caused him to be sick all over her whilst they were dancing at the after-meal disco. She had been a little drunk too, and she had hit him gently over the head with her handbag. She'd shouted, "Well that's just charming, isn't it?" And then she'd stormed off in disgust to the toilets. There had been a few laughs then, of course, but the two of them had made it up later that night. The following Monday it had been a joke around the office, but Colin had laughed it off, and now they were going quite strong.

Paul said, "Well I like Sarah, the red-headed one. She's absolutely gorgeous. Do you happen to know her surname?"

Michael replied, "Yes. I only know it from preparing the salaries. It's Morrison. Neither of them have been working here very long, and I've never been introduced to either of them."

Paul said, "Neither have I. I'll have a few drinks first, and then I'll make some headway with that Sarah bird later."

Michael thought, *He still doesn't mince his words regarding girls. For him, they are just objects of desire. I'm not saying anything more to him than I need to because he'll just jump onto me when he can.*

Paul then asked, "What drink would you like? I'll buy this first lot."

Michael answered, "Oh. I'll just have a pint of bitter please." It was not really his favourite drink, but all right as a starter.

Paul said, "OK. I'm having two pints of Foster's since I was born down there, mate." He said it as if he didn't know that Michael knew he came from Sidney. But Michael remembered that that was the first thing that Paul had ever told him about himself when they'd first been introduced.

"OK," seeing that most people were now sitting in their appropriate seats ready for the meal.

"Well, we better get seated. Who will you be sitting with Michael?"

"Oh, I'm between David and Julie." David Evans

was the senior accountant in his department, and Julie Green was one of the receptionists.

Paul said, "That figures. I'll be sitting with the same sales people again—Brian and Robert. At least you get to chat with one of the pretty receptionists who's rather easy on the eye. Oh well, it will give me time to get plenty of drink before meeting Sarah later." He picked up both his pints of lager and then said, "Anyway, I'll catch you later, mate."

As Paul made his way to the table. Michael said, "Yes. See you." Paul quickly downed half of his first pint. Michael thought, *Well, at least he'll enjoy himself now that he clearly has his night planned out. Most things go right for him, especially regarding the girls.* He knew that Julie would most likely be sitting next to her guest, Tony, whom she always talked about. Michael had never met him. As he approached the table, he saw that Julie was talking with a stranger. He was dressed smartly in a white shirt with a maroon tie and dark suit. Julie, who was a tall, blonde girl of five foot nine with light blue eyes, wore a light-blue dress with shiny black shoes. Her blonde hair was neatly tied in a bun on top of her head for tonight, where normally it was long and flowing down her back.

Michael drank some of his pint before sitting down. When he sat down next to Julie, who was seated on his left-hand side, she said, "Hi, Michael. How are you?"

"I'm fine. How are you, Julie?"

"Yes, I'm very well. This is Tony, by the way. I don't think you've ever met before."

"I don't think so. Anyway, how are you Tony?"

Tony stretched in front of Julie to offer him his hand. They shook hands, and Tony said, "Pleased to meet you. It's Michael, isn't it? Julie told me that you'd be sitting with us."

Michael replied, "Yes. I'm pleased to meet you too, Tony." He was a little apprehensive at meeting another one of her boyfriends.

Julie smiled and said to Michael, "I first got to know Tony through an internet dating site."

Tony said, "Yes, and it's a good one. You provide your profile, and they match you with someone who is compatible."

Michael thought, *Oh this is good. They both sound like promoters for this site.*

Julie laughed and said, "Well, it's given us a chance to meet each other, Tony, hasn't it? Anyway, Michael, I thought I'd let you know about it because I'm impressed with the service they provide." She then told him the name of the site. He thought back to when he'd chatted with her occasionally, but not surprisingly, there was always some other man interested in her.

Tony said, "Anyway, I understand you work in accounts."

Michael responded, "Yes. I've been working here for a year and a half now. It keeps me busy, and there's always plenty of work coming in. What is it that you do, Tony?"

He answered, "Oh, I work in marketing. I offer pensions and insurance products to people."

Michael said, "That sounds interesting. It must give you variety of things to do." He knew that Tony was most likely another of those cold-call canvassers.

Tony said, "Pretty much. It's more varied than that previous job I had in IT though."

Julie smiled and said, "Well at least you're on a steady income where you are."

David, who was grey haired and five foot eleven and in his late fifties, sat to Michael's right. He wore a dark-blue suit and a light-blue shirt with a red tie. He said to Michael, "Hi, Michael, how are you?"

"I'm OK, thanks. How are you, David?"

"I'm fine. I presume you got the salaries processed yesterday and ready to submit next week?"

Michael answered, "Yes. They may need adjusting before I submit them because I'm hopefully expecting to receive at least three amended coding notices this coming Monday. If I don't receive them by Friday, I'll send them as they are now."

"That's fine then. There's nothing else you need to tell me about, is there?"

"No, not that I can think of. Everything else seems fine so far. I'll see what other invoices arrive on Monday."

The waitresses then served the starter. Michael had selected the seafood salad with half a slice of warm buttered toast. David said, "Oh, I do like the seafood salads they serve here. They are very nice, aren't they?"

Michael replied, "Yes, I'm looking forward to it this time after having tried one last year." He remembered how tasty it was. When everybody had been served, they all started eating.

The wine was then handed round—a choice of medium white or dry red. David chose red and Michael had white because he preferred a sweeter wine. David tasted his and said, "I do like the red a lot because it's stronger than most and has a lot of body. The iron content is very good for you."

Michael said, "I do like red wine if it is medium or sweet."

"Well, most red wines are dry like this one."

"There are certain red wines that are sweet. Some of them are German, and I have sampled a few at the Yorkshire show in the past few years."

David said, "I've heard about a few of them, but in the supermarkets it's only the dry ones that tend to be available."

When they had finished their seafood salads, Michael said, "I've made sweet red homemade wine just by adding a little sugar near the end of the fermentation. That also helps to strengthen the alcohol content too."

David said, "I used to make homemade wine and have done that myself with elderberry. That was very nice, and I could make it very strong by just leaving it to ferment fully. I don't make my own now because I'm quite happy to just buy it. Wine generally isn't all that expensive anyway, and you don't feel you have to drink it so quickly then because you don't have to worry about it going off." He smiled.

Michael said, "That's true. I have quite a few bottles because I've also tended to just buy wines recently."

The waitresses collected the empty dishes, and David said, "Thanks. That was a very good seafood salad."

And Michael said, "Yes thanks. I really enjoyed that."

When David's main course arrived, he said, "This looks nice. I always go for the traditional turkey and stuffing with sprouts." Michael could see those items on his plate besides sausage meat, parsnips, potatoes, and a little gravy. Michael drank some more of his beer and was then served his meal. The waitress brought two gravy boats to the table. He said, "Well, this looks good. Would you like some more gravy?"

David replied, "Yes please. I always like a lot of gravy because turkey is a rather dry meat."

Michael said, "OK," and he passed the gravy to him and then helped himself afterwards. He then put a little salt on his meal and added some cranberry sauce, which had just been brought to the table. When he started to eat, he noticed that the food tasted lovely; he always liked the Christmas dinner.

David was chatting with his wife, Karen, who was sitting the other side of him. She looked to be in her early fifties. She was of medium build and had light brown hair. She leaned passed David so that she could see Michael and said, "Hi, Michael. It's good to see you again. How are you?"

"Thanks, I'm fine. Are you OK?"

"Yes fine. I always enjoy these occasions around Christmas. Did you receive our card?"

"Yes thanks. I liked it."

"Good. And thanks for the one you gave us. It was very nice, Michael."

"Thanks." She continued talking with David.

After a few moments, Julie said to Michael, "This is lovely. Are you enjoying it, Michael?"

"Yes. I always like a good Christmas meal. This is as good as it was last year." He looked at the table opposite where Melanie and Sarah were seated. He could see that Melanie was enjoying her meal whilst Sarah was concentrating on cutting her turkey. She seemed to enjoy her first bite, and he saw her quickly glimpse at him and then look away to continue with her meal.

Julie said, "Well, I always like Christmas. Are you doing anything special during that week off between Christmas and the New Year?"

"Well, I'll just be taking it easy and spending some of it with my parents and my brother. Are you doing anything special?"

She smiled and answered, "Well, Tony and I are going down to London to spend some time with his parents. It'll be a change from staying here as I normally do, and it'll be great because I haven't been down there in ages."

Tony, who had overheard them, said, "Yes, there is always plenty to do and see down there. We'll be staying at Esher where they live."

Michael said, "Well, there is plenty you can do with a full week off." He continued with his meal and then took a few sips of his white wine, which made him feel a little more relaxed. After that, he drank the rest of his beer and then had some more wine to wash the bitter taste away. By now he was feeling quite light headed. Shortly after they'd all finished their main course, the Christmas pudding was served with custard and brandy butter.

David said, "Some years ago when we had the Christmas pudding, it was quite a bit of fun because we had two of them and there was a two-pound coin in each of them. I blame it on both health and safety reasons and austerity as to why they've stopped that custom."

His wife said, "Well, I suppose hygiene was the issue, or the fact that the coin could damage your teeth if you bit unexpectedly on it."

Michael said, "Well, I'd have thought when you were eating your pudding, you would have had a little at a time so that would never happen! Those coins are too big to miss if you're careful." They started eating the pudding, and Michael enjoyed it.

David said, "Well, it could happen to those who may not be thinking too clearly because they've had too much to drink."

His wife said, "That's a good point, David."

He said, "Oh well, it was fun when they used to do it, even though I've never found a coin in my pudding. I'd have thought that, considering even the little bit of inflation we've been having these days, maybe a fiver would suffice. After all, that wouldn't be a problem even for hygiene if it was put in a bit of cling film or something."

Michael said, "Good point. That would be worth about three-quarters of an hour of work at the minimum wage."

David and his wife chuckled, and then David said, "Well one thing we needn't do then, Michael, if you'd won it, is to raise your salary."

His wife smiled and said, "Oh come on, David Scrooge. There's no need for that. That just spoils the Christmas spirit."

Michael said, "I wish I hadn't mentioned that now."

David laughed and said, "I'm glad you did, Michael. It'd have given me back pay for all the times I'd never won those two-pound coins." Michael forced a smile. They continued eating the pudding, and Michael enjoyed the banter, but he didn't want to say too much about salaries and such because David was effectively his boss, as he was the senior clerk above him.

After the Christmas pudding, they pulled the crackers. Julie offered to pull one with Michael, and he did so, but there was no crack. Julie laughed and said, "Oh well, at least we can wait and see how good the joke is."

Michael chuckled and said, "Or what the prize will be, if it is anything worthwhile."

David said, "Well, they should both be good because these crackers came from Marks and Sparks."

Michael said, to get in his bit of humour, "Well there was certainly no spark when we pulled ours, was there Julie?"

She laughed and said, "You said it, Michael."

That made him feel he'd lost ground on the banter again, after some of his own quips had worked against him. Michael thought, *Well, this extra drink hasn't helped me much. I'm saying all the wrong things as I try to be too witty, and it's all backfiring on me. I must wise up. I'll offer to pull a cracker with Julie this time and do my best to make it work.* He said, "Come on, Julie. Let's try this one."

She smiled and said, "OK then." He felt the chord inside and pulled so hard that she nearly landed on top of him. He was thankful she didn't, even though he fancied her and would have enjoyed it if she had, but that could have caused a bit of disarray with her boyfriend, Tony.

She laughed and blushed a little when he'd twice pulled her close to him and the cracker finally went off loudly.

A few people laughed, and Paul, from a nearby table, shouted, "Oh, well done, sport! Great one, Mike!"

Julie said, "Thanks, Michael, and I noticed the spark."

A few "Oohs" then went around the room, and Michael laughed and enjoyed it, wondering how Tony might take it, but he saw he was laughing with the rest of them. Michael said, "Thanks. At least this one went OK." He then saw some people preparing the equipment and lights for the disco in the next room.

Michael looked at what he'd won in the cracker. It was just a couple of metal loops hooked together, the object of the puzzle being to separate them. Julie had won a small plastic magnifying glass. She said, "Just give it a try, Michael. They're not too difficult and can sometimes be harder to put together again than take apart."

Michael laughed, wondering how long the challenge would take. He fiddled around with them for a bit, knowing full well that there was no point in forcing them because there was only one way to separate them. Julie joked with Tony a little by studying him closely with her magnifying glass, flirting with him. She pretended to examine his eyes and then gradually go further down, causing both David and Michael to laugh. Tony laughed a bit and said, "Steady, Julie. Let's leave all that for later!"

She giggled and said, "Sure. This isn't really the time or place for it right now." They both got up and went to the next room, most likely to start dancing.

As Michael saw a few more of the others leaving to work their way to the dance floor, the two metal pieces he'd kept moving around with his fingers finally came apart. David said, "Well done. You've done it at last."

Michael then wanted to put them together again so they would be in one piece instead of two. After a few moments, he was pleased that he'd managed to do it. He said to David, "Well, I think I'll get myself another drink and then have a dance myself." He wasn't really a keen dancer himself.

David said, "I think I'll just watch for a bit until Karen and I dance later." He smiled and left with his wife. Michael saw that she was smartly dressed in a long, dark-maroon-coloured dress with dark-blue shiny tall shoes that raised her to almost David's height.

4

OFFICE CHRISTMAS DISCO

Michael went to the bar to buy a pint of shandy because he felt that he'd had a little too much to drink for the time being. He was pleased to see Paul propping up the bar because he could now reciprocate by buying him a drink. He said, "Hi, Paul. I'll get you a pint of Foster's, unless you want something different."

Paul responded, "There is nothing else other than Foster's, mate. There might be if they'd served 4X."

Michael wittily said, "Well, they may offer you four eggs at the kitchen."

Paul laughed and said, "Well, that'd probably be better than some of the other choices of froth around here, sport. By! Some of it's so tepid, it's worse than drinking koala piss."

Michael laughed, expecting at least that sort of remark from Paul when he had half a skinful. He said, "Well, I shouldn't think kangaroo piss is much riper, and maybe a few extra dingo droppings would just enhance that." He waited to hear what Paul's next witty Aussie remark would be.

Paul cracked a smile but then assumed a straight face and said, "Well, you haven't heard the half of it, mate. I've seen some right butch sheilas get off on that sort of stuff. They couldn't piss more than twenty yards after downing eight pints of that tight swill."

Michael wondered where the heck this guy's ideas came from, but the way he expressed himself was quite entertaining. He then smelled some sweet perfume. Looking behind him, he saw that both Melanie and Sarah were there waiting to be served. Melanie was wearing a light-blue dress with black shoes, and her dark brown hair was cut fairly short. She wore a little red lipstick and light-blue eye shadow. Sarah wore a dark-blue dress with black shoes. She wore a lot of red lipstick and too much dark-blue eye shadow for her brown eyes. To Michael, they both looked stunning, even though they had make-up on, and he thought about that girl he'd seen at MVS, who looked so similar to him and to Melanie. He noticed that there was no sign of any blemish like his on either of her cheeks, so she couldn't be like him, positive or in reverse. He then wondered about how much they'd heard of what Paul had been saying.

Paul then said, "Oh, hi, girls. I've just been talking to Michael here about certain drinking habits the sheilas get up to in the part of the world I originally come from."

Sarah laughed and said, "I can just imagine, considering what I heard a moment ago, hey Melanie?"

Melanie responded and said, "Yes, that was quite

an eye opener. Some of them sound like they're up for anything."

Michael thought, *That's great! The first time I have with these girls, they hear all that from a work colleague of mine.*

Paul looked wide eyed and enthusiastically said, "You bet, girls. And that's just the starter. Those Aussie lasses, wow! They're not just broad, they broaden the mind too."

As Michael watched both Melanie and Sarah looking wide eyed and giggling a little at Paul's remark, the girl at the bar asked, "What can I do for you? What drinks would you like?" She was tall for a girl at around five foot ten and very good looking with deep-red dyed hair and blue eyes. She wore a sleeveless, plain, white blouse and blue cravat with black slacks and black shoes.

Michael answered, "Oh, I'll have a pint of bitter shandy and a pint of Foster's please." Then he looked at Melanie and Sarah and asked them, "Oh, would you like anything as well?"

Melanie smiled and answered, "Oh, yes, please. I'll have a vodka and tonic."

And then Sarah said, "Yes please. Could you make it an orangeade? I've had too much to drink already for the time being." Michael was pleased to buy Melanie and Sarah a drink.

As the bartender prepared the drinks, Paul laughed and said, "What sort of froth is that, sport? I thought you'd want to really get bladdered tonight." Then he tried to whisper prudently so Melanie and Sarah couldn't overhear him. But he whispered too loudly, saying, "So you could really get in with the beauties here tonight. I mean look at Melanie. I can see that you really have a chance there, mate. I can tell by the ways she's looking at you. She'll be really gagging for it, if you play it right. And I think I've got my chance with Sarah. She's a lovely bit of sheila, you know what I mean, sport?" And he smiled and winked at Michael, saying, "Let's go in there and get some, mate."

The drinks were finally ready. Michael handed Paul his pint of Foster's and picked up his pint of shandy. He could tell both the girls had got the gist of what Paul had just whispered to him. They were laughing together. And he thought, *By! He does put people in some tight and embarrassing situations. What will Melanie think about me now? And what will Sarah be wondering about his intentions after hearing all that from him? I don't know, it's either all or nothing now for me. If I'm myself, I'll be nothing because my intentions are no more than just getting to know her as a person right now, not for a bit of sex. He could think I'm a right wus if I don't do the crude thing.* He knew that was not what he was about anyway. His parents had not brought him up that way. He knew that a lot of what Paul had said was just macho Australian bravado. Michael then handed Melanie her V&T, and she took it in her right hand. He then gave Sarah her orangeade, which she took with her right hand too. They both thanked him.

Paul said to Sarah, "Would you like to have a dance shortly, Sarah?"

Michael realized that Paul was mainly all show. Sarah smiled and said, "Yes, OK. But I'll drink a bit of this first."

Paul responded, "Yes, OK then." They both walked

off together into the next room where the dancing had just started.

Melanie stayed with Michael near the bar and said, "Anyway, you and Paul seem to know each other fairly well." She smiled.

Michael, still being a little nervous even though he'd had quite a lot to drink, forced a laugh and said, "Yes. He can be a bit of a card sometimes. He's a great laugh though."

"Yes, I know what he's like. You just have to take him with a pinch of salt."

"Yes, I try to do that. Anyway, I've seen you around the office quite a lot. What sort of work do you do?" He asked even though he knew that she worked in computers in some capacity. He just wanted to hear a bit more about it from her.

She looked at him and answered, "Well, I'm mainly involved on the purchase side and stock control. I assist Sarah in ordering the right goods to replace the ones that have already been sold, besides giving her ideas about any possible new lines that we could buy and offer customers. Most of what I do is ordering online."

"That is quite a responsible area because it can have a great impact on the gross profits that can be made."

"Yes. I have to be aware of where the demand is regarding certain customers. A lot of it stems from what sort of wish lists you receive online."

He asked, "Are some of what you sell, software packages or computer games?" He wondered if that was how he'd received the DO program. He knew that it had somehow got onto his laptop when he had been using it in the office that day.

"No. We have never sold or marketed anything like software. I work only with the goods we sell."

He knew then, at least, that the DO program wasn't anything to do with something from work. He then asked her, "Have you come across any new sci-fi related games such as dimensional travel or puzzle games?" He didn't want to be too specific about DO because he was still concerned about how he'd come by that.

"I've never heard of any such games. Why should there be such a game? Most games are to do with war and fighting, or perhaps sports or board games such as Monopoly and chess."

"OK. I'm just wondering if you happened to have heard of anything like that."

"Not that I'm aware of—not yet anyway." And then she smiled and said, "Oh, I do like this track. Shall we both go and have a dance?"

He liked that song also and felt flattered that she'd asked him, and that made him feel obliged to say "Yes, OK then" even though he felt that he wasn't a good enough dancer, especially with such a gorgeous girl as her. They went to the floor whilst the track called "Dancing Queen" by Abba was playing, and Michael was pleased that most of the other people were dancing too, so he wouldn't be noticed as much. She danced near him, smiling at him whilst enjoying the music. That and the drink made him feel great; in fact, it was enough to help him forget about his inhibitions and just enjoy himself and her company as they danced to the rhythm of the good music. He felt that he should chat with her, but he was enjoying the moment too much for that, and he could also see that dancing was all she wanted to do. It went on like that for a few tracks, and then she offered him both her hands so he could hold her. He took her hands and felt a lovely tingling feeling whilst they danced together through the next two tracks by Oasis. He began to feel a little tense because he so wanted to say something nice to her, but he didn't know what, especially if he had to shout over the very loud music.

She said, "This is lovely. Just relax and enjoy it like I am doing. You don't have to say anything. I can tell what you're thinking, Michael."

That enabled him to relax, and he smiled and said loudly, "Thanks. It's never easy to chat with all this loud music. Anyway, I'm enjoying it."

She said, "So am I." She smiled at him, and that made him feel that she understood him. She was the first girl ever he'd felt like that about, and this was the first time he'd really been able to relax with a girl. With all the ones he'd previously met, he'd felt he had to give them a good impression and leave it at no more than that. And it was so difficult, he found he was happier to have his own company afterwards. A few tracks later when "Voulez-Vous" by Abba started playing, he became too hot and sweaty, so he left the floor to sit down and continue with his drink to cool off. He saw that Melanie smiled and dropped her arms, as if to know why anyway, but he still certainly didn't want her to start smelling his perspiration too much. It was thus another attack of him not wanting to give a bad impression to anyone. He then saw John Moore from the IT department move in to dance close to her. John was solidly built and very tall at six foot four, and that made Michael suddenly think, *Oh, Michael, you are down to Earth again, but this time with a very hard bang. It takes only one mistake as usual to put them off, and this time it is sweating too much. There could also be another—after all, I didn't say anything to her either. Maybe she was just tolerating me and thought I was amusing when she smiled at me. Imagine my silly notion that she admired me. I'll stick to what I've done all this time and that is to just keep up a good appearance. What the heck—I haven't done too badly so far by keeping things simple. I'll at least never let her know how I felt about her just now. That would lead to my total humiliation and give her a lot of satisfaction. Be realistic at least, Michael. Smell the roses or the sweat!* He saw John talking to her, and he wondered if they were maybe talking about him. Besides, maybe John and Melanie were sweet on each other. She wasn't smiling, though, so maybe they were serious about each other. He tried to put her out of his mind as no more than another fleeting fancy of his. He then noticed Paul dancing near to Emma Chapman who worked in sales alongside him. She was much shorter than he at five foot eight, and very pretty. She was very thin with short black hair and olive skin, and she had large, pear-shaped brown eyes. Her dress was green, and she wore black shoes. Michael thought it was all right for some and looked at his watch, seeing that it was just past eleven o'clock. He went to buy a last drink of lemonade to further quench his thirst. He watched the dancing a while longer and then saw Paul dancing close to Melanie and Sarah. He thought, *What's up with him? Isn't he satisfied just enough by coming from Australia. Does he have to have all the girls too?* When he'd finished his drink and had cooled down a bit, he went for another dance and saw Melanie walk off to go to the bar. He thought, *Oh well, she's seen me coming and left because of that.* He saw her wiping her brow as she queued up. Then John joined her and talked with her. Michael danced whilst watching them talk together, and then he saw her look in his direction. He quickly looked away, not wanting her to see him watching her with John. He continued dancing, looking at the people around him. He was very impressed by the way Emma moved to the beat and how lovely, thin, curvaceous, and stunning she looked even without make-up. He moved closer to her as she smiled and then danced closer to him. She took his breath away, and he just enjoyed it, not knowing what to say. After two tracks, she moved to dance alongside Paul. Michael danced a little longer and then walked off feeling too hot once again, whilst noticing that Melanie and Sarah were not far from him on the dance floor. He thought about joining them, but he was now just too hot and tired. He thought, *What's the point after what's happened earlier?* He decided that it was late and time to leave, so he went to say goodbye to David and Karen, as he felt he should do, saying, "I think I'll be on my way now. I've enjoyed this evening. I'll see you on Monday, David."

David said, "I'm glad you have. See you, Michael."

Karen said, "Nice chatting earlier. I'll see you sometime, Michael."

He said, "Thanks. See you too." And then he went to pick up his long, dark-blue raincoat so he could leave.

When he got outside to find a lift in a taxi, he found it had suddenly become very cold, and he was pleased to get home and have a shower before going to bed. He looked forward to a bit of a lie-in the following morning, just before going to church later that day.

5

Surfing DO

During the night, Michael woke up and had a brainwave. He decided to log on to his laptop. He then selected the alternative universe that he'd saved with the girl in it who was occupying his own room, whom he was certain was his alternate self because she looked so similar to him; in fact, she could almost be his exact twin. When the picture appeared on the screen, he could only just see that she was sleeping because the room was in darkness. The time in red lighted numbers on her digital clock, which was different to his, was the same as the red digits on his clock: 03:54.

He observed how similar she was to him and how lovely she looked without glasses. He looked at her left hand, which was flopped down beside her over the bed, and he saw that it was identical to his own left hand, which made him shudder a bit. He noticed her flowery patterned white cotton night dress. Her nose and facial features were the same as his, but as he had noticed before, her face was smaller and more feminine than his, making him remember how much bigger that made her eyes look. The more he looked at her, the more he realized that Melanie looked similar, but different. He was sure that this girl wasn't the same as Melanie, though, because he remembered that Melanie's eyes were slightly bluer. Although her eyes were a similar shape, they were not the same as this girl's eyes and his.

At that moment, the girl moved and briefly opened her eyes. She seemed to be looking straight at him, which naturally made him move away as though she could see him. She then yawned and went back to sleep again. Michael thought, *I wonder if she sensed that she was being watched for a moment. Anyway, she's all right now and seems to be sleeping OK.*

He glanced at the temperature gauge on his laptop. It read a moderate 20 Celsius, proving that she must have the radiators on. As he moved the computer anticlockwise, he saw the compass reading move backwards as it should do. He then looked at the things around her room and noticed that her CD collection contained albums by Coldplay and Keane like his, but then he saw that there were some albums by Bruno Mars, Abba, and Adele Adkins that he'd never bought. He thought, *More female taste, hey? They're good artists, but not exactly what I would buy.* He then looked at some of the books she had and found a number of unfamiliar romance novels by female authors. He preferred some of the Ian Fleming Bond books and science fiction thrillers, realizing that he could be living one of the latter right now. He took one last look at his near twin, hearing her snore for just a moment. He thought, *I hope I'm not starting to sound like that now.* He chuckled and closed the program tab. He then logged off and went to bed, thinking for a while about this girl to whom he had given the name Susan because that was the girl's name his parents had picked out before he was born. He then thought about how Melanie was nothing really special, being no more than any other girl he'd met. Nothing had ever come of those relationships. He then drifted off to sleep.

The following day, a Monday, he spoke to David only once to tell him that he'd submitted the salaries. They chatted a little about how good the Christmas dinner had been and how they had enjoyed the evening. At lunchtime he saw Paul, who said, "Hi, Michael. Why did you leave so soon on Saturday night?"

Michael answered, "Well, I just felt so tired and thought there was no point in staying any longer."

Paul said, "We all were tired. You could have at least stayed a little longer. Melanie even asked where you'd got to."

That made him feel a lot happier, and he wondered if he'd misunderstood her then. He said, "Well, I did enjoy it."

Paul said, "Not like you could have done, mate. I mean you could have missed out there, but I don't think you have because she asked after you just before we left."

Michael thought for a moment and said, "Well, thanks for telling me, Paul."

"No worries, mate. I'm just trying to help."

"Thanks again. Anyhow, how did you enjoy it?"

"Oh, it went bonza for me, mate. I couldn't hack it after all with Sarah, but I think I'm in there with Emma.

I've had my eyes on her for ages, but I didn't think she cared anything for me until later that night. You missed it all by leaving early. We kissed and hugged and then snogged each other like crazy after that. She was like a beautiful small kangaroo in my pouch and, wow, she's so gorgeous and stunning on top of all that. She's a real knockout, sport." He winked and then smiled, going a little red in the face in his enthusiasm. He then continued saying, "Anyway, I took her out for the day yesterday to Flamingo Land, and we had a great time there on the limited rides this time of year. I think I'm in there."

Emma then arrived and said, "Hi Paul." She looked at Michael and asked him, "How did you enjoy the party then, Michael?"

He answered, "Oh, I liked it very much." He knew that was the best thing to say after he'd just heard about Melanie asking after him. He thought that was great, but then he wondered if Paul could be making it up. He never thought that any girl had ever really been interested in him in that way.

Paul said, "Well, I'm pleased you did. Emma and I had best be getting back to work shortly. See you soon, Michael."

Emma smiled and said, "See you!"

"Yes, I'll see you both," Michael said. Emma was giggly as she walked away with Paul. Michael saw that it was nearly two o'clock, so he went back to the office. He hadn't seen Melanie or Sarah that day because they spent most Mondays travelling around to meet certain suppliers. He thought, *Melanie gets to go travelling around to meet prospective suppliers, and all I do is stay in the office all*

*the time, doing bookkeeping work and preparing salaries and
regular sets of accounts. I wonder what she thinks about that?
I should think she has thought about it when she gets out and
about with Sarah.*

That evening, he decided, out of curiosity, to check
out another inverse universe. He chose an origin date
this time of 31 January 1950, which was well before
this block of flats was built. He hoped to see a different
set of surroundings. The download took eight minutes,
and then the picture appeared. To his surprise, he saw
his room again, but with the elderly gentleman, John
Mitchell, resting on the bed. The reverse clock showed
the same as his own clock: five to eight. He thought,
*Well, it must be the luck of the draw that I'm here again. Maybe
this same building and everything was to be here anyway.* He
looked at the compass on his laptop to check out whether
it moved backwards whilst he moved his computer
clockwise, and it did. In this way, he knew he was in
a mirror-image universe. The room was the same as
before, and he saw a newspaper on one of the chairs.
He looked at his laptop screen through a hand mirror
and saw that the date on the newspaper was right—14
December. The headlines too were much the same as they
were in his world, except that there was a small article
about a dog suddenly disappearing whilst it was running
around in a farmer's field. Michael thought, *Well, it looks
as though there may be a few unusual things going on in this
particular unknown universe. You can think of anything once
again. That dog may have come into our universe or some other
one.* He saw the door was closed in the picture and he
thought, *If I open my door and walk out, I'll surely be able to*

effectively move through his door in the picture. He thought back to when he could move into a wall that he saw on the screen that wasn't actually there in his room. He did so, and as he walked through the door with his laptop, he saw the screen go black until he was through it into the lounge. He then walked into the narrow hallway with his laptop and opened the front door to the main hallway of the flats. He looked to his right on the computer, and it pictured everything laterally inverted to his left, just as if he was looking through a mirror. When he moved to the left towards the main entrance of the flats, he was clearly moving to the right in the picture of the mirror image world towards the main entrance of the flats there, so it was all relatively logical in the same space. He just hoped that nobody would come out of any of the flats right now and see him walking around stupidly looking at his laptop screen. Nobody did, and he went back into his room. He then looked at things for a few more moments before he closed the tab to think about it. *Why did he come back here again on an origin date of twenty-five years before these flats were built?* He remembered that, when he'd previously selected a later origin date to this one in a positive universe, the original building had still been there. He then selected 31 January 1950 again, but for the normal universe this time. When the picture came on after two minutes, it was the original building again. He closed the tab and then tried this same date again for the inverse one, and low and behold, the mirror image of his flat appeared on the screen again with John still in it, with all the same contents. Just then the old man got up to go to the toilet, and whilst he was in there, he made a lot of noise. Michael was relieved that at least he wouldn't get the smell of all that afterwards. He thought, *This is funny, and now I seem to have come to the same exact universe. Why on earth is that? What's so special about this particular inverse universe?*

He closed the tab and then tried a completely random inverse universe as he had done before when he had seen a picture from outer space. It took another long eight minutes to download, and that alone made him anticipate that he'd see John again in his flat. When the picture came on the screen, he saw John in the lounge watching an advert on television with all the writing in reverse, and he had left the toilet door wide open. The smell must have been bad, but John obviously didn't care much about it because he seemed to be happy enough as he drank from a can of lager that looked to be Heineken, with his shirt tail hanging out. Michael smiled and thought, *Well, I've always thought that John Mitchell could be a slovenly bloke. Now I know so.*

Michael closed the tab and wondered again why this was the only inverse universe he could see, when all the proper ones were still variable. He then selected an inverse origin date of two days ago—12 December—and selected a time speed of -1 to see what it would be like to go backwards in this fixed inverse universe. It took eight long, drawn-out minutes again before the picture came on the screen, and things weren't moving backwards when he saw John Mitchell still watching the same film as a mirror image on television. Michael thought, *What's up with this? I can't even see things move backwards. And images don't look like negative photographs the way I saw them before in space.* He then closed the tab and tried the same date in a normal universe this time, at a time speed of -1 and that worked. The picture took two minutes to download this time and showed another scene in outer space just as before. He saw the stars as black dots on a white background. There were only a few small red dots, presumably blue stars. As he moved his laptop slightly anticlockwise to see more of what was around him, he noticed the compass move backwards. He then saw a very large, bright-blue star taking up about a quarter of the skyline. Obviously it was a red giant. The temperature gauge read a very hot 857 Celsius. He thought, *That could be our red giant sun a few billion years from now. Maybe the fact that I've chosen a backwards-moving universe, the end of this one corresponds to the beginning of ours and here. The one on the screen is moving backwards from the end as opposed to ours, which is moving forwards from the beginning. An interesting thought, but it's possible that this red giant may not be ours at all. It may just be in a different solar system occupying our space.* He closed the tab and then logged off to think about things.

Later that evening, after he had been thinking, he decided to try the same origin date of 1 November this year, which was the one in which he had talked with himself, but this time in inverse to see whether the one with John Mitchell would still come up again. It shouldn't because this one was just recent and well after his date of birth. It took eight minutes to download again, and when the picture appeared, John Mitchell was watching the BBC news 24 channel with reverse writing running across the bottom of the television screen. Michael thought, *Well, it's just as I thought before trying this. Somehow my DO program has been adjusted recently in a certain way so that I can select only that particular laterally inverted universe. But how could that be done? Has somebody reprogrammed it online or by using my computer? Who could it be and why? Maybe it's true about somebody coming here from another universe, purposely or by accident. But why me particularly, unless it's somebody I know or maybe an alternative me? I did ridiculously converse with my other self about a female alternative of us, since seeing that girl that day. But it could, on the other hand, be another one or even a few of my selves. Perish the thought. One of me is surely enough. I think it's time for me to look further into this specific dimension so that I might just get some true answers.*

He listened to the news for a bit, but there was really nothing much different to what he'd already heard about half an hour ago on his own television. He then closed the tab, knowing what he would do next. He selected the origin date he had stored when he'd talked with himself. After two minutes, the picture came on the screen and he saw himself in front of it. He quickly said, "Hi, Michael, how are you?"

He heard his other self say the same a fraction of a second later and then ask, "How have things gone so far? How did it go last Saturday night? I presume you went to the Christmas dinner. I did."

Michael replied, "Yes I did, and it all went OK." He realized that was a rather dubious assessment when he thought back about Melanie.

DO Michael said, "I thought so. That Paul seems to be able to attract all the girls, doesn't he? He did well with Emma that night, and taking her out the following day to Flamingo Land."

Michael answered, "Yes. He told me he'd been interested in her for some time."

DO Michael said, "Yes, I got all that spiel from him too. Do you think he's genuine about Melanie seeming to be interested in us? Oh, excuse me, I know that's a funny way of putting it, but it just slipped out because it's so unusual talking to yourself."

Michael laughed and said, "Yes, and I know what you mean. Regarding Melanie, I'm not sure. I do hope so, though, because she's very nice, and it's the first time I've ever had a feeling like that just from shaking hands."

DO Michael said, "Yes, me too. I don't know quite what to make of that because we just seemed to gel at that moment. Anyway, since then, I've searched through nearly all the aspects of the inverse functions, and I always come out in that same universe. I suppose that's happened with you too, hasn't it?"

Michael answered, "Yes, it definitely has. I've tried lots of different alternatives this evening, and I find that I always come back to that same laterally inverted one. What do you think about that?"

DO Michael answered, "Well, probably the same as you. I think I'm going to have another look at that one again, but not in my room this time. I'm going to see what is happening outside for once."

Michael said, "Yes, I'll try the same. Tomorrow evening after work, I'm going to see how things differ in this one compared to ours. It'll work out well in the dark because people will be less likely to see me messing around in my car, looking though a mirror in front of a laptop." He smiled.

The Michael on the screen laughed and said, "Great minds, hey. I've just thought about doing the same as a start, and I'll take it from there, depending on what I find out and how it goes. I just hope no one spots us and wonders what the heck we're doing. I don't want to look any funnier than some of those train spotters."

Michael responded, "Certainly not. I'll be careful on that score."

DO Michael said, "Well, it'll be interesting to see what differences there are, if any."

Michael replied, "Yes, I'm very curious. Anyway, nice chatting. I'll try and contact you after a bit of searching around, depending on how it goes.

DO Michael said, "Yes hopefully. I'll see you Michael."

Michael said, "Yes, see you," and he waved to the image on the screen whilst DO Michael waved back. As he was about to press a button to close the tab, Michael saw DO Michael appear to log off. He closed his own tab, seeing the picture disappear. He then logged off to prepare for his supper.

6

MYSTERY OF THE
INVERSE UNIVERSE

The following lunchtime, Michael saw Melanie and Sarah as he left the office to go and play a frame of snooker for three-quarters of an hour whilst having his lunch with a friend called Andrew Thomas, who worked for the council. Melanie said, "Hi, Michael, how are you?"

He answered, "I'm fine. Are you OK?"

Melanie smiled and replied, "Yes, I'm OK. Did you enjoy the Christmas do?"

He answered, "Yes, it was good. Did you both like it?" He felt rather foolish and annoyed with himself that he'd brought Sarah into the conversation at that moment. He felt he was cutting off Melanie, especially since Melanie was working under Sarah.

Sarah smiled and said, "Yes. I very much enjoyed it too. It was a good evening out, wasn't it, Melanie?"

"Yes, it was OK."

Sarah said, "Well, nice chatting, Michael. I'll see you soon."

He felt she was giving him the cold shoulder. He said, "Yes, see you. I'm going for a game of snooker over lunchtime."

Melanie said, "Best of luck. I hope you win. See you later."

"Yes, see you both soon." He left the office feeling that he had not done very well with Melanie just then. He thought, *I hope there are plenty more fish in the sea.*

That afternoon after work, when it was dark, Michael left the office to go to his car, a blue Vauxhall Astra, which was in the office car park. He knew that he could get a broadband signal from the office hub, and he could access the internet there on his laptop. He was out of the sight of any CCTV cameras, so he felt OK to log in and then access the DO program. He selected the Inverse function and then chose Random, knowing that he'd get that same inverse universe anyway. After eight minutes, the picture appeared on the screen, and he saw that he was looking from the outside, slightly elevated off the ground as though his car wasn't there. The office building looked exactly the same as he looked at the screen through his hand mirror, and when he looked directly at the screen to see across the street over the wall, he saw a pretty young brunette walking her dog with the lead in her left hand. He then looked through his car window to see if she was actually here and she was, with the lead in her right hand. He thought, "Well, things are the same as they are here." He then saw Sarah come out of the office with Paul, and when he looked at the screen, neither of them was there. He thought, *Oh, there is a difference after all, maybe due to randomness.* He saw Sarah wave goodbye to Paul as she went to her car.

When he saw Paul coming his way, he quickly slipped the hand mirror into his jacket pocket and closed the laptop, not wanting to attract any questions right now because of the unusual thing he was doing. Besides that, this was the first time that he'd ever used his computer in the car, and he didn't really like overusing the battery unnecessarily. Paul came to his car when he'd caught sight of him and said, "Hi, Michael. It's not like you to still be here. Are you waiting for somebody? You're not waiting for Melanie by any chance, are you?"

"No, I don't reckon so." He didn't think she was interested in him after they had met earlier. He continued, saying, "I've just been looking through my work schedule to check a few things out."

"I wouldn't worry about that, mate. Why not check it at home where it's warm? It's freezing out here. Anyway, see you tomorrow."

"Yes, see you." As Paul went to his car, Michael looked around to see if anybody else might come out of the office and see him. There was no one, so he opened his computer again and saw an elderly man on the pavement in the picture. When he looked to see if he was actually there in the real world, he wasn't. Michael therefore saw that some things were the same and some weren't. He closed the tab and logged off before somebody else came along and made him feel foolish.

He started the engine and was making his way to the entrance when he saw Sarah in her car behind him through his driving mirror. She looked as serious as she usually did, and as he waited to turn left at the car park entrance, he saw the same elderly man that he'd seen on the screen. The man crossed in front of him. When it was safe to continue, Michael turned left to go home.

After his evening meal, Michael switched on his broadband and took his laptop into his car, which he'd parked just outside his flat away from where there were any CCTV cameras. He knew he didn't have to worry about being noticed other than by somebody passing. He logged in, selected the inverse function, and waited the usual eight minutes. When the picture appeared, he looked at it through his hand mirror. Everything was the same except that the light was on in his flat room, and John was in there. He then heard and noticed four girls pass by in the street. And when he looked at the picture without the mirror, he saw the same four girls walking in the opposite direction, which figured, so there was no difference there. He then looked through the right driving mirror on his side. There was a girl standing about forty yards behind him looking in his direction. She looked away and was too far away for him to recognize her. He thought, *I won't stay here much longer. I may be attracting too much attention and look stupid by being in my car too long without going anywhere on such a cold night.* Just then a stray golden Labrador puppy trotted along. Michael checked to see if the dog was on the screen, and it wasn't. He looked through his wing mirror again and saw the girl still there. He then looked back at the screen and couldn't see anybody there. Maybe she was just too far away to be seen in the picture, so he closed the tab and logged off. When he looked again, she had gone. He went back into his flat with his laptop to watch a film on television.

The following morning, which was Wednesday, Michael got through his work schedule fairly quickly. When he reached a convenient point in his work, he clicked onto the DO program and selected the inverse universe to see what things were like in this office there. Being aware that there was a CCTV camera above his door, he made sure that his screen was out of its range. When the picture appeared after the usual delay, he saw that things were quite different in the room. A lady was sitting in the same chair where he was, which gave him a shock. He thought, *No, no, that can't be me in this universe, can it? She looks nothing like me!* But then he realized that she was doing his job. She was blonde and quite plump and small in stature. She was dressed the way most of the ladies in his office dressed, and she looked to be in her late thirties. He moved out of his chair and moved his laptop so he could see the rest of the room on the screen. The door handle was the opposite way round, and he could see that she was typing in numbers with her left hand on a reverse keyboard, which still made him shudder a little, even though he knew full well that everything there was laterally inverted. He thought, *Well, I'm obviously not working here and not occupying my flat either. I wonder if I'm in this universe at all. I'm sure if I was, I would have seen myself before now, unless I'm somewhere else for some reason.* Just then he heard Sarah and Melanie go into the room next door to his. He listened closely to the computer to see if he could hear them there. He couldn't and thought, *Perhaps they are not are here either. This is proving quite interesting, and it doesn't look as though Paul's here either.*

He then looked at the screen to see what was on this lady's computer screen. Even though the image was backwards, he could see that the firm's name and the directors were the same. She started processing invoices on the computer, which meant that he couldn't learn any more for the time being. He saw a photograph on the desk. It could be her with her husband and children, but there was nothing else there that made him any the wiser. He closed the tab and continued with his next lot of work, which he wanted to complete before lunchtime.

That evening, after having had his evening meal, he decided to travel to his parents' house, wondering if, in fact, he was in this inverse universe. He thought that, if he was, and provided he was left handed there instead of being naturally right handed here, at least everything would be the same to him there as it was here. As long as his heart was on his right-hand side and his brain was laterally opposite, things would level out for him there and appear the same to him as they were here. It would be like two negatives make a positive, as do two positives. After driving for half an hour, he arrived. He stopped near the house and logged on to his computer, hoping that his parents would have their broadband switched on so he could get an internet connection. When he tried to open the DO program, he received the, "No connection found," so he knew that he couldn't go any further. He thought, *Well, it was worth a try, and I may have got somewhere. There is always Saturday afternoon, of course, because I think they'll most likely be out then to do some Christmas shopping.* He logged off and decided to pop in to see them since he was already there.

He knocked at the door, and his mother answered. She was fifty-eight with brown-grey hair and blue eyes. She was quite slim at five foot four. She wore a white blouse under her blue pullover with blue trousers and black shoes. She said, "Oh, hello, Michael! This is a surprise. It's nice of you to pop round."

"Yes. I felt like a bit of a drive around, so I thought I'd drop in. Anyway, how are you?"

"I'm fine. Come in, and we'll have a cup of tea. How are you?"

"Yes, I'm OK, and I'm looking forward to the week off between Christmas and the New Year. It's always the same at this time of year because there's more trade than ever and so many invoices coming in. I'm not objecting, though, because it means the business is doing well and we'll all get a better bonus in the spring."

"That's good. It's nice to hear that things are going well." They went into the lounge.

Michael's father was watching a western on DVD whilst stroking Patch, their female tortoiseshell cat. His father was sixty-four. He had grey hair and hazel green eyes. He was of medium build and stood at five foot nine. He wore a white, open-necked shirt with blue and red stripes under a grey pullover. His trousers were charcoal grey, and his shoes were black. He said, "Hi, Michael. How are you?"

"I'm fine. I just thought I'd call in since I felt like having a drive around. Anyhow, how are you?"

"I'm all right. We're just watching this film, if you'd like to join us."

"Yes, I'd like to. I'll stay and watch it." He had seen it before and knew he would enjoy seeing it again. It had only just started, so he hadn't missed much.

His father smiled and said, "Good, and we'll have a bit to eat later, if you like."

"Yes, that'll be OK."

His mother said, "OK, then. I'll put a pot of tea on so we can have a drink during the film." She went out to the kitchen to do that, and Michael watched the film with his father. The large, widescreen television set was to the left of the front bay window where the maroon curtains were pulled closed. Two bars of the electric fire kept the room very warm on this cold night. The carpet was a deep red burgundy pattern, and the walls were covered in gold-patterned wallpaper. The ceiling was painted a matte white. The Christmas tree with all the coloured lights, baubles, and tinsel looked lovely in the alcove to the left-hand side of the television set. His father sat in his own chair next to the hi-fi music system. Michael sat on the settee to his right. To the right of the bay window, there was a mahogany bookcase and DVD cabinet. On top of this was the family photograph that had been taken fifteen years ago. It showed his mother, who looked much younger then, with full brown hair. His father's hair was also dark, just like Michael's. In front of them in the photo, Michael sat on the left wearing glasses, and his brother, James, sat on the right. The boys had similar features, but James never wore glasses. At the time, he had been quite tall at five foot seven. Now at five foot eleven, he still had green eyes and dark brown hair.

Seeing that picture made Michael wonder if there would be any further differences in that inverse universe. His mother came in to join them, bringing the tea and biscuits. She sat on the settee, and they all watched the film and enjoyed it. After it had finished, they talked a little bit about it, and then his mother asked, "Michael. I'm still wondering what you would like for Christmas."

He answered, "I'm still not so sure. It may be best to give me the usual vouchers or just money."

His father said, "I think we'll do that, then, unless you let us know if you think of anything."

Michael asked them both, "Is there something you would like?"

His mother answered, "You could just buy me some more of those gift vouchers so I can choose something in the January sales."

His father said, "You could buy me some more of those woollen ankle socks and the razor blades I usually use."

Michael answered, "OK. I'll have a look sometime after work. Oh. Will you be in this coming Saturday afternoon?"

His father replied, "No. We'll be doing as much of the Christmas shopping as possible then, won't we, Mary?"

His mother nodded in agreement and asked, "Why? Were you thinking of coming to see us?"

Michael answered, "I may do, but a bit later, now that I know you'll be out."

His father said, "Fine. We should be back before six I think."

Michael got up and said, "OK. I'd better be going now. I'll hopefully see you then."

He gave his mother a kiss and a hug, and she said, "Yes, see you."

His father said, "Yes, see you then."

As Michael was walking down their driveway to his car, he waved to them and heard a dog bark a few times in the distance. He got into his car and drove home.

The following Saturday afternoon, Michael decided to go to his parents' house whilst they were out shopping. He arrived at about five o'clock, after having done some Christmas shopping himself. He let himself in with his own key and found that their broadband was already switched on, probably because they were recording something that afternoon. He logged on to his laptop and then selected the Inverse function of the DO program. It took the usual eight minutes to download again, and whilst it was doing so, Patch came in and rubbed up against his legs. He stroked her, and she purred loudly. The picture came on his screen, showing the mirror image of everything that the webcam was focussed on. He looked at it through his hand mirror; nearly everything in the lounge looked the same. He could see that the Christmas tree was slightly different, and then he noticed that the photograph wasn't exactly in the same place. And the photograph itself was different: His parents and his brother were the same, but there was a girl in the picture instead of him.

7

Observing Susan

Michael was shocked for a moment and, thinking of his conversations with DO Michael, he thought, *By! Our first thought may be right—a girl is there instead of me. How coincidental that we came to such a similar conclusion. Oh, surely not. It's too farfetched for me to expect that I, as that girl, could ever be here. It seems to add up, though, because I'm the only one who seems to have ever come across this DO program. Maybe, as we said to each other before, that is the reason I got the program—as a way for me to see her, as I'm doing right now. Oh come down to planet Earth, Michael. You're letting your imagination run away with you, again!*

Still looking through his hand mirror to the screen, he looked closely at the girl in the photograph, noticing that she was wearing glasses and looked almost identical to the way he had looked then, except for her dark brown hair that was long and straight. He also noticed the blemish on her left cheek. He looked at her on the screen as she looked in that inverse universe, seeing her to the right of his brother now, with that same blemish on her right cheek this time. He thought, *Wow, this is outrageous. This can't be real, I must wake up now.* He pinched himself and looked again at the evident truth in front of him.

Just then he heard the slight creek of a floorboard upstairs. Carefully, he put his laptop down on the settee. He walked upstairs with frayed nerves exacerbated because of these findings. Patch followed him, and when Michael went into what used to be his own bedroom, he saw nobody. He thought, *Oh, I'm imagining things again. It must be due to the central heating coming on.*

He went back downstairs and looked at the photograph again to double check it, wondering whether he'd imagined it. But it was no different. He thought, *Well there it is. This was worth it after all. I can't wait to see what she looks like now. She's certainly not at my flat because John is there instead. And she's not working where I'm working. Perhaps she's left this area altogether and is now married and working somewhere else.* He looked around a little further and could see that things were the same except that some of the furniture was in slightly different places.

Finally, he heard his parents arrive. He closed the tab and logged off. When they came in, his mother said, "Hi, I'm glad you let yourself in. How did you do with your shopping?"

"Fine. I've just about completed mine, and there's not much more to do. How about you?"

"Yes, we've nearly finished ours. There are only a few more things to do." Patch came into the kitchen for some food, which Michael prepared for her.

His father came in with some of the shopping and said, "Hi, Michael. You can tell we've been busy this afternoon. We've got the bulk of it done now. I see you've put our broadband on. Have you been watching television?"

Michael thought for a moment and truthfully said, "No, but I've been online doing a few things. It was actually on when I got here."

His father said, "That's funny. I'm sure I turned it off before we left. Oh, well, I must have thought I did."

His mother said, "Never mind. We were in a bit of a rush before we left because we didn't leave until just after three."

Michael said, "That must be why then." He wondered in the back of his mind if his father might be getting forgetful, hoping that wasn't the case. His father then started unpacking some of the bags, and Michael helped them put the food away.

His father said, "Well, we've got some chicken pieces to cook, and we're having them with potatoes and cabbage. Would you like that?"

Michael replied, "Yes, that would be nice. I'll do some gravy," Michael liked plenty of gravy on his plate whenever he had a roast-like meal.

His mother came into the kitchen and said, "OK. I'll prepare the potatoes and cabbage," and they all helped to cook the meal. When it was ready, they sat down to eat whilst watching the Saturday evening programs. They each gave Patch little bits of their chicken because she liked it so much. Michael thought about his father's oversight in leaving the broadband on, feeling that he wouldn't normally forget something like that. He was too meticulous at saving electricity as was Michael, who was a chip off the old block. Michael thought again, *Could she—Susan—have been here? I know that it's out of this world, but there is the very faint possibility that she could have been here.* He then thought about the things she would have gone through if it were true. It would be OK if she could come and wanted to, but certainly not if she came accidently. He bore that in mind and decided to be careful with her, if he ever met her, however improbable that could be. Michael then thought how ridiculously stupid his thoughts were. He laughed them off and then enjoyed watching television whilst eating. After the meal, they played some card games and watched a film until he went home.

That night, he woke up about half past two in the morning. His curiosity was provoked; he wanted to see that girl again who was occupying his flat—the one who looked so much like him. He switched on his broadband and then logged in to access the DO program. He selected the alternative universe that he'd saved with her in it. It took two minutes before the picture came on, and when it did, he saw her about to take off her white cotton night dress. That made him impulsively look another way, noticing the temperature gauge was 21 Celsius. But he just couldn't help himself. He glimpsed quickly at her. It took his breath away when he saw everything. She had a lovely thin and curvy figure just as he'd imagined. To him, she was absolutely beautiful. That aroused him. He watched her put on some tight, shiny, blue Lycra underwear and then kneel down as she caressed her thighs. She got into bed, and he saw her breathing heavily as she continued to satisfy herself further, which aroused him even more. He watched her eyes dilate and flutter a bit. He thought, *Wow, this is very engrossing. She's into some stuff, but I'm not much better because of some of those magazines that I look at.* He curiously looked at the temperature reading, which was now 25 Celsius. She finally calmed down. There was a slight glow on her face as she got out of bed to change back into her nightdress. He still couldn't help but admire her beauty. After she got back into bed again, she quickly fell asleep. He felt that he had invaded her privacy. He thought, *Gosh! How many times could I have been observed if someone had viewed me at any time? And when?* He closed the tab, logged off, and switched off his broadband. It took him a while to get to sleep because he kept thinking about what he had just seen.

That Sunday afternoon, Michael went online and opened the DO program. He chose the date of origin that he'd stored so he could talk with himself again. When the picture came on his screen, he saw that there was nobody in the room. Then DO Michael came in and logged on, which made him realize that the difference between their universes was gradually widening over the passage of time. When he saw DO Michael's face smile with acknowledgement, he knew then that DO Michael saw him. DO Michael said, "Hi! It seems you were here first. How are things?"

"OK." And he then thought for a bit and asked, "Did you happen by any chance to visit your parents yesterday afternoon?"

"Yes, I did, and it was interesting. I suppose you saw the same thing I saw?"

"By the sound of it, I did. I discovered that we're not there. There is a girl there instead of us."

"Yes, that's right. That was quite a surprise, even though we have talked about the possibility after we saw that girl who looked so much like us. Was there anything else that you want to tell me about?"

Michael answered, "Well, just after I spotted that a girl was there instead of me, I heard a floorboard creak, so I went upstairs to look. It was nothing, of course, because the central heating always makes creaking noises. But I was surprised to see the girl instead of me in the photograph. My nerves were rather frayed. Did you hear anything like that?"

DO Michael replied, "No I didn't, but I heard a few creeks a little later after I'd seen the photograph, just when Mum and Dad returned. I think it's just one of those differences again due to the further divergence of our universes as time has moved further on from 1 November since we spoke last."

"Yes, that seems to be it. These differences are interesting and could give us a better idea of what is happening here. One more thing—not that I want to sound like Columbo—excuse me! He chuckled.

DO Michael also laughed and said, "Yes, I like watching those programs too. They're good, aren't they? And I think I can guess what you were going to say next. It's about finding the broadband switched on when you arrived, isn't it?"

"Yes that is it. My dad was so sure that he'd switched

it off before they left for the afternoon. At least there's no difference there."

"Yes, that's more or less the same as it was for me too. It almost makes me wonder that if she—Susan as I call her—is here in our universe and was watching what we were doing then? I know it's a very tall order, but it could be true, especially as we have this DO program and all."

"You're telling me! I've wondered about that too because it's unusual enough for us to be able to talk together, especially with things diverging."

"Yes. What are you planning to do next?"

"I'm not so sure. I'll just keep my eyes open, I think, and take things from there."

"I'll do the same. We'll keep in touch, hey?"

"Yes I will contact you when the next big issue comes up. I'm sure whenever we do, we'll both be thinking about doing contacting one another." He wondered if he should mention what he'd seen Susan doing the previous night.

DO Michael smiled and said, "I think I know what you've just thought about."

Michael laughed and said, "You saw that too, hey?"

"Yes, I certainly did, and she was quite an eye opener."

Michael remembered how he himself had thought about that and how beautiful she was, and he had gotten off on that at that time and just afterwards. He said, "Well, we'll talk later sometime. See you?"

"Not if I see you first this next time."

Michael laughed and said, "How did I know you were going to come out with that one?"

"You didn't. Anyway, see you soon."

Michael said, "Yes, see you." He watched DO

Michael smile and look away, and then he closed the tab and stayed online to do some Christmas shopping before logging off.

That evening, Michael went to a carol service at the church with his parents and his brother, James, who wore a white-and-blue-striped shirt under a maroon pullover with blue jeans and black trainers. Michael felt rather uncomfortable when he remembered what he saw last night. James said, "I always like this carol service because it gives me the Christmas spirit. This is what it really is all about."

Michael said, "I know. I like this too."

His mother said, "Yes. It's nice to see so many people. And I like listening to the band playing the different carols." As they talked, the band was warming up with a medley of carols.

His father said, "Yes, they are playing them very well." The service started with "Away in a Manger," which Michael thought was a nice start for the children who were there. He looked at the lovely nativity in the corner as he was singing, which gave the song some meaning. They then sang "Silent Night". The minister said the prayers. After that, they sang some more carols and listened to Bible readings about Mary and Joseph entering Bethlehem and finding that they had to stay in a stable because there was no room at the inn. There was a short sermon followed by more carols. The service finished with "Oh, Come, All Ye Faithful," sung in harmony.

After the service, they went to the family hall to have a cup of tea and some mince pie. James smiled and said, "That was really good. I enjoyed it."

Michael said, "Yes. It was a nice service." He was thinking about how well the service represented the true meaning of Christmas.

John Anderson, who was an elderly gentleman that Michael knew fairly well at the church, approached them and said, "Hello. How are you? I'm pleased you all came. This is always a nice family occasion."

Michael's father said, "Yes. I like coming to this, and thanks. I'm OK. How are you, John?"

"I'm fine. I'm looking forward to the break this Christmas."

Michael's father said, "Yes, me too. I'll be retiring next year." Michael thought about his father's career as a life Insurance broker and accountant.

His mother said, "I'll just have a word with Margaret, now I see that she's better after that cold."

John said, "OK. She's just over there."

His mother said, "Thanks." She walked over to join her friend.

Michael and James chatted with a few of the others whilst they ate their mince pie. And when their parents had finished talking with some of the people they knew, they all went outside together. A golden Labrador puppy approached Michael and James, smelling them. He seemed to hesitate as if wondering whether to smell them both again. The puppy looked at Michael and ran off. James smiled and said, "Well, he seemed to take more of an interest in you than me, Mike. Have you put on some special deodorant or something?"

Michael laughed and said, "Not that I know of. I don't usually have that effect on dogs. Cats probably, but not dogs." Michael was very fond of cats because he'd always had them as pets when he lived at home. They'd never had a dog as a pet because dogs require too much looking after. Because Michael lived in a flat now, though, he couldn't have any pets. He remembered the golden Labrador that he had seen in the DO program walking about. He had thought it was a stray. He thought, *This one couldn't be that one by any chance, could it? That one I saw back then didn't seem to be in the other universe, unless of course it was there a little earlier or a little later like that elderly man I saw.*

James smiled and continued, "Well, you never know."

His father said, "Well, I've always thought about having a golden Labrador. From what I've heard people say, they are lovely dogs."

His mother said, "I like them too. A few of my friends have had them." Michael and James then went to spend the rest of the evening with their parents. Michael went back home to his flat before it got too late.

Two days later, at Tuesday lunchtime when Michael was walking around the shops in town trying to complete his Christmas shopping, he saw Sarah looking at DVDs in MVS. He felt that he didn't want to invade her privacy because he wanted to buy what was necessary. Besides, he was wary of her. She was one of the bigger cheeses in the firm, as head of the purchasing department. He thought to himself, *I certainly don't want that clever and technical blue stocking to criticize my taste in films and music. The way she talks so confidently sometimes, I wouldn't last the first round.* He believed that any lady who was the head of a department could be a stern battle-ax of a woman and somebody not to mess with. He thought, *I'm sure that Melanie could have it bad sometimes, working for her.* He kept his distance from her, and when he saw her gradually moving near to where he was, he quickly picked up the DVDs that he wanted and went to the CD section to pick up what he required there. When he'd gathered those and was waiting in the queue, she tapped him on his left shoulder and said, "Hi, Michael. I can see that you've been quite busy, and I can tell you knew what you wanted. Anyway, how are you?"

He was rather surprised that she had wanted to speak to him. Being in awe of her, he tried to cover up his nervousness as best as he could, but he still answered her rather nervously, saying, "I'm fine. How are you?" He didn't want to become too friendly.

She looked straight at him, smiled, and replied, "I'm all right." She sounded a little nervous herself. She then gulped a little and went silent for a few seconds before she said, "Well, it looks that I, like you, am doing some last-minute Christmas shopping. I've just bought some of these." She showed him a boxed set of John Wayne and Doc Martin DVDs.

Michael thought, *Well, she likes the same things I like. I bought those two recently for myself. I wonder if those are presents that she's bought for family members or friends. Or maybe they are just for herself. I can't really ask that. I don't want to risk getting too nosey and familiar with her.* He carefully said, "Well, they'll make good gifts."

She said, "These are for Melanie. These other two films I've bought are for me and my landlady, whom I know quite well."

Michael thought, *That must be only part of her Christmas shopping because a lady like her must have a large family and certainly a lot of friends.* He said, "Well, those are good. Melanie will probably enjoy them." He didn't want to say too much.

She looked disappointed, and then smiled, saying, "Well, they are good, and Melanie told me she likes them."

He finally reached the checkout feeling relieved because he still felt nervous being with one of the firm's senior workers. He paid for his purchases and, as he walked off, Sarah said, "Michael. We could walk back together if you like."

This made him feel obliged to wait for her near the entrance, thinking, *Why does she want to consort so much?* The situation suddenly making him think of that Michael J. Fox film called *The Secret of My Success*. When she had paid for her goods, she smiled at him and said, "Thanks for waiting. I always like this time of year. It'll be so relaxing, especially this year after I've been so much up to my eyes in everything because of this extra big turnover around Christmas time. By! It's certainly been a big job making sure all those computer orders are correct, so that we order the right stock to replace what's been sold. That is, of course, on top of all the new lines that we've had to order over the last few weeks before Christmas."

Michael wondered why she was sharing all this with him and said, "Yes. Christmas is always the busiest time. By all the invoices I've processed over the last few days, we seem to have done quite well."

She smiled and said, "Yes, I feel that we've done OK too, considering what we've had to replace. Anyway, there's more to do this afternoon because we've had quite a lot more orders this morning."

"Tell me about it. I've had an email from David about them."

She smiled and said, "Well, it's another nose-to-the-grindstone afternoon for us." She chuckled. "It's good, though, that we're doing quite well, isn't it?"

He laughed and thought, *Is it?* And then he replied, "Yes. It definitely keeps us busy." He knew that he'd need about an hour on the bed that evening to recover from his day before he completed the processing of the rest of the invoices at home.

When they arrived back at the office, she smiled and said, "Well, at least we'll have nearly a week off over Christmas to recover. I'll see you later, Michael."

"Yes, I'll be glad for that! I'll see you." He wondered if he'd said too much to her whilst they were walking back. He thought, *Why is she being friendly with me? Oh, it's only her way of being sociable I suppose.* Back in his office, he continued processing the invoices that had come in.

8

CHRISTMAS EVE

Two days later, on Christmas Eve, at about three o'clock in the afternoon, when the office was about to close, Michael decided to finish at a convenient point and then log off. He heard some of the other staff members gathering in the hallway outside the office rooms. When he left his room, Paul said, "Hi, Michael. I hope you have a good Christmas, mate. It's been busier than ever today, and we should all do well after this."

Michael could tell that Paul had had a lot to drink. He smiled and said, "Yes, I reckon so. I'm looking forward to the break at last."

Melanie came up behind them, looking a bit tipsy, and said, "Yes, so am I, and I have to rush to SVM to do some last-minute shopping. I mean MVS! Just joking. I think the drink has got to me somehow."

Paul laughed and said, "You must be seeing things back to front, like us Aussies do over here. Down there, love, the sun appears to rise anticlockwise, and it's strange here when you're used to that."

Melanie smiled and said, "I never thought of that. I suppose that is where that saying comes from, 'going down under', isn't it?"

He said, "Not quite, love. That came about when a bloke looked under a busty blonde sheila's tight, black, PVC miniskirt when she had gone commando." He was smiling, and obviously enjoyed saying this.

David, who was in the vicinity, laughed and said, "You're in cracking form today, Paul. That's one more Aussie joke I'll have to enter in my album."

Paul said, "Yes. That's a Bonza one, mate, and it's certainly great that she had a big enough one to fit in two small bottles of 4X. Nothing's too big to fit mine in, though, sport."

There were hoots of laughter in the hallway, and Michael laughed too, noticing that Melanie was blushing as she looked at him. That made Michael wonder if he'd given her a bad impression of himself by laughing so much at Paul's dirty joke.

David said, "Now, now. That's gone far enough, Paul. There are ladies present here, and I know you've had a skinful."

Paul said, "Not far enough for me, and I'm nowhere near, mate, to what I'm going to have later. This tank is only a quarter full so far." Then he loudly said, "You sheilas on the town tonight, just wait. Paul, here, is going to give you a bonza time."

David said, "OK then. Beware, the girls in town."

Paul said, "Too right. Half this town will be of Australian decent when I've finished."

David said, "Well, whatever. I'll take your word for it. Anyway, I hope you all have a good Christmas. See you all next Wednesday."

Because David was Michael's boss, Michael said to him, "Yes, and you have a good Christmas, David."

David said, "Thanks, Michael, and I'll see you all." And then he left.

Paul smiled and said, "Oh, I'd best be getting off then to prepare myself. You're welcome to come along, Melanie, since you see things the way I do."

She smiled and blushed again, saying, "Well, I'll know where you'll be, if I can make it."

Paul said, "Oh, be a sport. Give me a chance."

She said, "No promises. Maybe I will."

He said, "Oh well, the option's open. You have my mobile number. I'll see you all soon. Have a merry Christmas like me. See you!" He left the office.

Melanie said, "Wow, he's so above himself, isn't he, Michael?"

"Yes, but it's all bravado. He does go too far when he's had a drink, but he's a good laugh."

"Yes, but he'll certainly be way too much for anyone with that much plonk he's talking about. Oh, excuse me. He's got me talking his lingo now."

Michael laughed and said, "Yes, that Aussie stuff can rub off a bit, but I think if he has too much, he'll fall asleep instead."

As they both walked out into the car park, she smiled and said, "Yes, I think that'd be the case and then she wouldn't get any. Oh, excuse me. That just happened to slip out. You can tell that I've had too much to drink now. His humour has rubbed off on to me." She blushed again.

Michael said, "No worries. Now, I'm talking like that, and I've had nothing to drink yet. You'll be wondering now what I might say with a skinful." He was trying to impress her with a little humour.

She laughed and said, "Yes, that does makes me wonder. Anyway, I hope you enjoy your Christmas, Michael."

"Thanks. And I hope you do too, Melanie." He felt that he'd like to see her before work again. He thought, *Well, she's not interested in me now anyway. I can tell by the way she's just said, 'that does makes me wonder' and then changed the subject to wishing me a good Christmas. I suppose it's because I was too amused at Paul's jokes and then said too much about what I'd be like with too much drink. She has therefore fended me off, as she did with Paul. It's been the same with every girl that I've been close to inviting out—one mistake and I'm finished.*

Melanie said, "I'll see you next Wednesday then."

"See you, Melanie." He felt satisfied that they'd ended on good terms, as he saw her walk ahead of him towards town. He thought briefly in the back of his mind about how Melanie could be Susan from that inverse universe by the way she'd referred to MVS as SVM, which, coincidentally, would be how the store name would look in a mirror. He slowly walked into town behind her, feeling that it was best, under the circumstances, to let her get well ahead of him so they wouldn't bump into each other. Anyway, he always liked to have a look around there in the afternoon of Christmas Eve to get a little bit of the spirit as he listened to the usual Christmas pop songs being played and watched the people who'd had a lot to drink.

As he made his way towards the main shopping centre, listening to "Last Christmas" by Wham, he watched three giggly girls, who were in their early twenties, walking into the shopping centre. Two of them were quite pretty—about his height with dark-brown hair. They were both wearing T-shirts and blue jeans. The other one was a small, pretty blonde girl who was clearly dressed to have a good time. They stopped at an open café and asked for some coffee. They had been singing carols in slurred karaoke style. Michael chuckled as he walked by. He could smell their perfume. The small, busty platinum blonde came up to him and said, "Oh, come on, love, join in with us. It's Christmas!" She spoke in quite a doolally way, as she snuggled up to him. She held on to his arm, reminding him of a loafer he'd seen quite frequently and not so long ago. This girl clearly wore no bra under her loose-fitting, colourful, flowery blouse. She wore a faded denim miniskirt over shiny pink Lycra leggings. Her outfit showed off her thin legs and rounded backside.

He was rather taken by surprise as to why this girl, who was so pretty and dressed to please, would want to single him out particularly. He felt really fantastic when she pressed herself against him. Feeling her took his breath away. He could smell a mixture of mint and alcohol on her breath when she just managed to stand up high enough to kiss him on the lips whilst holding him very close. He felt her warm breath go into his mouth, and suddenly felt her very warm tongue brush along his for a moment, which was quite arousing. He withdrew, realizing that this wasn't really the thing to do with a complete stranger. Besides, he wondered if he could catch something. One of the other girls laughed and said, "Ooh, Susie. If we'd brought the mistletoe with us, this would have really meant something."

The girl who'd just kissed him said, "Well, he is … Oh, I'm Susie by the way … What's your name, love?"

Feeling a little hard, he answered, "Oh, it's Michael."

"Well, Michael. I loved that! You're so fit!" Her large, light-blue eyes looked straight into his. Susie then asked, "How come you're on your own on this great occasion? You taste so good, you could have anyone you want."

He blushed and said, "Well, it's how things are I suppose." He became flustered, wondering what to say next.

"Well, come with me and join us. The evening is so young."

One of the other two said, "Yes, Michael. Come with us and enjoy yourself. Let your hair down." It was now getting a little bit too much for him, being picked up by this strange girl. But he suddenly thought, *If Paul were here instead of me, he'd really be in his element. That would be three women with buns in the oven. Hello, Australia!* Michael chuckled at that thought.

Susie said, "I know you're thinking about it. Please come, if only for the fun of it."

He said, "Oh, I'd like to, but I've got something else on." The situation was too much for him now.

She said, "Oh, well, I've tried. You don't know what you're missing. Have a good Christmas, anyway."

They all chuckled, and Michael automatically said, "And I hope all of you have a good time."

As he walked on, he heard one of the others say, "Oh, that's sweet." They giggled at his inadvertently suggestive remark.

He then felt very hot and embarrassed, wondering whether anybody he knew had seen all that had just taken place. He thought, *Well, it seems I could attract a girl, but they were probably just taking the piss anyway. I can tell by how drunk they were.* He quickly came back to reality. He thought, *If Paul had seen me just walk away after an offer like that, he'd have looked totally gone out at me and said, "What a drongo and Pommie idiot you are." It would be terrible if anyone saw me then. I'd never live it down, whoever it was.* He nervously looked around and saw nobody he knew, but he then noticed that very familiar girl that he'd seen at MVS. She was looking in his direction. She was Melanie's height and was wearing that same woollen hat that he'd seen her wear before. He saw her walk into a crowded store, and he curiously followed her but couldn't see her anywhere. He thought, *Well, if that is Susan, she must have disappeared back to her inverse universe to have gone as quickly as that.* He began to feel a little tired, so he looked around a few more shops whilst listening to the continuous Christmas music. As he was walking back to the office car park, he saw the three girls again in the distance with a group of lads who must have just joined them. When he got back to his car, he drove back to his flat.

That evening after his meal, he logged onto his laptop to talk with himself. When the picture appeared, he saw himself. DO Michael said, "Well, we must be diverging even more because I've been waiting for about five minutes to talk to you. Anyway, how are you Michael?"

"I'm OK. Quite a bit happened today, so I thought I'd get in touch again. So how are you at the moment?"

DO Michael replied, "Yes, I'm OK too. You can tell me a bit about it."

"I don't know whether it happened to you, but … how shall I put it? It's rather embarrassing to talk about afterwards, but it was lovely at the time."

"I think I know what you're talking about. It was about those three girls in town I saw, wasn't it?"

"Too right." He chuckled, thinking he sounded like Paul again for the moment.

DO Michael laughed and said, "Yes, I can tell what you've just thought, and you did sound a bit like Paul for a moment then. Anyway, if it's those girls you're referring to, one of them approached me near the entrance to the shopping centre and asked me if I wanted a good time, but as usual I declined. I just hope at that moment that Paul didn't see me because I know he'd slumped into town after work."

Michael thought, *Well, he hasn't had near enough the full works that I've had*. And then he said, "Well, my experience was slightly different to yours then. That blonde girl actually came up to me and kissed me for a bit."

DO Michael looked gobsmacked and said, "Well, Michael, I got nothing like that. Things are quite varied between us. What exactly happened? Oh, excuse me for wanting to pry too much." He smiled.

"Don't worry about it. You are excused because we

are, after all, the same, if not brothers. But it would be funny if I asked James such a question." He laughed and then continued, "Well, it didn't happen there. It happened just outside a café nearby. She approached me, and it went no further than a hug and a kiss. I did feel her tongue for a short moment, but I then withdrew because of what I thought I might catch from her."

DO Michael laughed and said, "Well, I now have some idea of what I've just missed. She did seem naturally attracted to me, and I was just too careful."

Michael, then feeling a bit disgusted with himself for letting it happen even though he'd enjoyed it, said, "Well, she was just onto me, and I went with the flow up to that point. Anyway, again it's randomness and luck I suppose. When she was at the café, she must have been more easy going than where you saw her. Maybe it was due to the coffee she had."

DO Michael said, "That must be it, because I saw a wet brown mark down one of those girl's jeans. They must have had a lot to drink to spill hot coffee over themselves. Well, according to the service you had, you seem to have been in the right place at the right time. You didn't reciprocate by buying her a coffee, did you?" He laughed.

"Well, I should have bought her fifty coffees for what she did for me." He chuckled.

"I think I could have got closer if I'd accepted her offer, not that I would, of course, because of being too careful. I thought they were just having a laugh and everything."

"Well, there was a bit of that in it with me, but it was still a fair experience though."

DO Michael asked, "Is there anything else you want to mention?"

"Yes, there is something. After leaving those girls, I naturally looked around to see if there was anybody I knew who may have seen all that."

"Was there then?"

"Fortunately, no. But I saw that girl we both saw who looked so similar to us. I saw her walk into a shop, so I curiously followed her in there, but then she was nowhere to be seen. If she is Susan, I wonder whether she can keep travelling to and fro from her universe to ours and so on?"

"Well, if she came here, that could be feasible."

"Did you see her too, today?"

"No I didn't, probably because of randomness again. It's clear that we're doing different things at different times now. Oh, and speaking of Susan, I've just remembered something about what Melanie said today. I don't know whether it means anything, but when we were chatting at the office just after finishing work, she referred to MVS as SVM. It may be one of her jokes or just a slip up that means nothing, but it could indicate that she has come from that inverse universe. Did she say that same thing when you were there today?"

Michael said, "Yes, she did, and Paul made a rude joke about it after she'd likened it to going down under."

DO Michael laughed and said, "Yes, the same was said here. Paul joked about a busty blonde going commando in a PVC miniskirt."

"Yes, it was the same here. There's been no difference between us regarding that then. It may mean nothing, but we should consider the possibility that Melanie may be Susan. We should keep our eyes open. Surely, if something similar happens again, it could be proof of something." He thought about that lovely tingling feeling he experienced when he had held Melanie's hands whilst dancing with her at the Christmas party.

DO Michael said, "Yes, we'll watch her with an open mind. Anyway, are you going to the midnight service tonight?"

"Yes. My parents are going, and James is I think, so I'm going to go. By then, I should think town will be empty because of all the usual late-night drinking taking place during the day on Christmas Eve. Last year when we went at about half eleven, it was a little noisy, but when we left at about a quarter to one, there was hardly anyone around."

"Yes, that was the same for me of course. Are you staying over with Mum and Dad after that? I am."

"Yes. I'm going round, too, straight after the midnight service to stay with them."

"I'm wondering how Susan will be celebrating if she happens to be stuck here."

"I've thought about that from time to time. I wouldn't know. It won't be nice for her here, though, if she is and isn't here by choice."

DO Michael said, "Yes, that thought has crossed my mind too, but it's just too remote to even consider. It's nigh to impossible. Anyway, we'll chat soon, and I'll wish you a happy Christmas for me." He smiled.

Michael laughed and said, "Yes, that reminds me of

The two Ronnies, and I think they're on tomorrow, so that should be good."

"Or *The Two Morrows*, meaning you and me!"

Michael laughed and said, "Don't wonder. I've thought about that too. Tomorrow, hey? I always look forward to Christmas."

DO Michael smiled and said, "Anyway, you have a good one. I'll see you."

"Yes, and you too. See you soon, Michael" He saw DO Michael close the tab. Michael closed his tab and logged off. He then wrapped up some more presents whilst watching television. Then he packed his bags for his overnight with his parents. When he was finished, he packed the car and drove to the midnight service.

9

CHRISTMAS DAY

The following morning, Michael's family members opened their presents after breakfast and then they all helped to prepare the Christmas dinner so it would be ready for half past one. They had turkey with stuffing and sausage meat and plenty of sprouts, potatoes, and parsnips. There was a lot of gravy flavoured by the juices from the turkey. With it, they shared bottles of white and red wine and then had some Christmas pudding with nice tasty custard and brandy butter. They finished just in time for the queen's speech at three o'clock and then settled down to watch an afternoon film whilst recovering from the drink.

At a quarter to six, they heard the front doorbell ring. Michael's father said, "Who could this be at this time?" He went to the door to answer it, and Michael heard Sarah's voice.

Michael thought, *Why on earth has she come round now?*

He nervously went to see what was going on. He was nervous because she was office hierarchy!

When she saw him, she smiled and said, "I do apologize, Michael, for disturbing you on this day, but my car has two flat tyres, and it just happened to happen one street away from where you live." She was wearing a smart white blouse and blue trousers with white trainers.

Michael thought, *She looks to be a bit more endowed than I'd thought. Oh, it must be due to the fact that I've had too much to drink.*

His father said, "Oh. You know each other, do you?"

Michael quickly replied, "Yes, this is Sarah Morrison, who works at the same firm that I work at. She is head of our purchasing department."

His father smiled and then shook her hand, saying, "Pleased to meet you, Sarah, and I'm John, Michael's father. I'm a little surprised you came here, though, because I'd have thought you'd have used your mobile to call a breakdown service."

She answered a little tearfully, "Unfortunately I couldn't because I've run the battery right down just now while trying to ring them."

John said, "Well, come in then. You can use our phone. They'll be on a free phone number anyway."

Michael curled up a little bit as his father had just exhibited himself as being so careful with money.

She came into the hall and Michael, still rather apprehensive and nervous about her, said, "Well, you were fortunate to break down near to somebody who knows you. How did it happen exactly?"

She answered, "Well, I was just on my way home

when I saw some glass in the road. When I swerved to avoid it, I hit the curb which punctured my two left tyres. They may be repairable, but I don't know. Anyway, I'll just ring them now, Michael, and see what they say. Then I'll just wait in my car." She picked up the phone and slowly tapped in the phone number and waited for a reply. She told them about what had happened and that her car was an automatic. Then she gave her location.

Michael's mother came into the hall and said, "Hi, and happy Christmas by the way. I'm Mary, Michael's mother, and I overheard you talking out here. It sounds to me that you may have got it sorted." Michael noticed Patch come in from the kitchen and rub up against Sarah's legs. His mother said, "Well, our cat seems to have taken to you. Usually when she sees strangers, she keeps her distance."

Sarah said, "Um. I've sometimes had that effect before on animals."

Michael said, "Well, it seems you are privileged today."

Sarah smiled and said, "Who knows? It's probably because it's Christmas. Oh, I'd better go now and wait in my car because the chap told me that, if I'm not present in the vehicle when they arrive, they'll just leave and go to their next emergency."

Mary said, "Well, they could be a while, couldn't they? You could have a glass of wine before you go, if you like. We've got some left over after our dinner."

Sarah smiled and said, "OK, thanks. That'll be nice, but I must get out there soon."

Mary went to the kitchen, and then James came into the hall and said, "Hi, I'm James, Michael's brother."

Sarah hesitated for a moment before she shook his hand and said, "I'm Sarah Morrison. I work with Michael. I've only popped in because I happened to have a breakdown in your area and I couldn't use my mobile because it's run out of power."

James said, "Well you've done the right thing, then, by knowing Michael." He smiled.

Michael thought, *Well I don't know her all that well, James, as you put it*. He then smiled and said sarcastically, "Yes, we're here to help, especially with it being Christmas." He then thought, *Oh no, I've gone too far with the sarcasm and shown my true feelings about people higher up in work than me.*

Sarah chuckled and looked down at her feet, saying, "I know how you must feel. I want to get away from work, too, on Christmas day." She wiped an eye and said, "Oh, excuse me. I had too much onion with my Christmas dinner."

Michael said, "Yes. Those things can repeat on you."

Sarah smiled and said, "You're telling me. Oh, I'm forgetting the time. I must get to my car."

Mary came in and said, "Not until you've had your drink." She handed Sarah a glass.

Sarah took it in her left hand and quickly drank it. "Thanks very much for that. I'll go to my car now. Thanks for everything, and enjoy the rest of your Christmas. I'll see you, Michael. Thanks." She rushed to leave.

"Yes, see you, and enjoy the rest of yours."

She shouted back, "Yes! Thanks again!" Michael saw her trot back to her car.

His father said, "She's a nice lass, Michael. Haven't you thought about getting to know her better?"

Michael rolled his eyes and thought, *Oh no, not again. He's trying to match me with another girl. This cookie, though, is way, way, way above my league. She earns far more than I do to start with, and she's an office manager for heaven's sake. There's absolutely no way I could ever reach her level. Purchasing— that's a bloody high skill. You have to get everything right with that or you're out on your ear with your P45. If a humourist and salesman like Paul can say, "I can't hack it with her," then what chance do I have?* Michael responded to these thoughts and said to his father, "She has a higher position than I do in the firm, and besides that, there are a few other people at work interested in her."

His father said, "Well, maybe, though she does seem to like you. Give her a try at least and remember, you do all your bit on the accounts for David and do all right, so think about that."

Michael thought, *I want somebody at my own level, or somebody who can look up to me; not somebody who's way ahead of me.*

His father said, "Well I've said my piece now. It's up to you, Michael."

Michael responded, saying, "OK then." He didn't want to go any further into it.

His mother said, "I wonder how long she'll have to wait until they arrive? Why don't you go out, Michael, and make sure she's OK?"

Michael said, "She'll be OK. They'll probably be there by now, or will be at any moment. It's her business really." He still felt that he didn't want to consort any further with work hierarchy.

His father said, "Oh, go on, Michael. At least keep her company until she is sorted."

Michael thought, *Oh, perhaps I should*. It would be a good Christmas gesture to be with her until they arrive. He smiled and said, "OK then. I'll take a couple of glasses and some lemonade because she is driving." He felt better about doing that.

His father smiled and said, "Good. I hope it goes OK."

Michael forced a smile and said, "Please, Dad." He picked up the bottle and glasses before going outside. He thought, *Oh, I'll just go and keep her company. I'll make sure, as I have with every other girl I've met, that I give her no more than a good impression of myself. I'll try and have a few laughs at the same time, of course.* He turned right at the end of the road and then noticed her car. He looked in the road behind it and saw what was left of the fine glass fragments after they had been swept up. He then saw her sitting in the driver's seat with the engine running. She seemed to be looking through her vehicle documents. When he tapped on the window on the passenger side, he saw her smile as she beckoned him to sit in there with her. He noticed the two flat tyres on that side as he got in and said, "I hope you don't mind. I couldn't very well leave you on your own. Do you have any more indication as to when they might arrive?"

"No. I'm afraid not. It's so annoying this had to happen on Christmas day of all days."

"I think I know the feeling. You haven't got anything specific on this evening, have you?"

"No, I was just on my way home."

"Oh." He didn't want to be nosy with this office VIP. He smiled as he sensed the oncoming awkward silence. He felt the tension for both of them and looked at her, noticing that she was deep in thought and trying to think of something to say.

She finally said, "Well, I hope they get here soon. Christmas day I suppose is the worst time for this to happen because all these breakdown services, I should think, will be on a skeleton staff, besides the fact there'll be no repair places open."

"Yes, I suppose that's it. You'd have been all right, though, if it had only been one tyre that had been affected. It's a pity that it had to happen to two of them."

She rolled her eyes and said, "Yes. If it was just the one, I'd have been able to cope. Anyway, one good thing is that we've done very well with the takings this Christmas, even though it will be the spring by the time we get our Christmas bonuses. Oh, excuse me, Michael, I shouldn't be talking shop again especially on this day." She laughed.

He laughed and said, "It don't matter. At least it's more cheerful than having to sort out this annoying breakdown. I bet all your plans have been dashed for this evening. I mean, you'll be missing some good programs like *The two Ronnies* and *Coronation Street*, or anything else that is on."

"Well it don't matter, and it won't have to in the circumstances."

He smiled and said, "Very philosophically put for somebody working in purchases."

She laughed and said, "Hey, you're cheeky. Stop that now, or else I'll claim your bonus for myself."

He thought, *I hope she doesn't mean that. She could be powerful enough to.*

She looked at him and said, "Oh, don't worry. You don't have to take me literally. For the way you've helped me today, you deserve some of mine." Her eyes became a little watery.

He thought, *Surely this breakdown hasn't been as bad as all that, but perhaps she had plans after all, and I don't know what great thing I've done to help. It was my parents who let her use the phone.* He said, "Oh, it's not that bad. You didn't have to be somewhere after all, did you?"

"No, it's just me. I'm just wondering about how much of this day I'll have to wait for these people. You can go if you like. I can see this could be spoiling the rest of your Christmas day."

He thought, *Well, it isn't great.* But he was quite enjoying being with her, even though he thought of her as an office bigwig. He said, "You're all right. I'll stay until they arrive. Oh, I'm forgetting. Let's have a glass of lemonade each."

She looked at the bottle he held up and pursed her lips. Then she smiled and said, "OK then. I'll have some, please." He poured some out for each of them and saw her look into his eyes. He passed her a glass, which she took in her right hand as she said, "Thanks, Michael."

He smiled and said, "Cheers, Sarah. This is to wish you a happy Christmas."

She smiled and said, "Yes, thanks, and the same to you. Happy Christmas, Michael." They touched their glasses.

"Well, at least we still have the Christmas spirit."

"Me likewise!" She turned the heat up slightly and said, "Yes, and at least we can keep warm in here." She glanced in her driving mirror and said, "Well, it looks as though they're here at last. I'll go and see to them." She got out whilst he noticed the flashing amber lights. He gave her a couple of minutes and then got out. She was telling the man about what had happened. He was quite tall at about six foot and looked a bit sweaty as though he'd been quite busy before this. Michael watched him look at the two flat tyres.

The man then looked at her and said, "Well, it's not so great I'm afraid. You'll need two new tyres because they've been damaged too much. There's nothing I can do while I'm here right now, so we may as well leave it here until somebody can tow it away to a place that's open tomorrow where they'll be able to replace your tyres. If it was only one that had gone, I'd have put on your spare and you would have been fixed for the time being."

She said, "OK then. What happens now?"

He said, "Well, I'll take you to the nearest guesthouse and then somebody will contact you there tomorrow when they're ready to pick you up and take you to your car. Because your car is an automatic, it will have to be loaded onto one of our trucks and then be taken to the nearest repair place."

She then looked at Michael and said, "OK then."

The man said, "Fine. We'll go now then. You may as well take what you need from your car and then secure it."

Michael, being in a benevolent mood, said, "If it's OK with my parents, you could stay over with us, Sarah."

Sarah looked at him and smiled, saying, "Thanks, Michael. That'd be great, if your parents are OK with it."

He then thought, *What am I doing? Why did I just say that? What a stupid and silly thing I've gone and done. I've just invited an office VIP bigwig round to spend the rest of Christmas with me and my family. Oh dear, the rest of my Christmas now is going to be ten times more unbearable than being at work. At least when I'm there, I'm working by myself and not having to converse with any boss every five minutes. This'll be like spending infinity with them! Shit! Over the next twenty-four hours I'll have to continuously give a good impression. If I do anything wrong, I may no longer be working for this firm in the new year! This is terrible! I can't even relax or let my hair down now.* Michael sighed deeply to himself and said, "I'll go and ask them, then, Sarah, and come back to tell you."

She said, "Thanks, but you don't have to if you don't want to."

He said, "Oh, you're OK. I will." He felt he had to ask, having offered already. As he walked back to his parents' house, he felt as though she was watching him. He looked back to see that she was, even whilst she was still talking with the man.

When Michael got back to the house and went in, his father asked, "How did she get on then? Have they been repaired?"

He answered, "No. They're damaged too much. They'll have to be replaced tomorrow sometime."

His father said, "I suppose that means they'll arrange some accommodation for her then."

He said, "I hope you don't mind, Dad, but I just

suggested the possibility that she might stay here overnight until she gets sorted."

He said, "Well, you could have come and asked me first. It will be all right though."

His mother said, "Yes, of course it will."

Michael said, "OK. I'll go and tell her that she can come. If I hadn't said anything, she'd have just gone to a guesthouse because she was about to collect some of her things from her car."

His father said, "Oh, you're all right. Just go and tell her."

Michael said, "Oh, I'm going." He left to walk back to where Sarah was.

The man smiled and asked, "Is she all right to stay over then?"

Michael answered, "Yes, it's OK."

The man said, "Well, don't do anything I wouldn't do then." He winked at Michael and said, "She's quite hot. You could be in there, mate."

Michael thought, *Not another lad like Paul. He can't be any relation though because of that broad Yorkshire accent.*

Sarah laughed and said, "Oy, you! I am here you know."

The man said, "Yes, and looking lovely. Anyway, I hope you enjoy the rest of your Christmas. Like I say, Sarah, somebody will ring you on your mobile sometime tomorrow afternoon most likely. Take care, both of you."

Sarah said, "Thanks, Gary, and I hope you enjoy the remainder of yours too."

Michael then said, "Thanks, and happy Christmas."

Gary got into the van and smiled, saying, "Cheers."

Sarah said to Michael, "Nice chap. He's certainly a leg puller." They walked to his parents' house.

Michael looked at her and thought, *Well, she is rather nice looking for an office VIP, even though she looks a bit top heavy and wears too much of that blue eye shadow around those deep brown eyes.* He said, "Well, he seemed to like you."

She smiled and said, "Oh, come off it. He's just one of those blokes who likes to be charming—a bit like Paul."

Michael, knowing that Paul had been serious about her, said, "Well, whatever. You want to give somebody a chance."

She said, "I like to be careful. Anyway, thanks for letting me stay here."

When they went into the house, Mary said, "Well, we're pleased to help you out. It'll be nicer for you to stay here rather than at a guesthouse on Christmas Day."

Sarah said, "Yes, and thanks. It all went rather well really. I thought that, because of the way I hit the curb, those tyres would be a write-off."

Mary said, "Well, that's what can happen. At least you know that something will be done about it. Anyway, we've been waiting for you. We were just going to have some of the turkey leftovers from dinner along with some potatoes and sprouts that are left. Is that all right?"

Sarah said, "Fine. That's what my family always have for the meals that follow the Christmas Day turkey. We ate that until it was all finished."

Mary said, "OK then. It's almost ready now, and we're just in time for *Coronation Street.*"

Sarah smiled and said, "Yes, I keep up with that too. That's what I was wanting to get home for in fact."

Michael thought, *She could've told me that when I'd brought it up with her, but I suppose she was too embarrassed to admit to me that she watched it because of her high reputation at the firm.* He said, "Well, we've been looking forward to it because something always dramatic happens on the program on Christmas Day."

Michael's father came in and said, "Yes. They always hold a lot back until then to keep up the viewing figures. Anyway, I'm pleased you're staying until you get those tyres replaced, Sarah."

Sarah said, "Thanks."

Mary said, "Well, we'll get served up now." Michael's mother and father shared out some of the food onto the plates, which they all carried into the lounge. They watched *Coronation Street* and accompanied the main course with another bottle of wine. As Michael was eating during a very dramatic part of the program, he watched Sarah eat two bites of turkey from her knife.

She noticed he'd seen her, and she blushed slightly, smiled, and said, "Oh, do excuse me. You can't take me anywhere."

James said, "Oh, you're all right. Just let your hair down and relax."

Michael laughed and said, "You're in good company, and I can see you're enjoying yourself." He wondered if he'd said too much just then because of her position at work.

She looked at him whilst flitting her eyes a little and said, "Yes, too much I think by the look of it."

John said, "Oh go on—just indulge for once. Enjoy yourself."

She said, "Thanks." And then she laughed as she licked some gravy off her knife. After their main course, they had some Christmas cake and watched a few more programs on television until just after eleven o'clock when they decided to play a game of brag, using marbles to represent the stake money. John said, "I don't know whether you've played this before, Sarah, but if you haven't, I think you'll enjoy it."

She replied, "Yes, I have played it before with my parents occasionally. I haven't seen them since they moved to Melbourne in Australia last January."

John said, "Well, I should think that that's a nice place to live."

She replied, "Yes. From what they say, it is. They're celebrating this Christmas over there with barbecues, sunbathing, and swimming I should think."

James said, "That sounds great! Imagine it's summer over there at the moment."

Sarah smiled and said, "Yes, tell me about it."

John said, "OK. I think we'll start playing brag now before it gets too late."

Sarah smiled and said, "Yes, I'm looking forward to it." They started with twenty marbles each, and John dealt out five cards to each of them. They each put in one marble to pay for their hands.

Michael picked up his cards and looked at them as he watched, out of the corner of his eye, Sarah fiddle around with hers. He thought, *What's she up to, doing that? She's either got a good hand or is trying too hard to bluff.* He could only make a pair of threes, so he folded to cut his losses, leaving himself with nineteen marbles. Sarah put another marble in, and John said, "I'll raise you all by two."

James and his mother folded, and Sarah put in two more, saying, "I'll continue."

His father put in three marbles and said, "I'll see you then, Sarah." He laid down a king, a queen and jack of hearts running flush.

She smiled and said, "Well, I have a prile of eights." As she showed them, she took her marbles.

John said, "Well done! That was an exceptional hand for only five-card brag. You did well to start with a hand like that, and mine was a rarity! Do you all want to continue with five-card or go higher?"

James answered, "Yes. We could try with seven to give ourselves more likelihood of getting something better than king high."

Mary said, "Why not? You'll be less likely to want to throw your cards in then."

Sarah said, "Let's try that, then, on this next hand."

Michael said, "Yes. I'm quite happy to do that after all I've had." It was Michael's deal, so he dealt out seven cards each and had only a flush. They each put one marble in to start off with, and Sarah immediately started by raising it to two. John folded, and James and Mary both put in two. Michael said, "Oh, I'm folding." Sarah raised it to three. James paused and put three in.

Mary stacked them and said, "Oh, that's enough."

James then put four in and said, "I'll see you, Sarah." When she showed her running flush with the ace, king, and queen of spades, James showed his mixed run of ace, king, and queen. She'd won again!

John said, "Well, that is rare, Sarah, to have two such good hands one after the other."

She smiled and said, "Yes, I could get used to this!" As it was her turn to deal, she asked, "I presume we're continuing with seven-card?"

James said, "Yes, why not?" John nodded. She paused and then dealt quite slowly. James said, "I hope you're not dealing like that on purpose and sharping us all."

She blushed slightly and then smiled, saying, "Of course not. Would I do a thing like that? As you've seen already, I don't need to cheat."

James said, "Ooh, we'll soon see." His father looked at his cards, paused, and put just one marble in. James and Mary did the same. Michael had only a two, three, and four mixed run, so he folded, and so did Sarah. When James raised it to two, John and Mary folded and James said, "Well, you could have continued."

John said, "Not with my hand. I want to remain in the game for some time, if I can." After that, the game continued, and they each won a hand or two. Suddenly, it was midnight.

10

BOXING DAY

After the next deal, Michael, to his surprise, had a running flush with the king, queen, and jack of diamonds. He immediately raised it to two, thinking, *Surely Sarah can't have another good hand at the same time I do. I mean, there's only two running flushes and a prile that can beat this one.* To his relief, Sarah folded and so did his father, but James raised it to three. His mother then threw hers in, and Michael kept it going at three. James kept it going with another three, and so did Michael, until James paid four to see him. Michael then showed his hand, and James threw his in and said, "Well, that's enough to beat mine!" Michael breathed a sigh of relief whilst collecting his marbles.

Sarah said, "Well done, Michael. If only all of you would have gone like that when I'd had one of my good hands."

John said, "Well, I suppose that's the disadvantage

of having a good start. The players are more careful at the beginning of a game when they don't know who they're up against."

Sarah said, "Well, I'm not that great."

John laughed and said, "Well, we're not to know that."

She responded, "Hey, cheeky, you're not supposed to agree with me. I'm your guest here, and you should at least back me up."

John said, "Well, not in this game. This is serious stuff, and I'm here to win."

Sarah said, "Well, there is something to consider called sportsmanship, and just taking part."

Michael was enjoying their banter, thinking she was a feisty one.

John said, "That's just it. It's important to take part in order to win."

Sarah said, "Wow, you have an answer for everything." She smiled.

John laughed and said, "Too right. It comes with being in business, and I can see that a little of it has rubbed off on to you, by what you do."

Sarah answered, "Yes, and I see I could do a lot better... John."

Michael felt that he wanted to chip in and said, "I don't think so, Sarah. You seem to be doing all right so far."

Sarah said, "Thanks, Michael. At least I have some support around here."

John smiled and said, "Well, that's very cosy then. We'll continue playing."

Sarah looked at Michael and caught his eye. Michael thought, *He still seems to be trying to get us together. I don't know why because it will never happen. I'm the underling here, and surely since she is so feisty, she'll be interested in somebody even higher up the ladder than herself, such as one of those top directors at the firm.*

They continued playing the seven-card game, and James was the first to be out because of what he'd already lost to Michael. James had told them that he had had a running flush then, which would normally have been a winning hand. It happened because Sarah had the winning hand with a prile of tens when all those who were still in had to show their hands as soon as James had no marbles left. He said, "Oh, well, I tried, and it could have worked. I should have been back in the game."

Sarah said, "Yes. It was worth a try if your hand wasn't far behind mine."

James laughed and said, "OK, OK … I'll go and put some tea on now."

John said, "Yes thanks. That'll be nice." After that, the game kept going back and forth. When it was nearly one o'clock, they counted up. Sarah had the most marbles. Michael was in second place, and John was in third.

They then discussed the sleeping arrangements. Sarah would sleep in the guest room next to Michael's original room, where he would be sleeping. John said, "Well, I'm ready for my bed. This has been great fun, and I hope you've all enjoyed it. I'll see you all in the morning, and goodnight, Sarah."

Sarah said, "Thanks. Goodnight, John."

Michael said, "Oh, I think I'll head off as well. I'll see you all in the morning. Goodnight all, and goodnight, Sarah. I hope you enjoyed it here, Sarah."

Sarah said, "Thanks. I enjoyed the company. I'll see you in the morning, Michael. Goodnight."

Michael went upstairs to his original room. Just after he'd changed into his pyjamas, he heard a girl shouting outside, "Merry Christmas, Michael, James, and all!" She sounded very much like Melanie. He went to look through the window and saw nobody outside. He thought, *I wonder if that is Melanie, who is really Susan?*

About ten seconds later, he heard a knock on his door and heard Sarah say, "Michael. Did you hear that?"

He answered, "Yes, I did. We do get some rowdy people around here occasionally."

She said, "Well, whoever it was, they seemed to be talking to you."

He said, "Yes, it sounded a bit like that. Oh, it's just someone having some fun I suppose."

She said, "Oh, well, I'll see you in the morning. Goodnight, Michael."

He said, "Yes, see you. Goodnight, Sarah." He heard her walk back into the guestroom. Later on during the night, he woke up and felt curious about seeing Susan again. He selected the origin date for her on the DO program and saw her sleeping in bed in his room. He thought of Sarah next door to him and then closed the tab, as he imagined her suddenly bursting into the room whilst he was watching the screen. He then selected the Inverse option, and when the picture came on after the usual eight minutes, he could see that there was nobody in the mirror-image room of where he was. He thought, *Well, she's not here. Maybe she has gone away somewhere, such as where I am now.* He then closed the tab and logged off before going back to bed.

The following morning after breakfast, they all played Monopoly except for Michael's mother, who decided to prepare the lunch. After setting up the game and dividing out the money, James, as usual, chose the car whilst Michael had the ship. Sarah selected to play with the iron, and his father, the boot. When they shook the dice to see who would go first, James got the highest total of eleven, so he started. Sarah said, "I'm wondering whether we could start buying sites immediately, since I might not be here too long this afternoon if they ring me."

John said, "I don't see why not. It'll certainly move the game on faster."

James said, "I'd quite like that too, since we'll get into it quicker." He shook a double four to land on Euston Road. He bought it and took another move, having got the double, and then landed on Vine Street. He smiled and said, "Oh, I'll buy that as well."

Sarah said, "No doubt you will. You've had a good start, James."

Michael said, "Yes, he's been very lucky at this game before."

Sarah laughed and said, "You're probably right according to by what I've already seen."

John said, "Well, I'll see what I can do then." It was his turn. He landed on Pentonville Road and bought it, which made Michael feel better because now James couldn't immediately acquire all the blue sites. Sarah took her turn and got twelve, enabling her to buy the electric company. She shook the dice again and landed on Marlborough Street. James shook his head as she bought it because that stopped him gaining the full group of the orange sites. When it was Michael's turn, he landed on Pall Mall and bought it.

A little later, when Sarah landed on Mayfair just before she first reached Go, she giggled into her hand and then bought it. Michael thought, *What's so funny? Does she have to laugh so much when she's doing so well, especially when she's bought the key site on the board? Yes, she's good at purchasing, but she certainly doesn't need that amount of luck to go with it.*

Sarah said, "Oh, excuse me, I didn't expect to land on that one so soon and for the first time round."

Michael said, "Well you did, and you've got four good sites now."

She said, "Well, the game's only just started, and there's plenty of time for you, Michael."

He responded, "I hope so."

The next time it was James's move, he landed on Bond Street, and Sarah chuckled a little as he bought it.

Michael thought, *What's up with her? She's certainly enjoying herself very much ... having the giggles and all. Winning must be so important to her. I suppose it goes with the job.*

A little later, when she shook a seven to land on Community Chest, she picked up the card that said, "You have won second prize in a beauty contest. Collect £10." She laughed and said, "It should surely be worth more than that nowadays."

Having had too much to drink in the last hour, James laughed and said, "Well, with your beautiful looks and your lovely red hair and big … you should certainly have the first prize."

She blushed slightly whilst laughing and said, "Wow. You are getting quite personal, James, and thanks for that."

Michael looked at her. He saw her smiling at him, and he thought, *Well, she would look a lot better with less of that make-up on and if she wasn't so oversized, besides being over confident and too perfect.* And then he said the first thing that came into his head, which was, "Well, whatever turns you on, James."

James responded, blushing slightly, "Well, she is very hot and stunning."

Sarah said loudly, "Oh, excuse me, you two. I am still here you know." Then she quietened down whilst saying, "And, James, you are beginning to sound just like Paul from work." She turned to Michael and smiled, saying, "You know who I mean, don't you Michael?"

Michael laughed and answered, "Yes, and you don't have to tell me too much about him. I know what he can be like."

She said, "Well, at least you've got some idea about him then."

John said, "Now you're making me a little curious about some of your work colleagues."

Michael said, "Paul is a typical chap from Sidney, Australia, who is proud to be such and loves a joke. He's told us many a story or two, about things down under."

Sarah laughed and said, "You're not the only one then, Michael?"

He responded, "No. He likes to tell everyone a little something about it." He smiled.

John said, "Anyway, here's your ten pounds for coming second with such flair." He laughed.

She laughed and said, "Thanks, I'm honoured. I should be first. I won't bother doing a speech because if I did, we would never finish this game."

Michael smiled and said, "Probably not, with the amount you'd have to say." He'd let his tongue run away with him again because of how he felt about her over perfection and confidence.

She said, "Well, it's a good job that I'm not going to then." She looked at him and then laughed when she saw him smile.

They then continued playing, and when Sarah landed on the square that advised: "Go to jail. Move directly to jail. Do not pass Go. Do not collect £200," James said, "You're in my jurisdiction now since I'm a policeman."

She chuckled and said, "Oh, is that so? I'd best be careful then."

James said, "Yes, you'd better. I'll be watching you." He smiled whilst clearly admiring her.

Michael thought, *Well, if my brother is serious about her, he'll have a handful there, considering that a few of the lads at work are also interested in her.*

After a few more rounds of the board when nearly everything had been bought, except for some unwanted sites because they did not complete a full site for anybody, Sarah landed on Park Lane. She chuckled and then mortgaged two of her cheaper sites to buy it, saying, "That's a stroke of luck for me after all of you missed it."

John said, "Well, Sarah, you're the only one now who can possibly win this game. We'll have to barter with each other now if anyone else is going to have a chance."

Sarah said, "Oh, do you have to? We could continue as we are." She smiled.

Michael said, "Yes, and it'd be your game. I think we should negotiate now whilst we still have a chance, before she accumulates more money and puts houses on each of those full sites."

James said, "OK, what shall we suggest?"

John said, "Well, I have Leicester Square and Piccadilly, and I could exchange my Old Kent Road and Liverpool Street Station for your Coventry Street."

James said, "That would give me only the two brown sites and all the stations. You would have all the yellows then, which charge much more rent."

John said, "Yes, but you would have six complete sites once you put hotels for very little cost on Old Kent Road and Whitechapel, with the stations needing no development. It will cost me £150 per house on my yellow sites."

James thought for a bit and said, "OK then. At least I'll have six full sites and only the danger of paying street repairs on two hotels." They swapped sites and continued the game. Michael could see that he was out of the game because he didn't really have anything to barter with compared to what the others had. Just before they broke off for dinner, Michael landed on his father's Coventry Street and was out, after having previously landed on Sarah's Park Lane. At that point, she paid what was required to put a hotel on each of her dark-blue sites, and then it was dinner time.

They had some more cold turkey with the remainder of the stuffing and sausage meat, with some warm potatoes and cabbage and gravy, followed by Christmas pudding. They watched a film and talked a little bit about the news and politics whilst eating. After the meal, they continued with the game, and shortly after that, James was out once he'd landed on Mayfair, enabling Sarah to put hotels on her dark blue sites. A few moves later, she landed on Vine Street, which was originally owned by James. She bought it so she could control all the orange sites, and before her next move, she bought as many houses as she could afford to develop those sites. A few moves after that, she landed on a Community Chest square and picked the card saying, "Pay a £10 fine or take a chance." She smiled and said, "Oh, I'll pay the £10 fine."

John said, "Oh, go on, take a chance. You may have won a hundred pounds in a crossword competition or something."

Sarah said, "No. I can't risk it with those five built-up sites that I have." She paid the fine.

When John was the next one to land on Chance, he picked out the card saying, "Go to jail. Move directly to jail. Do not pass go. Do not collect £200." This pleased him. He smiled and said, "Well at least I'm out of danger for a little longer, Sarah. That could have saved you for a bit."

She said, "Well it was worth paying that ten pounds, since there are two street repairs cards in the Chance deck." He stayed in jail until his second move, when he shook a double four and then sighed, noticing that he would land on Marlborough Street with three houses on it, which gave her the upper hand against him when he had to mortgage some of his houses. She then put hotels on all her orange sites. After the breakdown company had rang her just ten minutes later, John said, "I'll concede. I only have to land once more on any one of your properties and it'll be over."

She said, "OK. It's been a good game, and any one of us could have got the run of the dice."

John said, "Yes, it's been fun, though. The game could have worked out differently if we hadn't landed so often on your sites, enabling you to develop them quickly."

She said, "Yes. Anyway, it's been nice to stay with you, and I hope you enjoy the rest of your Christmas."

James said, "Yes, it has been nice seeing you."

Mary said, "We've enjoyed your company. You're welcome to come again."

Michael cringed a little at that, again because of her position at the office and her air of sophistication. He said, "Yes, it's been nice having you. I hope it goes OK with the tyres, and I'll see you next week."

She looked happy but a bit tearful and said, "Well, I've enjoyed it—the banter and everything. All being well, I'll see you soon." She picked up her things and said, "Bye for now. See you, Michael."

Michael said, "Yes. I'll see you next week, Sarah."

John said, "See you probably sometime. All the best

with the repairs, and enjoy the rest of your Christmas." They all waved as she walked to her car.

Michael thought, *Phew! I can now relax, unwind, and enjoy the rest of Boxing Day.* He'd seen the last of one of the office hierarchy until next Wednesday.

John said, "Well, she is a nice lass, and I've enjoyed the time she's stayed with us."

Mary said, "Yes, and I'm sure I remember hearing her voice before. Oh, yes, last January or February a woman came round to ask directions to our local library. That person's voice sounded very similar to Sarah's. It wasn't her though because she was thinner and had matted, dark-brown hair. Also, she looked unwashed and in a bit of a state. I felt worried about her, but I was concerned about what she could be up to, looking like that. She looked so much like you, Michael, that she could have almost been your identical twin. I thought I'd mention it, now that I've just remembered it."

James said, "I noticed some very familiar things about Sarah too. Some of her mannerisms were also like yours, Michael. I wonder if she purposely put on that act to flirt with you." He smiled.

Michael thought, *I also could see similarities to myself, and now I think about it, a lot of the things that she said in response to me are things that I could have thought of. This just can't be so because we are complete opposites; she is in a top job, and I'm just an office boy. I'm not going to let my imagination run away with me about her because she is too good at everything and way above my league.* He said, "Well, I don't know how you can think that. She has a top position at the firm I work for, and we're nowhere near alike."

John said, "Well, we're only telling you about what we noticed."

James said, "Yes, and I notice a fair amount of things in my job. She's worth a thought, Michael, at least, and I think she likes you." He smiled.

Michael said, "OK then. I'll have a think about it." He said it just to get off the ridiculous subject—that he would ever consider her in that way.

Mary said, "Well, good. We'll put on another pot of tea shall we, before the late afternoon film?"

John said, "Yes, I'd like that."

Michael said, "That'll be fine." He was looking forward to the rest of the day because, now that Sarah had gone, he could relax. He thought, *I think I gave her a good impression of myself except when I occasionally and stupidly let my tongue slip. I hope things will be all right at work after all this.* He had a couple of glasses of red wine to calm his nerves, knowing that he had to limit himself because he'd be going home later on. He then relaxed and enjoyed the film.

Later on, just after eleven o'clock that night, after he'd arrived home and packed his things away, he logged on to the DO software to speak to his other self. He was the first one on, and he waited for ten minutes before DO Michael saw him on the screen and they started talking.

DO Michael smiled and said, "Hi, Michael, how are you? Did you have a good Christmas?"

"Yes, some of it was nice. I spent it with my parents as I'd planned to, and then, believe it or not, Sarah Morrison turned up yesterday after having had two flat tyres. She stayed over with us until the middle of this afternoon."

"Yes, the same happened with me. We played brag last night and Monopoly this morning. I didn't feel great about it, as probably you didn't, but we had a few laughs, perhaps too many considering where she is in the firm."

"Yes, me too. I felt that I had to be on my best behaviour, but did let some things slip a little due to the drink. Anyway, I'm curious. How did those two games finish for you?"

"Well, Dad won the brag game with the most marbles, and Sarah came second. I came in third. Dad had some good hands, though, and Sarah seemed to bluff quite well. Did it work out like that for you?"

Michael answered, "No, it was quite different. Sarah won in our game, and I came second. That just proves things are random, and you can't bet on anything with certainty. In Monopoly, Sarah won because she had Mayfair and Park Lane and all the orange sites."

DO Michael said, "Well that was different, too, then. James won that game, and I came second. He won by owning the pink and orange sites all on one side of the board. I had Mayfair and Park Lane and couldn't develop them fast enough because I landed on his sites too many times, and Sarah and Dad had no full sites at all. That also shows you just how random things are."

Michael said, "Yes, it does. The thing that Mum said about this girl having brown hair, though, leads me to still believe that she could be Melanie, if she's here as Susan."

"Me too, because my Mum said that she was in a very poor-looking state with a bad cold. That was probably why her voice sounded deeper, like Sarah's then."

Michael thought again about the ease with which she could catch things, if she had come from an inverse universe and said, "Well that's it, then. Melanie must be Susan because my mum didn't mention any of those exact details."

DO Michael said, "Well it now looks pretty certain, doesn't it, that Melanie is the one—*pretty* being the apt word."

Michael laughed and said, "Too true. Have you had a bit to drink since you got back?"

"Yes, I have."

Michael laughed and said, "I thought so."

DO Michael laughed and said, "Yes. I know what you mean. It's because of my comment about Melanie. I had to have something heavy after spending most of these last two days around Sarah."

"Me too. I haven't had that much yet. There is another thing that I should mention that also backs up my hunch that it's Melanie. I heard a girl shouting out 'Happy Christmas Michael, James, and all' outside our mum and dad's house that sounded so much like her."

"Yes, I heard exactly that same thing, and so did Sarah. She knocked on my door and asked me about it. It does back up our idea."

"Yes. She knocked at my door too, after having heard it. Anyway, I'm going to put a comedy on shortly and then have something to drink myself."

DO Michael said, "I've thought about that, and I'm going to do the same. Anyway, I'll speak to you soon, Michael. See you."

Michael said, "Yes, see you soon." They both closed the tab and then logged off to watch the late-night film.

11

BETWEEN CHRISTMAS
AND THE NEW YEAR

During that night, Michael woke up feeling a little aroused after having a dream about Sarah. He thought, *How could I think of such a perfect and superior girl in that way?* He decided to have another look at Susan, and when the picture appeared on the screen, he saw her kneeling down wearing what looked to be white silk underwear. She breathed heavily whilst feeling herself, and then he heard a slight noise. She continued until she seemed to climax. Then she took off the underwear, revealing all of herself, which again took his breath away and aroused him further. He could see that she was a little sweaty where she had worn the bra and briefs. She went for a shower. He felt that he had invaded her privacy again.

At that point, he heard somebody shout out "Hi,

Michael", which made him jump because he was still flustered. He went to look out of his lounge window, which was where the sound seemed to have come from. As he peered through the curtains, he saw the same girl he'd seen before. She was still wearing the woollen hat. She waved to him with her left hand and then walked off. He thought, *Well, she's playing games with me. I think I'll start and have a bit of fun with her too, but subtly, bearing in mind that she could have come here accidently, considering the way Mum described the state she was in.* He thought of her as Melanie.

He went back to his laptop and couldn't help but watch Susan in the shower for a short moment. When he saw that she had a dark blue bath towel wrapped around her, he went close up to where she was on the screen and put his right hand where her left shoulder would be, as a kind of greeting. There was nothing there, and as he wondered why he had done that, she walked straight through where he was on the screen, and that made him wonder if she could have caught some particle bombardment, at the point of walking through where his laptop was. He thought, *Well, it should be no different to when I hold a mobile phone close to my ear or when somebody wears a tracking device.* He respected her privacy while she dried herself and put on a cotton nightdress before going back to bed. He closed the tab, logged off, and then went for some sleep, but with all his mixed thoughts and everything, he just couldn't sleep for the next few hours.

The following day, on Monday afternoon, just before meeting Andrew to play snooker, Michael went into town to look at the bargains and spend some of the

Christmas money he had been given. He saw Melanie go into a supermarket and followed her. She was wearing a white raincoat with a black-and-white-patterned skirt over her blue Lycra leggings with white trainers. He noticed that she seemed to be naturally right handed by the way she was putting some tins into her trolley. He thought, *She's had enough time to practice with what is her left hand since last January. Putting myself in her shoes, I would have done the same because of the differences any doctor would find in my anatomy.* He kept his distance because he didn't really feel ready to talk to her just yet. He felt that he needed more time to work out his strategy of detection, which suddenly made him think about Columbo and then some hapless detectives such as Inspector Clouseau and Johnny English. He saw her go to the till and fetch out her purse with her right hand. She paid by entering the PIN number with the same hand. He then quickly left the store before she could see him. He made his way towards MVS to look at some cut-price DVDs and CDs. As he was looking around the store, he thought, *There surely must be a more definite way to find out, other than being left handed. I can surely think of something before too long. I have to remember that, if she is here, she'll obviously be well ahead of me, having been in this predicament for so long, possibly since last January. Besides that, she'll think like me too.*

At that moment, he felt somebody tap on his right shoulder. He looked behind him, and to his surprise it was Melanie. She smiled and said, "Hi, Michael. How are you? I saw you in front of me, so I thought I'd head out this way, since I like to look at DVDs and CDs here. Did you enjoy your Christmas?"

Michael, who was rather shocked at being caught off guard, answered, "Yes, I'm fine, and I had a good Christmas. Did you?"

She replied, "Yes. I've been given quite a lot of money to spend from friends and relatives. Now's the time with all these sales."

Michael, wanting to pull her leg a bit, said, "Well, you should be all right with that, as you work in purchases."

She looked straight at him whilst her eyes were flitting between his and she giggled, saying, "Why you? That's quite funny. You're on reasonable form today."

He caught a slight smell of alcohol on her breath, besides her perfume. He said, "Yes, I try to be. I always enjoy comedy."

She said, "So do I. It'll be interesting, now I'm here, to see what's on offer. I tend to price the things in the shops first, and then I try online later for better bargains."

He said, "I often do the same, but I have some vouchers to spend here, so I'm curious as to what there is here now."

She said, "OK. On the way in, I noticed there were a lot of DVD boxed sets for knockdown prices."

He said, "Thanks. That sounds interesting. I'll take a look." They looked over the sale items, and Michael saw a boxed set of films that he noticed were cheaper than they were online, especially considering the cost of postage and handling.

He picked them out, and Melanie said, "Oh, I'll have one of those too. I've seen nothing cheaper than that."

That made him think, *She is the one. Melanie has to be Susan because, besides our great similarity in looks, we seem to think the same way and say similar things. I'll bide my time and then subtly test her out when an opportunity arises.* He said, "Yes. We'd better buy these quickly before they sell like hot cakes."

She smiled and said, "And I'll have this one too."

He said, "You've done well there. I bought that online a couple of weeks ago for a bit more."

She said, "Well, you should have been in purchases like me. I had an inkling that this would be cheaper after Christmas."

He smiled and said, "Well done. I'll know who to ask whenever I want to price the market before I think about buying something." They went to the counter to pay, Michael observing again that she did everything with her right hand.

They left the shop and she said, "I think I fancy a drink. Would you like one as well, Michael?"

He thought, *This is too soon. I need time to think out my strategy. I don't want to get too familiar with her right now and do something silly, which might blow my cover or spoil things. She's a lovely lass, and I want to just keep up with giving her a good impression, especially since she works alongside the formidable Sarah, who is her boss.* He couldn't help but say, "Yes, I'll join you. I could do with one." But he thought, *Now I'm going to have to pad this one out and very well, if possible. There must be no awkward silences here.*

She smiled and looked straight into his eyes and said, "Thanks, I'd like that. Shall we go to that café over there?" She pointed it out.

He answered, "Yes, that'll be OK." They walked in and he said, "Well, I'm going to have a lemonade. Do you want one?" He wondered if she'd ask for an orange drink of some kind, knowing that it would taste like lemon if she was him from an inverse universe. He preferred lemonade to orangeade.

She answered, "I'll have a tango, I think, please."

This made him think, *Bingo! That's just proved it. First test affirmative that she is Susan.* He chuckled and said, "OK, I'll buy them."

She said, "Thanks." She went to sit down after taking her coat off. She was wearing a plain, long-sleeved blue blouse.

After he bought the drinks and sat down with her, he said, "Well, Sarah came unexpectedly on Christmas Day. She happened to have scraped two of her tyres against the curb, having avoided some glass in the road. We let her stay the night since she couldn't get them replaced until the next day."

Melanie said, "Well, that was a nice gesture. It must have been nicer for her to stay with somebody she knows rather than in a hotel overnight."

He said, "Well, I hardly knew her anyway then, and I still don't really. We played brag later that evening and Monopoly the following morning, just before they replaced them."

Melanie said, "That must have been enjoyable."

He said, "Yes, I enjoyed it, and we had a few laughs. My mother and father seemed to like her, and so did my brother, James." He almost said that his parents had seemed keen to want him to get to know her. He certainly didn't want to admit that because that could spoil his detection ploy!

She smiled and said, "Well, she likes to give a good impression. I can see that by the way she says certain things."

This stirred his attention, especially after his folks had said how similar they were. Again he thought, *How can I be so similar to such a perfectionist and somebody who is so sophisticated and in control, and even a boss?* He said, "I got that impression, too, about her. She's not all that bad, though, and I had to laugh. Our James actually had a bit too much to drink whilst we played Monopoly and almost came out with the 'big word' when he passed a rather nice comment about her. You know ..."

She giggled loudly and said, "I could just imagine what her reaction would be to that. She didn't blush did she by any chance?"

He answered, "She actually did, and I was amused." He almost told her he'd nearly wet himself," but he said, "Yes. She said loudly, 'I am here you know.'"

Melanie laughed and said, "Yes, I can just imagine her saying that. It's one of her standard lines when Paul has got close to the knuckle about her red hair and cleavage, excuse the expression. I've had to laugh at how he goes on at her, as though she could be his fancy piece. It's so hilarious."

Michael said, "I can just imagine it myself. She takes it well." He felt a bit aroused then, at how she may secretly feel about those comments. He continued to say, "Yes. She actually did comment then about James being like Aussie Paul."

She laughed and said, "Really. She gave a good account of herself then as she always tends to do! Pardon the pun."

He said, "Yes, she's OK." As he finished his drink, he said, "I have to be going in a moment because I agreed to meet Andrew at about a quarter to four to play snooker."

She said, "That's fine. I'm going to have a meal with Julie Smith later. I've known her as a school friend for a long time."

He said, "I hope you enjoy it."

She said, "OK, and I hope your game of snooker goes well and you win. How was it with brag and Monopoly?"

He smiled and answered, "Well, you can guess. She won at both of them."

"Yes, I thought she more than likely would."

He thought about the alternative outcome in the other universe and said, "Yes, I could tell that she was pleased, but her comment about the Monopoly was admirable. She said that any of us could have won; it's a lot due to the dice. She just happened to have got Mayfair and Park Lane to start off with before anybody else had anything, and when James was out, she acquired all the orange sites and beat my dad."

"Yes, that'll be just like her. I know that not much will get past her in that game."

"Well, I suppose that goes with her job of purchasing."

She smiled and said, "Yes, tell me about it."

"Anyway, nice chatting. I'll see you soon, Melanie."

"Yes. See you, Michael." They waved to each other as he left to go and see Andrew.

Two days later, on Wednesday morning, when Michael arrived at the office, he saw Melanie and Sarah talking in the hallway. Sarah said to Michael, "Thanks for having me stay. I really did enjoy it."

Michael, determined to be on his best behaviour with Sarah due to his previous slipups, said, "You're welcome. I enjoyed it too. Did it go smoothly, with replacing your tyres?"

She replied, "Yes. It was all sorted out after about half an hour, and then I went home and watched some films."

Melanie said, "Well, it sounds like you both enjoyed yourselves."

Michael said, "Yes, it was good. Anyway, I'd best get started on all the work that I have to do. There's quite a backlog after we've been away for these last few days. As usual, there'll be a lot to account for with all the after Christmas sales."

Sarah smiled and said, "Yes, you're telling me. It's nose to the grindstone until New Year's Eve tomorrow. I just hope everything goes OK today. See you later, Michael." She winked at him.

He thought, *Why did she do that?* He said, "Yes, Sarah, I hope so, and I'll see you, Melanie." He smiled at her and then at Sarah, who smiled back at him.

Melanie grinned and said, "Yes. See you Michael."

"Yes, see you." Then went into his office to start the day's work.

The following day at lunchtime, when they'd finished work and Michael had left his office, he saw Paul chatting with Melanie and Sarah in the hallway. They were all laughing. Paul said, "Hi, Michael. I've been trying to get Sarah to come over to my place this evening just before we hit the town and paint it red. Oh, pardon the expression." He pointed at her hair.

She smiled and said, "Oh, very droll, Paul."

He said, "Yes, that was a bonza one, love." Michael could see that Paul was already half tanked up before the afternoon. He could tell by the way Paul was looking at Sarah's chest.

She shrugged her shoulders and said, "Do you mind not being so obvious and doing that?" She blushed a little.

He laughed and said, "I can't help myself. It's just something you bring out in me, Sarah. You are what my dreams are made of. Please come later and give me a chance. I'll behave myself. It is, after all New Year's, and I'm missing the warmth, though not right now." He smiled whilst looking goggle eyed at her.

She said, "Oh, you're just incorrigible. I'm making no promises."

He smiled and said, "Fine. I'll take that as a yes then, Sarah." He turned to Melanie and said, "Yes, and you can join us if you like. The more the merrier, you know what I mean." He laughed.

Michael smiled and said, "Yes, and the other half of the girls in town too probably."

Paul said, "Yes, mate, you've got it, and I'm going to get a load of it from the other half of the girls that I didn't get acquainted with last Thursday."

Sarah said, "Well, that'll be enough for you then. You won't need me."

He said, "I will, to break myself in."

She said, "Well, you're not with me, Mr. Studley." She mentioned the name of a street in the red-light area, to say, "Wherever that is." She forced a laugh.

He said, "OK, then, and you'll know where I'll be later when you change your mind. Bring Melanie along with you, Sarah, and I'll see you soon. I'm now going to hit the town to get the first bite at the cherry. See you, sports. Happy New Year's, if I'm too inebriated to see you later." He then left.

Sarah looked wide eyed and still a little red faced, but laughed and said, "Wow! He's absolutely full of that Aussie blarney, isn't he?"

Melanie answered, "Yes, with the drink and everything."

Michael said, "Well, he can't get a lot more explicit than that, and I can tell that, if he drinks much more, he'll only be fit to sleep, and then it won't be hello, Australia." He laughed.

Sarah chuckled and said, "Please, Michael. Don't let it rub off onto you."

He laughed and said, "Sometimes I can't help it. He certainly gets the mind going."

Sarah asked, "Are you doing anything special this evening, Michael, to see the New Year in?"

He answered, "No, not really. I'm going to my parents' later, and my friend Andrew Thomas will be joining us. Are you two doing anything special?" He felt a little nervous asking them that.

Melanie answered, "Well, I'm meeting a group of friends later in the afternoon, and then I'm going to spend the evening with my parents and my friend Julie."

Sarah said, "That will be nice. I'm just going to have a quiet night in I think, but I may decide to go and see a friend later." She looked at Michael and smiled.

He thought, *Might she drop in and see me again? I don't particularly want that pressure on New Year's Eve. I want to enjoy some drinks with Andrew and my family.* He said, "That should be good. I hope you both enjoy yourselves." He heard Sarah sneeze.

Melanie said, "I hope you're not getting another cold. You had quite a bad one when you first started working here."

Sarah responded, "Yes. I thought I'd at least get away with that for a bit longer. Anyway, I'll get going. I've got some things to sort out. I wish you both a happy New Year."

Melanie said, "And I hope you have a happy one too, Sarah."

Michael said, "Yes, and I hope you have a good one," thinking about what he had just said then.

Sarah smiled and said, "Thanks, and I'll see you both soon."

After Sarah left, Melanie smiled and said, "She can be quite a cough drop, you know, and Paul does take her too far sometimes. It's not quite such a blessing for her to be so thin and big. She can attract too much attention looking like that."

Michael smiled and said, "Yes. Like I said, my brother was quite impressed, too, and I must say I was, except for the fact that I had to watch my p's and q's because of the position she holds here at work."

Melanie said, "Yes, I feel pretty much the same way. I was on tender-hooks wondering if she'd want to spend this evening with me. I prefer, as you probably do, to let my hair down a bit with family and friends."

Michael thought, *A girl after my own heart*. He said, "Yes, me too. Anyway, I'll get going because I want to go home and change, and I want to have a little bit of a look around town before this evening. Have a happy New Year Melanie. I'll see you."

She said, "Yes, see you, Michael, and I wish you a happy New Year too!" He went to his car to drive home.

Later that afternoon whilst Michael was in town amongst all the revellers, he saw that girl again with the woollen hat. She was sitting by herself near the window in a café drinking what looked like a cup of tea, which she held in her left hand. She was wearing a dark-blue blouse with blue trousers, and he noticed her navy-blue raincoat lying on the chair next to her. He hesitated and thought, *Shall I try to meet her?* She then saw him and acknowledged him by waving. He gave her a quick wave and felt obliged to go in and see her.

When he went in, she wasn't there, and then he felt a tap on his left shoulder. She said, "Hi. Are you enjoying yourself?" She spoke in a fairly slurred and deep husky cracked voice, as though she had a cold. According to the amount of alcohol he could smell on her breath, he thought she also was drunk. He then nervously said, "Hi, Melanie. Is that you?"

She laughed and said, "Not quite, but I'm whoever you'd like me to be. Oh, excuse me, just a joke of mine. Actually, my name is Claire." She looked straight into his eyes, her glance flitting between his eyes. He noticed that her eye colour was the same as his. Because she didn't wear any make-up, he also recognized the blemish on her cheek, which was in exactly the same place his own was when he saw himself in a mirror. He thought, *Well, she is my inverse double, and my parents told me that the name Claire was a possibility after Susan. That's obviously her name here instead*. He was then tongue tied for a moment in deep thought. Finally he said, "Hi, my name is Michael. I've seen you around before and I am wondering who you are."

She said, "I suppose you are. Let's just say that I'm somebody who's very interested in you." She then appeared to be nervous, and she got tearful as she said, "Oh, now's not the time or the place. I'm too drunk at this moment, and I don't know why the heck I've even got near to doing this right now." She took her hat off with her left hand and revealing her hair, which was straight and dark brown with quite a lot of mottled grey in it.

He thought, *Yes, I've got a few grey strands like that, but nowhere near as many as she has. Goodness, she must have come here accidently after all. That's what accounts for that extra grey hair. By! I must be careful how I handle her and not take things too quickly.* To him, because of their similarity, she looked absolutely stunning.

She got herself into more of a state and ran off saying, "Excuse me, Michael, bear with me. Sorry about this, I'll see you soon."

He thought, *Well she's tried to reveal herself, but only by drinking too much. By! She certainly was close to wanting to tell me everything, I think. What now? There could actually be two of them—Melanie and the so-called Claire now, because everything about her is just like Melanie, except for her hair and only a slight difference in her eye colour, probably only due to randomness between the two universes.* He was then so stunned and deep in thought that he walked through the shops in a daze before returning to his car. He drove home and then had a couple of hours on the bed before going to his parents' house where he met up with Andrew. They played some computer games and then had some drinks whilst watching television and seeing the New Year in.

12

THE £10 NOTE

Michael and his family were joyous and then wished each other a happy New Year just at the turn of midnight. After that, they watched one of the early-morning comedy films and then went to bed. Andrew stayed the night in the guestroom, and Michael slept in his original room.

The following evening when Michael arrived home, he logged onto his laptop to speak with himself. When the picture came on the screen, he could see DO Michael waiting to talk. DO Michael said, "Hi, Michael. Happy New Year, by the way. How are you?"

"Fine. Happy New Year to you. Are you OK?"

DO Michael smiled and answered, "Yes, as usual. I don't know about you, but quite a lot has happened since Monday, especially yesterday."

"Yes, you're not the only one. It seems that that girl, Susan as we called her, is actually Claire. What about you?"

"Yes. She told me that her name was Claire too, and she seems definitely to be a mirror image of me. I can tell by the way she looks and the way she uses her left hand, which to her would be her right hand. How did you come by her, when you were there then?"

"I was walking past a café window when I saw her drinking tea or something, and she waved to me. I went in and didn't see her there, but suddenly she tapped me on my left shoulder."

DO Michael said, "Well, it happened differently for me. I remember walking passed that café. A few minutes later, I got a tap on my left shoulder. As I turned around and saw her, she immediately took her woollen hat off. When I looked at her and then her hair, I was stunned. When I looked at her eyes and that blemish on her cheek, it was exactly like looking in a mirror, but a lot of her hair was mottled grey."

Michael said, "Yes, I saw her like that too. That makes me certain that she came here by chance or accidently, which I think would have been a massive shock to anybody who suddenly found everything laterally inverted. I should think that, seeing all that, a person would first imagine he or she was on an alien planet and, goodness me, what would you do in a situation like that?"

"I don't know. Go mad or something probably. It would take me some time to turn myself around to even accept that. To her, I should think it would be like Alice through the looking glass."

Michael saw DO Michael shudder a little. Michael said, "Yes. It would certainly make the hairs on my head stand up. Just talking about it makes my hair stand on end. We must go easy on them, assuming that Melanie may be another one who's come here by accident, though by her hair colour it doesn't seem so because she still has pure, dark-brown hair, unless of course, in her case, she's dyed it. If that's so, there are two of them who could have come here from two different parallel inverse universes. This is quite complicated stuff now. I mean, just think where they've come from. There will be two missing persons from there."

"Yes. I'm curious about that too. What effect will that have had on their mums and dads, and James. We wouldn't be there, of course."

"Yes, that's something else I think I'll look into. I'm going to change the subject slightly so we can pause on it while I remember this—how did your game of snooker go on Monday?"

DO Michael laughed and said, "I'm surprised you can suddenly change the subject to that, rather than Claire and Melanie—ooph! How did your game go, then?"

"Well, I beat Andrew three nil."

DO Michael smiled and said, "Now I know why you asked me that. He actually beat me two one, by potting the black ball when it was the decider in the last two frames. How did you win your last two then?"

"Well, the second frame was a black ball decider. He was lucky on the black, but the white ball then went into the opposite pocket."

DO Michael laughed and said, "That nearly happened to him in the second frame. It just clipped the jaws of the pocket, and he breathed a sigh of relief then. How did you win that last frame?"

"Well, I potted the pink and black in one break."

"I did get the chance of potting the black then, but fluffed it, leaving an easy shot for him, which won him the session. It certainly makes you think about the different possible outcomes for some of the closer tournament matches. Anyway, do you have any ideas about how to find out more about these two lovely girls—especially where they may have come from?" He smiled.

"I'll have to think about that. I don't really have any ideas at the moment, except to maybe test out Melanie's reactions on something in that area. There's no point in thinking about Claire now because she's gone AWOL. That's something we'll have to take as it comes, if we see her again. Anyway, that's my only suggestion for the time being."

"That sounds like quite a good idea. I've just thought about perhaps testing her out on her rights and lefts to see how she reacts to that. I won't ask her something silly, though, as to whether she's all left or half right, politically of course." He laughed.

Michael smiled and said, "Yes, I've thought about that same thing, too, and could easily ask her that. On a serious note, though, I'm not going to take it too far because we have to bear in mind the trauma she's most likely been through."

"I agree. I'll do something that's not going to make it too obvious as well. I'm not going to give the impression of being too obsessive about this because that'll alert her too much. Besides, other people at work may overhear and get curious about her, which could lead to intervention from medical people, and we have to bear in mind the differences in her organs. You only have to put yourself in her position to realize that. Remember that she'll surely be thinking like us. Anyway, I'm going to have a meal now. I'll speak to you soon. Oh, I've just thought—because I had to wait for quite a bit before you came on, I'm wondering if we could talk at a specific time, since the divergence between us is increasing."

Michael thought and answered, "Yes, that's a good idea. Will Tuesday evening at ten o'clock be all right?" He didn't want it to be Monday night because of all the backlog of work he expected that evening.

"Yes, that'll be fine I think. I'll see you then."

"OK. See you then, and nice chatting." He saw the screen go blank after they waved to each other. Michael closed the tab and logged off to have his meal.

The following Monday morning, Michael purposely arrived at work early and sat in his office so he could overhear anything that Melanie said once she arrived. He heard Sarah arrive in the hall first when he heard Paul say to her, "Hi, Sarah. Happy New Year, by the way. Where have you been all my life? I was waiting for you late on in the pro-area. I was already for your dessert after having a great bonza time with so many sheilas there. By! They certainly kept me going, and if it wasn't for my thoughts about you, I wouldn't have lasted the pace."

Sarah said, "Ooh, what is it with you? Are you still tanked up, as you put it?"

He laughed loudly and said, "Yes, you bet I am. And I've got plenty here to put in you, Sarah."

Michael thought that Paul was taking it too far again, as he tended to do frequently, especially after her unfortunate choice of words, which fuelled the situation. He thought, *Should I put a stop to this? I will if necessary, but I think it's only his bravado.*

Sarah said, "Eww, that's disgusting."

"Absolutely. It will be when I can't turn off the tap."

"Ooh, you're incorrigible!" And she huffed and went into her office and closed the door.

"Well, I'll keep some for you later then."

"Well by then, the cork will have probably blown off."

"Ooh, it's about to go off now. Oh no, it's just gone! Oh dear." He laughed and said, "Never mind. Maybe later."

Michael then heard Paul talking with Melanie now that she'd arrived. He said, "Happy New Year, Melanie. I had a bonza one with Sarah. She was a real goer, know what I mean?" Michael heard Paul laugh.

Melanie said, "I'm sure I do. Anyway, happy New Year to you, Paul."

"Thanks. Cheers, Melanie. You'll hear all about it from her when you go in."

Michael then heard Melanie go into Sarah's office next door, whilst Paul went into his. Michael heard Sarah say, "Hi, Melanie. You'll have to excuse him. He's been at the humour again. Anyway, happy New Year. How are you?"

"Fine, and thanks, and I wish you a happy New Year. Did that cold develop into anything worse?"

"Not really. I soon knocked it out with some medicine

and just took things easy then. Anyway, we'd best get on. Can you process those requisitions and check to see if the orders are on their way? I'll get on the phone and sort out these other ones."

"OK, I'll do that." And then Michael heard Sarah start her telephone calls. He began to concentrate on processing a further backlog of invoices that had piled up after the bank holiday weekend. Soon he heard Sarah stop talking on the telephone, and he heard them both leave their office to go on their usual day out of visiting suppliers.

A little later, David popped in and said, "Happy New Year, Michael. How are you? Did you enjoy the New Year celebrations?"

Michael answered, "Yes I did, and I'm OK. Happy New Year to you, David, and how are you?"

"Thanks, and I'm fine, except for this slight cold. Anyway, here are some more invoices and several order notes to process. There are some more due at lunchtime, which I'll give you later. See you soon."

"Yes, see you." David left. Michael then sorted out the paperwork and processed the transactions on his laptop. After doing that, he went into Sarah's office and left the order notes in a tray on top of all the other ones she had. He then took the opportunity to look in some of the drawers of Melanie's desk. When he looked through the third drawer, which was her top left-hand one, he saw a couple of desk pads, and when he took them out, he was stunned when he saw a laterally inverted £10 note and a small hand mirror tucked between the pads. He picked up the fairly well-used note and blew a little powder off it as he looked at it carefully through the mirror, seeing that it was real legal tender with the watermark and thin metal strip. He thought, *Well, well, well, that answers everything besides the joke about SVM. She has to be one, besides Claire. There are two of them, and maybe they even know each other and are in collusion together. Crikey, we've got aliens amongst us. This couldn't be the invasion of the body snatchers, could it? Are we gradually being taken over by our reverse selves? Sci-fi—it does get you wondering. Oh, calm down, Michael. There is now lots to think about.* He put the £10 note and the mirror back between the two pads and put them back in that drawer where they came from and then went back to his office to continue working, with one eye open on the door.

Just after midday, Michael heard someone knock on his door. It was Melanie. He smiled and said, "Hi, Melanie. And how are you? And happy New Year, by the way. Did you enjoy it?"

"Yes, thanks, and I'm OK. And a happy New Year to you. Are you OK?"

"Yes, I'm fine. Are you back at the office for the rest of the afternoon?"

"No. I've just come back to collect a few more things we require for this afternoon from Sarah's office. And now I'm here, I may as well give you these invoices I've got." She smiled and said, "I'm sorry to be the one to load you up with even more work now."

He laughed and said, "Oh, don't worry. I'm used to it. Besides I need the pay. That's what I'm here for!" He knew a lot of his evening would be taken up completing this backlog.

"Anyway, I hope you're all right. I'd best be going now to collect those things Sarah needs. See you later, Michael."

"Yes, see you. Don't let her work you too hard, Melanie."

She laughed and said, "That's what I'm here for too. See you, Michael." She waved and smiled at him before leaving the room. He heard her go into Sarah's office to collect those things, and he heard her leave and lock the door behind her. When he left his office at about lunchtime, there was nobody in the hallway, so he curiously checked to see if Sarah's door was locked. It was. He thought, *Wow, I think Melanie might have left that unusual £10 note there by mistake. She must have come back to pick it up before somebody else noticed it. Though it might be possible, because I saw powder on it. She could have left it there on purpose to see if anybody—such as me—had been through her drawers. She then, of course, would have come back to collect it before anyone else could spot it, such as Sarah. If that's the case, that's why she's locked the door—to stop me going in and looking again and not seeing it there. If that is what's happened, then she's thought about it very deeply just as I am doing right now, so nothing would surprise me.*

Later that afternoon, Michael decided to work quite a bit longer than five o'clock to finish at a convenient point before taking the rest of the work home with him so he could hopefully complete it after his evening meal. He heard somebody go into Sarah's office at about quarter to six to collect a few things before leaving. He then curiously looked outside his office window into the car park to see who it was, and he saw Sarah carrying her document case and still wearing the office uniform.

She put the case into the passenger seat with her left hand and then got in. Five minutes later, she drove off.

He continued working until just after ten past six and then left with the bundle of work he needed to complete, stopping off for some fish and chips near to where he lived. Whilst he was waiting in the queue, he saw a yellow Labrador come up to him and then back off. As he looked at it, it looked straight at him and pinned its ears slightly. Then it came up to him again, smelling him to pick up his scent. Michael remembered the dog he had seen outside the church at the carol service. The dog backed away again and sniffed a blonde girl who was standing behind him, and then it came back to him to smell his legs. Michael patted it on its head, and the dog became quite friendly. Michael enjoyed making a fuss of it, even though he preferred cats to dogs, as he thought of Patch.

The girl said, "Come on, Fido, that's enough now." She sounded very much like Sarah, except she spoke a little slower. She held her dog back slightly with the lead in her left hand.

Michael looked at her and said, "It's OK. We seem to be getting on."

She was thin and stood about five foot five. She had deep-blue eyes with gold flecks. She was well proportioned and had wavy platinum blonde hair. She wore a white raincoat and smart blue jeans with black shoes and had quite a bit of make-up on. She smiled and said, "Yes, I remember seeing my dog go up to you before, just after that carol service. I was there and saw you with someone who looked as if he could be your brother."

He smiled and said, "Yes, I remember your dog. He's quite a live wire, isn't he?"

She smiled and said, "Yes, he's up to anything."

"Well, that was my brother you saw me with. Did you enjoy the service?"

She smiled. "Yes. It was nice and very festive. It's a pity it's all over so quickly. I always enjoy this season, but it never lasts long enough."

"Yes. I feel the same way."

Jack, who was at the counter, said, with a deep voice, "OK, Michael. What would you like to order then?"

Michael answered, "I'd like a portion of cod and chips with some curry, please."

Jack said, "OK, just the usual then?"

Michael smiled and said, "Yes please. That'll be fine." He handed Jack a ten-pound note, which reminded him of Melanie's funny one.

Jack said, "Well, it shouldn't take too long." And he went to the till to pick out Michael's change.

The girl said, "Well, I suppose It's been a busy day and all that, for you today?"

Michael answered, "Yes, it has, and I've still got a little more to do at home later. I have lots of invoices to process. It's part of my job in bookkeeping." Of course, the "little more" was an understatement.

She said, "Well, never mind. Once that's done, you can relax."

Jack handed Michael his fish and chips and smiled saying, "Hope you enjoy. See you later, Michael." Then he said to the girl behind him, who was waiting with the dog, "Hi, Sophie. Is it the usual for you then?" He smiled broadly.

She smiled and answered, "Yes, please. I'll just have the cod and chips, please."

As Michael left the shop, he looked back at her and saw that she was looking at him. He went to his car and drove home where he had his meal whilst watching a little television. After that, he had a rest on the bed, and then he completed the processing of the invoices just after eleven o'clock.

13

DO Expired

The next day at lunchtime, when Michael came out of his office, he saw Melanie talking with Sarah and Paul. Paul said, "Hi, mate. Happy New Year, Michael. How are you?"

"Thanks, I'm fine. Happy New Year to you." He was polite even though he didn't like how far Paul had gone yesterday with Sarah, despite her being a boss.

Paul smiled and said, "Thanks, mate." He then turned to Sarah and said, "I have to say, Sarah, that I did rather overdo it with you yesterday. I did have a bit to drink before work. I felt I had to pull myself up a bit after all the New Year celebrations, and I do get carried away sometimes. I hope you don't mind too much."

Sarah answered, "OK, then. I like humour, but there is a limit, and I was wondering who may have overheard you." She looked at Michael. He didn't really want to say he had overheard, feeling that he could let himself down by not having done or said anything about it, so he kept quiet.

Melanie said, "Well, I didn't hear very much between you two when I arrived, except when you said, 'Oh dear' about something, Paul."

Paul said, "Well, it was what I'd said before that. Anyway, it's all water under the bridge now. I'll have to watch my drink a bit more from now on, though I can't go so far as making any New Year's resolutions on that. Anyway, I had a bonza time over Christmas, and I hope you all did. Now it's back to work again, and I wish I was back down under right now, since it's so beautiful and hot down there this summer. Anyway, I'm going to hit the town now, but I will stay sober of course. See you, sports." He smiled and left.

Melanie said, "Well, he's still a cough drop. I'm curious about what he said, though, Sarah."

Sarah rolled her eyes and said, "I'll tell you later, when it's just us two. I'm sure Michael's not interested." She laughed whilst looking at him.

He said, "Well, I did overhear it a bit, and he was a bit too much. I was concerned until you replied to him very well."

Sarah smiled and said, "Thanks for that, Michael, but I'm not so sure whether I did or not. Oh, I've just remembered. I have to buy some more stationery stuff. I'll see you." Before she left, she said to Michael, "Oh, by the way, happy New Year, Michael."

He responded, "Yes, thanks. Happy New Year to you, Sarah."

She smiled at both Michael and Melanie and said, "Thanks, Michael. I'll see you both later."

They both said goodbye as she left. Melanie then said, "She seems to like you, Michael." She smiled at him.

"Yes, probably. She's all right." Michael was trying to play it down, knowing her position and how well she could handle things. He then thought, *Now's my chance to test Melanie out.* He said, "I'm going into town. Shall we go for a bite to eat?"

She replied reticently, "Yes, I could do with something." As they walked into town, he was thinking about how he could force some feedback from her—anything that would indicate that right for her would be left for him. He said, "Shall we just turn left at the clock corner to go to the markets to see what snacks they have on offer?"

She laughed and said, "You mean right, don't you? You're not drunk like Paul now, are you? I hope you're not going to start talking like he sometimes does with Sarah."

Michael thought, *Well, she's seen that one and bluffed me. I'll have to try something a little subtler when I get the chance.* He said, "Oh, I meant right. What's got into me? Anyway, do you want to try the markets?"

"OK. We'll see what's on offer there then." They walked towards the market. He watched her carefully as she took some money from her purse with her right hand. He noticed that she wore her watch on her left hand and saw that her vein patterns on that hand were nothing like his on his right hand. There was no similarity at all, not even to a mirror image, so she didn't appear to be anything like him, although her left hand was similar to his left hand. He then thought, *That could be something random again—maybe due to the randomness of the differences between this world and hers, that would be different anyway. I'll try something else when I can.* He looked at a stall where there were some readymade sandwiches for sale, and he bought a ham salad sandwich. Then he had a thought and asked her, "Would you like some orangeade?"

"Oh, I'm not too keen on that. I'll have a cola I think."

He thought, *Well, that ploy has now gone by the wayside. I know for a fact that, like before, if she was the inverse version of me, she would prefer orangeade to lemonade because that would taste more like lemonade. Oh, I can't ask her anything more now for the time being or else I'll just be too obvious. She clearly knows that I'm probing her now and is ready for anything else.* He said, "OK. I'll have the same." And he went to buy them. He thought, *Shall I come straight out with it and just ask her whether she's come from a mirror image world? I can't do that because, if she hasn't, she'll think I'm absolutely barking mad, having probably been released from a looney bin or something. I must be patient and think deeper on this.*

When he'd paid for the drinks and brought them back to their table, she smiled and said, "Thanks for those. I've noticed that Sarah prefers orangeade to lemonade, but she likes tea most of the time." Michael remembered her drinking orangeade at the office party. Melanie then said, "Well, talking of Sarah, I didn't particularly want to mention it in front of her earlier, but, apparently, yesterday Paul was dressed down by one of the directors who'd overheard what he said to her, regarding what we'd talked about earlier."

"I'm not surprised really. What did you hear?"

"Well, he told Paul that what he'd said was tantamount to bullying and more. Paul said that he hadn't meant anything like that, and he said that that was the last thing he ever wanted to appear to be. He then apologized and admitted to having drunk too much. Mr. Smith said, 'Well, OK, but don't let it happen again. We won't tolerate such behaviour here, especially to hard-working members of staff such as Sarah. That'll be all.' Paul apologized again and went back to his office. I felt for him a little, but he's bounced back now, and I think he'll be all right from now on."

"He seemed to be OK today, and he sounded genuine." He finished his sandwich and then they walked back to work.

"Well, things aren't quite as busy now as they were before Christmas, but the January sales are certainly keeping us going. The discounts, of course, mean that the margins aren't as high." She brushed her hair over her forehead with her right hand as she smiled at Michael.

"Yes. The Christmas period is the most important one with the retailers." He was coming to the conclusion that she may be flirting with him, besides perhaps being naturally right handed. He then thought, *Perhaps she's staged that too, or again by randomness she may be left handed in her world, thus appearing right handed here. Those are perhaps the only possibilities now.* They arrived back at the office, and Melanie went to join Sarah in her office after she and Michael said their usual goodbyes. Michael then got himself a cup of tea before continuing with his work.

The following evening at ten o'clock, Michael spoke with himself as he'd promised to. He saw DO Michael waiting. DO Michael said, "Hi! It's good to talk again. How are things?"

Michael said, "OK. I've had a try with some of the left- and right-hand ploys, but none of it's been really conclusive. She's either been ready for it and put a good act on, or she is naturally left handed by randomness from wherever she's come from. I don't know, but the key thing is, I found an odd laterally inverted ten-pound note yesterday with a mirror. I think she could have anticipated somebody looking for it because there was a slight film of powder on it. I don't know. I could be imagining it."

"Yes, I noticed that too, and when she came back and locked the office, that made me wonder further as to whether it was planned."

"Well, we've now seen something concrete from an inverse world. I will probe further into that, I think, from now on. Anyway, just to recap about the snooker again ..." He wondered if he could maybe be talking to a different Michael, even though the origin date was the same at 1 November at midday.

DO Michael quickly said, "I think I know what you're going to say. You're wondering if I'm going to give you the same result for the outcome of those frames that I played a week ago with Andrew. I've thought about that too."

"Yes. Like I said when we'd last talked, I won three nil. Had you?"

"No, I won two one. Was that the same score you heard me say last Friday?"

"Well what do you know, it wasn't. You, or should

I say, *he*, told me that he'd lost two one. I thought there could be that possibility about each one of us being different. How did you lose your odd frame then?"

"Well, it was the second frame that I let slip. Andrew had potted the deciding black in that one. Anyway, turning away from the snooker back to New Year's Eve. What happened there when you bumped into Claire?"

"I saw her in the café, and when I went in, she wasn't there then. She then tapped me on my left shoulder, rather surprising me."

"Yes, it happened similarly for me too. Though it surprised me when she called herself Claire, after I overheard her parents in her universe referring to her as Susan. I'm wondering if there are three of them due to that, unless of course she's pretending to be called Claire for some reason or other."

Michael, who was rather surprised, said, "Well, I'd never seen her parents when I was there on that Saturday afternoon before Christmas. When my parents got back, I felt that I had to click off the tab immediately because I didn't want them to see that I was looking at a mirror image world. What you've just said is, therefore, new to me."

DO Michael said, "Well, it's that random element again. Her parents arrived just before mine did, and I got to hear only a little bit from them. It was very sad because her mum, or my mum, said, "It would be really lovely, and there would be nobody happier than us, if Susan could suddenly walk in through that door right now and could spend Christmas with us." The way she said it bought a tear to my eye. I then heard a sniffle upstairs just as my parents arrived, and then Patch came downstairs to greet them wanting some food."

That made Michael's spine tingle, and he felt a tear come to his eye as he said, "Well, that's fascinating. At that time, I only saw the photograph of her there instead of me and was hoping to find out more from what other things I could see. I did hear a creaking sound upstairs, though, and went to have a look, but I saw nothing. I just put it down to the radiators coming on. You say you heard a sniffle?"

DO Michael replied, "Yes, I did, but I thought it could have been Patch sneezing before coming downstairs. It did cross my mind, though, for a moment that somebody may have been up there."

"Well hearing what you've just told me means I don't have to look into seeing her parents as much. I will still though, if I can, because this coming Saturday they'll be out shopping in town in the January sales."

"I thought about seeing them too, to maybe get some more information about what they're like, besides Susan. I'm also interested in how different James will be if he has a sister instead of me."

"What you've just told me about her parents makes me think deeper now on things."

DO Michael paused and said, "Did you hear the way Paul talked to Sarah first thing yesterday morning? At least he's admitted to going too far with her now and has apologized."

"Yes, I heard it when I was in my office. He had drunk too much, and she made a rather unfortunate reply adding to the situation." Michael gave DO Michael the gist of what Paul had said to her.

DO Michael said, "Well, it wasn't quite as explicit as that. He said something like just wanting to share it all with her. It sounds, according to what he said to her with you, that he could be reprimanded by going to those lengths, if he'd been overheard."

"Well he was. Mr. Smith had a serious talk with him according to what Melanie told me today. Did it go as far as that where you are then?"

"No, it didn't. He wasn't that bad. He just teased Sarah in a friendly way, and she accepted it. He obviously likes her a lot."

"Yes, he does here too, and she seems to have accepted what he said today."

"Anyway, I'd best get off now. It's late, and I need some sleep. Do you want to decide on another definite time when we can talk again?"

Michael answered, "Yes, why not? We could chat, say, at around six o'clock on Sunday evening."

"OK, I'll see you then—or another of you. It'll be interesting anyway."

Michael said, "I agree! See you soon." DO Michael closed the tab, and then Michael did. He then put on a short comedy DVD before going to bed.

The following Saturday afternoon at about half past four, Michael went into his parents' house with his laptop to look there at the inverse universe. When the picture came on the screen after the usual eight minutes, he saw the same laterally inverted room. The photograph of Susan, James, and his parents was still there along with everything else, except the Christmas decorations, of course, which would have been taken down on the twelfth night. He went upstairs to look around his original room, which would more than likely have been Susan's here. It was more or less the same as when he'd quickly glimpsed in there before after hearing that floorboard creak. The bed was in a slightly different place to where his was, and he saw a mirror-image poster on the wall of Coldplay. He thought about his full collection of their DVDs, but he'd never gone as far as to have a poster of them on his wall. He remembered the poster that he had there, which was of Girls Aloud.

Michael looked around the house on his laptop screen for some more clues, but there wasn't much since she clearly would probably be living somewhere else now. He thought that she may have been occupying the flat where he lived now, until John Mitchell had moved in after she'd disappeared. He could go no further than seeing what was lying around there because he couldn't move anything. He was effectively like a ghost there that could only observe things.

He looked in the other rooms and didn't learn much from them either. He then sat down in the lounge and read a book. Soon Patch came to sit on his lap. He made a fuss of her as she purred, and then he felt relaxed. He peered at the screen again and saw Patch sleeping on the sofa. The cats looked the same, except that the smudges on their faces were on opposite sides. He thought, *Melanie can't be Susan because she's too different. Everything I've seen in DO is exactly the same, and when it is laterally inverted, it is exactly laterally inverted. I must search further than Melanie now. It can only be that girl I saw as Claire, but why did she call herself that if her real name is Susan, unless there are two of them? No, I don't think so. She's probably just too apprehensive and wants to cover up, wondering what I might do if I found out. I wouldn't do anything to harm her in any way, but she won't know that. She must have had a very traumatic time to be that doubtful.*

At that moment, he heard voices on his laptop, and he closed his book to listen and to see what was happening. He heard his father's voice say, "Here's some of the stuff from the boot. I'll go and fetch the rest of it." His mother said, "OK. I'll just get some of these things put away." He then heard James ask, "Are you two managing to cope all right?" James spoke just as he normally did, enjoying pulling their leg. Michael thought, *Well, he doesn't seem to be that much different from having a sister.* His mother then answered, "Hey you, Michael, stop that. I am coping actually." Michael then thought, *Well, James is called Michael. That makes sense because Claire's here instead of me, and James has got my name.* He guessed that the voices came from the kitchen and said, "Sorry, Patch, I have to go now." He placed her on the sofa next to him, and she settled down to sleep.

Michael took his laptop to the kitchen while watching the picture on the screen. He saw a couple of laterally inverted shopping bags on the kitchen table. As he saw his mother putting some of the things away, his father came in and said, "As soon as we've packed away, it will be about time to chat with Susan, won't it? She'll be interested to know about some of these bargains that we've got." His mother answered, "Yes. She'll be through in about ten minutes." Michael noticed that it was twenty-five to six, and he thought, *Well-well-well, they seem to be in contact. That girl who called herself Claire must be Susan, and somehow she's returned back since New Year's Eve because I haven't seen her since then. That's good news for them, and things have definitely worked out for her.* He felt pleased for her and smiled whilst speaking out in glee, "Well she's back. I'm pleased for her and them."

He watched them a little longer, and when he heard his parents' car arrive, he closed the tab and then logged off. He went to look through the kitchen window and saw them collecting their shopping bags from their car boot. He then noticed Sophie walking Fido on the pathway just outside their house, and she briefly looked in his direction. She looked lovely, wearing the same jeans that she had worn before, but with a white T-shirt under her small blue raincoat. He felt like going out to meet her, but his shyness stopped him. Besides, his parents had just arrived. He thought, *If I could do, it wouldn't amount to anything because she's just too stunning for me to invite her out, and I wouldn't make anything of it anyway.* His father came in with some bags and said, "Hi, Michael. I see you've beaten us to it."

Michael said, "Yes. I'll give you a hand." And he helped them pack the things away. They prepared the meal and watched some television whilst eating, and had a lazy evening in. Michael stayed the night, and they went to church the following morning.

That evening at about six o'clock, when he logged onto his laptop to speak with himself at the usual origin date, he saw himself immediately on the screen. As he said, "Hi Michael, how are you?", he heard DO Michael say exactly the same thing. He thought, *How can this be happening? I thought we were diverging and not being the same again, where we can't talk with each other*. He said, "Hello, it's me, Michael." Again, DO Michael repeated the same exact words at the same time. The screen then flickered off and came back on for a moment, showing DO Michael. Then went off completely. A message came on: "The DO program expired at 00:01 on Sunday, 10 January."

Michael was very surprised and startled at that, thinking, *Oh no, why now? What bug have I just got in my system?* He immediately switched his broadband off and then checked his control panel, but he saw no Dimensional Observer program on it. He thought, *I've lost it all now. I won't be able see DO Michael anymore or be able to observe Susan as she is, and I'll never see her as she is in her laterally inverted universe. It's as though I've lost some friends. I'm on my own now.*

He then got hot under the collar and did a system restore back to before he'd last spoken to DO Michael. This took about twenty minutes, after which he saw the usual message: "None of your files have been affected." He checked his programs, but the Dimensional Observer program still wasn't there. He thought, *Well that's it. It's all over, and I'm on my own. Perhaps it's for the best. Susan's back now and hopefully can live a normal life, and I can move on with mine like everyone else. Oh well, it's been enjoyable while it lasted, but now I'll move on.*

He logged off and watched some television. He went on his laptop again later, wondering if he might still have

DO, but he didn't. He tried one or two more things after that, but the DO program still wasn't there. He then had his supper before going to bed, trying to put all this out of his mind so he could move on. He wondered again about how Melanie had come by that reverse £10 note, thinking that she may have received it purely out of coincidence. Maybe it had been in circulation or a fake. No. It was too real for that. He thought, *That powder on it may have been a bit of her face powder or something, to prove if anybody had seen it. I had.* He then wondered about why the program had expired at that particular moment, thinking, *Perhaps I had it only temporarily. Or, as I thought before, it was a way for Susan—or Claire as she'd called herself—to make me aware of her existence here. Now she's back, of course, she must have removed it from my laptop because it's no longer required.* He then felt relaxed, and he drifted off to sleep. But he woke up in the middle of the night thinking about the possibility that she might have observed him whilst he used the program before she went back. He thought, *What does it matter now? It's all over.* And he fell asleep again.

14

SAINT VALENTINE'S DAY

A month went by. Michael just continued with his work and played snooker with Andrew regularly. He visited his parents occasionally during the week and saw them at weekends. He hadn't seen Sophie since he'd seen her walking her dog that afternoon outside his parents' house, but he'd thought about her. He had talked with Melanie and Sarah occasionally, but it was mostly about work and when they checked invoices. He felt that they just wanted to keep their distance, and Paul had just started taking Sarah out.

It was Friday, 12 February, now and Michael thought, *Well, Paul has mellowed a lot, and they seem to be an item. They like each other's sense of humour and are on a level regarding work.* That evening after work, he went to Jack's fish and chip shop and saw Sophie there. She smiled and said, "Hi, Michael. How have you been?"

He answered, "OK. I've been busy as usual." He

felt a little nervous at getting tongue tied again because of how beautiful she looked. Her hair was the same, and she wore slightly less-dark-blue eye shadow that matched her eye colour. She had red lipstick on and wore a tight white T- shirt with a black-and-white patterned skirt over blue Lycra leggings, which showed her thin legs. She wore black shoes.

She smiled and said, "Well, I have too. I'm working on the computer mainly in my job, doing the processing of order notes so we order the right goods." This sounded similar to the work that Melanie was doing for Sarah.

He said, "Yes. A lot of what I do is processing invoices for order notes and also keeping up with the sales records."

She smiled and said, "It sounds like you have a lot on and that the firm you work for is similar to ours. We sell things on the internet and also deliver to customers."

He said, "That's more or less what we do." He told her the name of the firm he worked for. She told him who she worked for, and then Jack asked them what they wanted. Michael said, "I'll let you go first."

She smiled and said, "Thanks. I'll have cod and chips with a curry, please."

Jack smiled and said, "OK, Sophie. Coming right up." She said thanks and started looking through her purse with her left hand to collect some change to give him.

Michael said, "How's Fido, by the way?"

She answered, "Oh, he's fine. I'll be taking him out for a walk later. I just hope it doesn't rain. It does so often in February, it being February fill-dyke." She chuckled.

"Yes, I know what you mean. It's just started out there now."

She giggled and then said in a bit of a higher pitched soppy voice, "Oh no. It would have to do that when I haven't brought my coat!"

He imagined what she would look like sopping wet in that T-shirt without a bra. He said, "Well, we can wait until the worst of it is over."

Jack said with a broad smile, "Yes, I would. I wouldn't go out until it's at least cleared." He handed Sophie her fish and chips. Michael was able to tell what was going through his mind.

She giggled and said, "No, I'll take your advice I think." She passed the exact change to Jack with her left hand. Michael felt a little intrigued now with lefthanders after having seen and thought so much about inverse universes.

Jack said, "Anyway, what is it that you want to order, Michael. Is it the usual?"

Michael answered, "Yes, please. I'll have a portion of cod and chips with a curry, please."

Jack smiled and said, "Yes, the same as Sophie's order."

She laughed and said, "Great minds, hey?"

Michael smiled at her and said, "Yes, I always tend to have this."

Jack said, "Yes, it's nice cod straight from Grimsby. It's a good regular order for lots of people." He worked at preparing their meals. Michael got a £10 note out of his wallet to pay him. Jack passed him his fish and chips as Michael handed him the money. Jack gave Michael his change and said, "Thanks. Hope you both enjoy them. See you later."

Michael said, "Thanks," and followed Sophie out. He said, "It's been nice seeing you again, Sophie."

She looked straight at him for a moment and said, "Here's my card. You can get in touch with me if you want to. I'll see you around," as her eyes flitted between his.

He smiled and said, "Yes, thanks. See you. We'd best get moving because of this rain." He felt great about what had just happened.

She said, "Me too." As he rushed to his car in the downpour of rain, he looked back and saw her rushing around the corner, presumably going back to her car. He then got into his car, which quickly became steamed up because of the moisture. He put on his lights and the windscreen wipers on this fairly mild night and then drove home whilst thinking about how lovely Sophie looked.

Michael ate his meal with a stiff drink of vodka as he relaxed and had an evening in watching one of his favourite comedy DVD films. He decided to send Sophie an anonymous Valentine's card the following day. It would arrive on Monday, since Valentine's Day fell on the Sunday this year. He looked at the business card she had given him and saw that her full name was Sophie Kaye. Her home address was on it, as well as her landline and mobile phone numbers with her private e-mail address.

On Monday morning when Michael was in his office, he received one anonymous Valentine's card amongst the post. It read, "Michael. I've really been admiring you a lot," mentioning the pub that she would be at after nine o'clock on Friday evening. It concluded, "I'll hopefully see you there." He thought at first that it could be from Melanie and felt a little guilty for not sending her a card, after having thought about it, especially the way she looked at him sometimes. He had decided not to though because he didn't really want to become overly familiar with any girl in the office because, recently, everything there had just been work related.

The following Friday evening he had a few drinks to help him develop some Dutch courage before leaving his flat to catch a bus into town. He wore a plain, long-sleeved blue shirt with charcoal-grey trousers and black shoes. When he went into that pub at about a quarter to nine, it was very crowded and warm with a lot of loud music playing. He saw Melanie and Susan there talking with Paul, and he thought, *Yes, it can only really be Melanie now who sent me the card*. He queued up to buy a pint of lager and lime, and it was a quarter of an hour before he was served because so many taller lads in front of him were being served first. He thought, *By! This is why I don't like these busy places too much. Besides taking forever to get served, they're very hot and sticky and so loud that you have to shout at the top of your voice down somebody's earhole. You then get showered in return when they reply to you, and mostly you have to guess what they've just said because you can't hear them properly. Sometimes before, when I've asked something in these places, I get an answer that doesn't even match the question I've asked. It can be embarrassing, and you just get fed up repeating yourself, trying to get your point over. It can be very hard work sometimes.*

After he finally got served, he went over to join

Melanie, Sarah, and Paul. Paul, who was wearing a white T-shirt under a black leather jacket with blue jeans and brown trainers, said, "Hi, mate. You took a long time to get served. You should have climbed over them!" He laughed, and Michael knew that he was taking the mick.

Michael responded by having to shout above the noise, saying, "No, that's not it. I should have brought my own cans of lager with me so I could have joined you twenty minutes ago."

Paul said, "Too right, mate. Bonza idea. That's what I've done already. I could've downed ten pints in a tenth of the time it's taken for you to get served, sport!" He laughed.

Sarah, who was wearing her white, long-sleeved blouse from work with dark blue trousers and black shoes, said, "Yes, I've got some tips for next time."

Paul burst out laughing and said, "Yes. You said it, gal!"

She slapped him quite hard on the shoulder with her left hand whilst laughing and saying, "What is it with you? I know what's going through that mind of yours."

He laughed and said, "Too right, love. We'll save it while later" He then shouted in Michael's ear, "She thinks I mean it, but it's only my usual banter. I really love egging the girls on, to get them going. It's great fun."

Michael laughed and said, "Yes, I can see that. Sarah makes a really good sparring partner."

"Yes, a bonza one, mate, besides everything else. She's lovely."

Sarah shouted, "What's all this you're saying about me now, Paul?"

He said, "Oh nothing, love." He turned to Michael

and said, "Yes, and it really gets the sheilas going when they know you've said something about them and you leave them guessing. That's another bonza one sport!" He laughed.

Melanie said loudly, "What am I missing here?"

Paul laughed and said loudly, "You don't want to know, love. It's just something between me and Sarah. I'm now going for another one, sports. Dunny first though, to powder my nose." Paul went off in the direction of the toilets.

Melanie came over to Michael, and he saw that she, too, was wearing her white, long-sleeved blouse from work with smart blue jeans and black shoes. She said, "Well, hi, Michael. How are you—except for this overloud music and Paul of course."

Michael said, "Fine, and I know what you mean. It is difficult to talk here, let alone hear some of the things people say, especially Paul." He chuckled.

Melanie said, "Yes. I've had that problem all night so far with this loud music and Paul. He's been good fun, though, but I just wonder how Sarah will cope later after he's had a few more jars of what he's been having." Michael suddenly laughed when he thought of what Paul might say to that if he'd heard her. Melanie laughed herself and said, "Oh, do excuse me. That's not meant to sound like it did. I'm pleased that Paul hasn't heard that one. That will be a double bonza in his books, I should think. Oh, excuse me again, his humour's making me see too much now. I'm beginning to get a disgusting mind." They both laughed.

Michael said, "Me too now. With Paul, you can

twist anything. Oh dear, I've just come out with another one now."

She laughed and said, "That actually sounded like a few, Michael. I'm at it now, and I just can't stop!" She giggled.

Sarah smiled and came over to them, asking loudly, "Now, what have you two been talking about, especially you, Michael?" She smiled and looked straight at him.

He answered, "Nothing really. We've just been chatting about some of the music being played here."

Sarah said, "Oh, come off it. I know by your looks that there's more to it than that. You've both been laughing your heads off at something."

Melanie laughed. "It's just Paul. There's just a funny side to everything we say when we imagine how Paul would respond to it all if he heard it."

Sarah said, "I know what you mean. He's had that effect on me too."

Paul then arrived back with another pint and said, "Hey you, Michael. You've had that same pint in your hand all night so far. When are you going to blow the froth of some more?"

"Well, I blew the froth off quite a few before coming here. I'm quite tanked up already."

"Well clearly not as much as me, mate, and I'm still only getting started. Them lasses in that nightclub will taste some from the great Australia shortly. Oh, excuse me, Sarah. I'll save the best for you later, after breaking myself in."

She slapped him in on the back with a fairly hard

left one again, bursting into laughter as she said, "Can't you ever control yourself?"

He said, "No. Not me, love. At the office, yes, but there's no stopping me here, sport."

Sarah said, "Oh, you're incorrigible."

He said, "That's me! Anyway, I'll finish this and let Michael finish off what's left of that warm tepid froth at the bottom of his glass, and we'll all head to that nightclub."

They all laughed, and Michael said, "OK." And he drank up that little tot and then said, "Yes. It was just about corked after all this time." He wanted to sound witty at his own expense.

Paul laughed and said, "I say it would be, mate." He drank his pint down quickly, and then they went a few doors away into the nightclub.

Melanie said, "I've been looking forward to some dancing. You should have worn your white John Travolta suit, Paul."

He said, "Not tonight, sport. I've got some more crucial things on my mind, or should I say ..." He looked at Sarah.

She said, "Oh, please don't. We can all imagine what that could be."

He said, "Imagine what? I'll be doing the stuff."

She said, "Oh, you're disgusting."

And then Paul said, "Just watch me." He danced John Travolta–style around a small group of pretty girls.

Sarah said, "There's no controlling him, is there? I'll join him for a while." She went for a dance. Paul joined her, and they danced close to each other.

Michael thought for a moment and then asked Melanie, "I'm just going to buy myself a cola. Is there anything you would like?"

"Yes please. I'll have one too, and thanks, Michael." As he went to buy them, he saw Melanie join Sarah and Paul on the dance floor. He watched her dancing quite well, near to them whilst he waited to be served, and when he'd bought the drinks just over a quarter of an hour later, he went to sit down. Melanie joined him and said, "I just thought I'd dance for a bit whilst you were being served. I thought it might have taken a bit longer. It seems so busy."

"You're all right. You did right to join them."

"Yes, thanks, and thanks for the drink." There was a bit of an uncomfortable silence mainly due to the loud music and the fact that Michael felt a little tired after his day at work, besides the amount he'd had to drink. He thought about maybe thanking her for the card, but he couldn't because it may not have been her who sent it. Besides, he felt awkward about saying such a thing, especially since she was a work colleague whom he thought could be more superior to him if she progressed to Sarah's position. Melanie said, "Well, I suppose it's been a hard day for you, hasn't it?"

"Yes, it has quite. What's it been like for you?"

"It's been OK. There's been the usual amount of processing of the order notes on the computer. Sarah tends to leave most of that to me when we're together in the office. She does some when I'm there, but she's on the phone most of that time."

"Oh. Perhaps she's just wanting to let you get used to using the computer."

"Yes, I suppose so. I shouldn't really complain because it does keeps me busy, and it's all important work. Anyway, shall we go for a dance?"

"OK then." And they went to dance close to where Sarah and Paul were, Michael keeping a fair distance away from him because of his occasional fast arm movements whilst the Bee Gees' "Staying Alive" was played. He saw Sarah holding back a laugh as she managed to dodge away from his right arm just in time, and Melanie enjoyed watching him too.

Paul shouted, "Come on, why don't you try it?"

Sarah said, "I think one is enough. We have to leave some space for the other dancers here."

Paul said, "Never mind them. They can join in too."

Michael saw a fairly tall, plump, middle-aged woman with wavy black hair come onto the floor to try it out. When she started dancing close to Paul, a lot of the dancers left the dance floor to just watch them as they laughed and talked about it. One of the girls near to them, shouted, "Go on, Julie! Get in there!" This made Paul laugh.

Michael thought, *If it were me, I too, would have been off before now.*

Melanie said, "Good luck to him, if he lasts the pace."

And Michael said, "Surely this is the moment when he can say, 'Hello, Australia!' She does have a lot of energy."

Melanie laughed and said, "Yes. Probably from the Sanatogen tablets!"

He laughed and said, "Or the tonic wine."

Sarah came off the dance floor to join them, laughing. "Well, I don't know where she came from. Just look at them. And look at her swing her arms around. She could almost be an aerobics instructor!"

Melanie smiled and said, "Yes. She could be giving a lesson right now."

Sarah laughed again. "Well, he's got his work cut out the way she's going at that. She could actually be one of those long-lost girls that he may have met on New Year's Eve."

Michael said, "Well, they do seem to maybe know each other quite well."

Paul then chatted to Julie, and then they continued dancing for a bit longer until he left the floor to join Sarah. Melanie said, "He's obviously giving her the spiel about possibly knowing her."

Michael said, "It seems so."

Paul came over to them with a bit of a lather on and said, "Hi, that was quite a bit of fun. I know her from coming here before with some mates. She's great company and likes all types of dancing, especially jive," panting slightly.

Melanie said, "Yes, she danced very well to that. You two gave quite an exhibition."

Paul laughed and said, "Thanks, sport. I like to entertain."

Michael said, "Yes, it was enjoyable, and she knows her dancing." Paul said, "Thanks, mate, and, yes, she really likes the different moves."

Paul went for another drink, and Michael went to do some more dancing. Melanie and Sarah joined him, doing the usual moves to some of the eighties and nineties tracks. Paul chatted with Julie and her group of girls who joined them a little later on the dance floor. Michael chatted occasionally to Melanie and Sarah about some of the music whilst dancing to it.

When it got fairly late, Melanie and Sarah ordered a taxi as Michael was dancing, and they waved to him before leaving. He left a little later and waved to Paul on his way out. Paul was sitting and chatting with Julie and her group.

Michael walked home since it was a dry and fairly mild night. As he walked, he thought, *Well, it doesn't appear that it was Melanie who gave me that Valentine. I didn't really get any positive indication from her, but somebody sent it to me and suggested that we meet there. Perhaps it was done as a joke between the three of them to get me there, but why? Unless whoever it was couldn't make it?*

15

SOPHIE'S STORY

A few weeks later, on a Saturday afternoon, Michael decided, out of curiosity, to drive around and find out where Sophie was living. When he arrived near to where it was, he nervously parked the car on the other side of the road and thought, *Why the heck have I done this? I don't know what I'll say to her if I see her. I could put myself in a funny situation too.* He felt a bit like a stalker. After a few moments, just as he decided to drive off, he saw Sophie with Fido in his rear view-mirror rushing gently towards his car. Through the mirror it appeared that she was holding the dog's lead in her right hand. He saw that she was wearing a white T-shirt under her white raincoat with a blue jeans skirt over her blue Lycra leggings with black shoes.

She knocked on his window with her right hand as he thought, *Now I'm committed. What have I done by coming here?* He felt that he'd got cold feet. As he turned the window down, she smiled and said, "Hi, Michael. Have you come to try and see me?"

He answered, "Sort of. I happened to be in this area, so I thought I'd have a look." He cringed a little at what he'd just said.

"Well, I'm glad you've come. Do you want to come and have some tea?"

He smiled, feeling a little better and said, "Yes thanks, I think I will." He stopped the engine and got out of the car feeling a little embarrassed and flustered, thinking, *I'm now back to having to give a good impression again. What now? I just have to try and relax and go with the flow.*

"OK, that's good. I live just a few houses down there on the … um left." They crossed the road to the left-hand side and walked to her house as Fido kept smelling Michael's legs and jumping up at him with his left paw.

Michael wasn't so keen on such boisterous dogs and said, "By! He's certainly friendly. Too friendly I think. I don't mind as long as he doesn't think I'm a tree or something."

Sophie giggled loudly and said, "Oh, you! He's not like that, are you Fido?" She smiled and petted him saying, "Oh, Fido, don't worry. He doesn't mean it. You're not that kind of dog, are you?" She bent down and made a fuss of him, making a few cooing noises in a soppy voice, which Michael thought was quite lovely. She then said, "After that comment, you're lucky that he didn't oblige you!" She looked straight into Michael's eyes and smiled.

He laughed and said, "Would I mean such a thing? Sorry, Fido."

She smiled and said, "Well then, Fido, I don't think he means it." Fido then smelled Michael's legs again, instinctively causing Michael to back off slightly.

Sophie laughed and said, "Well, Michael, I think he's forgiven you. You've both made up."

They arrived at her front door, and Michael was enjoying how soppy she sounded with the dog's name and everything. He said, "I'm not so sure about that. He may be ready to do it now."

She looked seriously at him whilst tutting and shaking her head. Then she laughed and said, "Oh, Michael. Your sense of humour! He won't forgive you now." She removed the lead from the dog and patted Michael on the shoulder with her left hand.

Michael said, "Probably not."

"Oh, he will. I'm sure that he'll have forgotten by tomorrow ... well, hopefully." She chuckled. They went in, and she said, "Hi, Maureen. I happened to bump into somebody I know slightly and thought I'd invite him round. This is Michael."

Michael saw Maureen, who was a late-middle-aged lady with brown eyes. She was wearing a dark-grey, long-sleeved blouse under her-red-and-green-patterned pullover with blue trousers and white trainers. She was a little plump and stood around five foot six. She had dark-brown-and-grey mottled hair. Maureen said, "Hi, Michael. It's nice to see you."

"Yes. I'm pleased to meet you, Maureen." He shook her hand.

She had a firm handshake, and she said, "Thanks. I'll put a pot of tea on while you two chat."

He said, "Thanks."

Sophie said, "Well, it's lucky you came today because I only come here on Saturdays. This is where I used to live for a bit, but recently I've had nothing permanent. That is why I left you this address."

He asked, "Where are you living now then?"

"I'm only just down the road in temporary accommodation, so I'll be moving again soon, but I don't know exactly where yet."

Maureen came in and said, "Sophie first came here from overseas just over a year ago. She was in a bit of a fix like most people coming over from the Ukraine."

Sophie said, "Yes. I was over there for just over five years and lost all my identification, so I had to come back here and start from scratch. I originally lived here before that, of course, and my family are still over there."

Maureen left to prepare the tea.

Michael said, "Well, that must have been a bad experience."

Sophie said, "Yes. I had to replace a passport, driving license, National Insurance number, and everything else once I got here. I hardly had any money and only the clothes I was wearing."

Maureen returned and said, "And when she arrived at the Salvation Army where I work, she was really in a bad state with a very nasty cold. I helped her over the next few days until she suddenly disappeared just when I brought a nurse in. She arrived back that evening, though, and gradually got better after that on her own accord."

Sophie laughed and said, "Well, at least I recovered after a week."

Maureen smiled and said, "Well, just about. It was actually a little longer than that, but anyway, she helped us out in the soup kitchens after that whilst I gave her board and lodgings here to get herself back on her feet."

Sophie said, "Yes. It was quite a long haul before I got all my documentation sorted out, before I could find work." She told him the name of the supermarket that she worked for. She continued, "I stacked shelves for a time there, until I progressed further. I then moved on to where I'm currently working."

He said, "Wow. It's been quite an uphill task for you. You've done well to come out of it and lead a normal life. It's an eye opener to know what it must have been like to come over here with nothing and then get started."

She said, "Yes. Fortunately, I've done quite well on the stock market over the last few months. I've made enough money to buy myself a reasonably good second-hand car so I can travel to work. And I've been able to afford other things."

He said, "You've done well then. My father's had plenty of experience making money on the stock market. It's not all been plain sailing though. There have been some losses and write-offs."

She said, "Yes, I had one or two losses, but fortunately kept my head above water." She smiled.

Maureen, who had just returned with the tea, said, "Well, you've come out of it fairly quickly, and it's good you're doing OK now."

Michael wondered if this was another girl who was too good for him. He thought, *Maybe she's even more capable than the magnificent Sarah could be. After all, she had just shown how quickly she had progressed.* He said, "I guess it was necessity that got you to where you are now, Sophie."

Maureen said, "Well, they say that necessity is the mother of invention." She smiled and handed Sophie a mug of tea, which Sophie accepted in her left hand.

Sophie dropped two sugar lumps into her mug and stirred it whilst saying, "Yes, it's been interesting. Thanks for the tea."

Maureen said, "OK, you're fine." And she gave Michael his mug of tea.

He said, "Thanks, Maureen."

She responded, "Yes, you're welcome." And she turned to pick up hers.

Michael thought to ask, "I'm curious. What happened when you moved on after stacking shelves there?"

Sophie looked at him a little nervously and answered, "Yes … After that, I went to help with the accounts, and that's when I thought about dabbling in the stock market to give myself a head start money wise. I was rather fortunate—call it beginner's luck I suppose. I made some money, but it wasn't all a bed of roses, as I said before. I did lose some, but by having a reasonable spread of investments, I did more than cover those fairly quickly on other things."

Michael said, "Yes. My father had a very wide spread of investments in different areas to cover the risks of certain categories that didn't perform well, by hedging a bit."

She said, "Yes. I adopted some of those principles."

He said, "Well, by the sound of it, you did very well in such a short space of time to make enough to buy a car and do other things. You are good." He felt awed by her, possibly more so than with Sarah. He now had enough and felt that he was wasting his time with her, feeling that she was definitely too good for him, but there was something intriguing about her that made him want to stay a bit longer and ask her some more questions.

She said, "Don't get me wrong, I'm no genius. A lot of it was luck, probably due to the right timing." She smiled.

He said, "Yes like my father said timing is of the essence, and if you can buy right, you can always sell right."

She said, "Yes, I learned that. Certain books that I read taught me."

He thought, *What a smart girl. She's ahead of most people*. He was now getting cold feet, but he was still interested. He asked, "Did you go any further there, other than helping with the accounts?"

She looked straight at him, but then looked a little concerned and tearful. She paused and answered, "Yes, only just. I did a little of the type of work I'm doing now. I helped process order notes and had a hand in helping with the some of the buying orders. That's how I progressed to the job I'm doing now, which is a bit of buying, besides doing some of the bookkeeping linked to purchases."

He said, "Well done. It sounds like the kind of the work that two of the girls where I work at do. They are both very good at what they do. As I told you, I do a lot of the processing of their invoices besides all the other expenses and sales invoices, but I work as an assistant to David Evans, who is the head of my department. It's mainly all on the computer though."

She smiled and said, "Well, we're similar. We all have significant roles to play."

Maureen said, "Very interesting, both of you. You're both experts in your own different fields."

Michael finished drinking his tea and said, "Anyway, I'd best be getting off. I've got certain things I need to do before the end of the afternoon." As he looked at his watch, he thought that he knew enough about how good she was now and didn't particularly want to know any more. He got up and said, "It's been nice chatting." He wanted to leave her with a good impression and get on his way before he said anything silly.

Maureen said, "It's been nice chatting too. You're welcome to come again."

He noticed Maureen prod Sophie with her right hand. Michael thought, *Well another Melanie and Sarah. I'll go quickly. I thought Sophie was so lovely and about my type, until she just showed me how great she is*. He said, "OK. I'll probably see you around." And he left to walk to his car.

Sophie came behind him and said, "Come on, Michael, I'd like to see you again. This was just something I had to do, and I got lucky I suppose, a lot of the time."

He said, "Well, I could do with a bit more luck sometimes." He thought of that saying "You make your own luck," and he felt a tear in his eye. He thought, *Pull yourself together, Michael. Not in front of Sophie now*. He looked at her, and she seemed a little nervous and tearful as he said, "OK, I'll keep in touch."

Sophie smiled and said, "Good. I'd like that! And, from what you say, you are good at what you do. Please believe in yourself. See you again, Michael." She took his right hand into her left. He immediately felt a tingle that was similar to what he'd felt with Melanie.

Sophie looked straight into his eyes, her gaze flitting between his eyes for a moment. Then she smiled and said, "Thanks for that."

He felt joyous and said, "Yes, I'll definitely see you again."

She jumped up slightly whilst smiling and said, "Great! I'll see you sometime."

He then got into his car and waved to her as he drove off. He thought, *Wow, that's the second time I've felt like that about a girl. What's with it with those two, Sophie and Melanie?* He then did some shopping and stopped off on the way home to buy a chicken takeaway for the evening. He ate whilst having an evening in, having a few drinks and watching a film on DVD. That night he thought, *Be realistic, Michael. Don't get your hopes up and let your imagination run away with you. Sophie is just like any other girl—like Melanie and Sarah, who are way above my league. They are all beautiful and clever in different ways. I'll just keep to what I'm doing at work and hope the right one comes along someday.*

Two weeks later, on Easter Sunday morning, Michael went to church and sat with his brother. He saw Sophie come in and sit behind him and thought, *I didn't think she'd be here. Oh, it makes sense because I remember her telling me that she'd been here at the carol service when she'd talked about Fido being with her that night, the same night that he'd seemed interested in me.*

After the service was over, Michael felt nervous and

not too keen about meeting her again. He said to James, "Shall we leave now and go for our dinner?"

James replied, "Yes, why not? It was a good service wasn't it?"

Sophie, who was sitting directly behind them, answered, "Yes it was. The sermon part was very interesting, especially what he said about the resurrection."

As Michael noticed her quite strong perfume, James looked round and said, "Yes. It was quite informative." He smiled at her.

She said, "Oh, I'm Sophie by the way. I know Michael just a bit."

Michael looked round and then quietly coughed coyly and said, "Yes, we happened to meet a few times at Jack's fish and chip shop not far from where I live." He saw that she was smartly dressed in dark blue trousers with a white, long-sleeved blouse. It looked just like what Melanie and Sarah wore at work. He thought, *Our work uniform isn't the new fashion, is it?*

Sophie smiled and said, "Yes, and we happened to get chatting once on the off chance." She smiled at Michael.

Michael said, "Yes. I happened to see her when she was walking her dog." He didn't want to use Fido's name because it could show too much familiarity.

Sophie said, "Well, it's been nice chatting. I'll leave you two friends to it. I've got someone to meet."

James said, "Well, I'm Michael's brother, James. It's been good talking to you … Sophie." Michael could see that James's breath was taken away. He thought, *Goodness me, we're in church. This is too much. We should be having religious feelings. Come on, Michael, think properly. This is not the time.*

She said, "See you around, Michael, and maybe you again sometime, James."

As she walked away, Michael thought, *Oh! What's James going to think now?*

James said, "Well, Michael, she seems OK. Anyway, I'm ready to go when you are."

Margaret, a family friend, approached them and said, "Hello. It's nice to see you again. The service was good, wasn't it?"

Michael answered, "Yes, it was quite interesting, and it helps us put things in the proper perspective."

She said, "Yes, it does. If only everybody could think like that, we wouldn't have the problems that we have in the world today."

James said, "True. I've got lots of those sorts of things to deal with in my job on the police force."

Margaret said, "Yes, it must be a tough job."

James said, "You're telling me—and with all the paperwork it creates."

Michael said, "Yes. There's too much unnecessary bureaucracy. It takes us away from some of the vital things we have to do."

Margaret said, "Well, it comes in all walks of life these days. Anyway, nice chatting. Take care! See you again." She went off to meet some of the other people she knew.

Michael and James went outside to walk to their cars. James said, "Well, I'm sure I've spoken to somebody similar to Sophie before. She looks completely different but sounds very similar to how I remember Sarah."

Michael said, "I've noticed the same. Sometimes, come to think of it, some of her mannerisms are similar to Sarah's too, but she isn't ... She works for another retailer or should I say e-tailer. She does a little accountancy work, though, some of it which is similar to what I do."

James said, "Well, I noticed that she was definitely left handed, and some of her mannerisms remind me of Sarah's. Oh, I must be imagining it. They're nothing alike."

As James arrived at his car, Michael said, "I'll see you shortly at Mum and Dad's."

James responded, "Yes, see you there." As James got into his car, Michael waved to him and then went to his car to drive to his parent's house for their turkey dinner.

16

A Game of Pitch and Putt

Two days later, on Tuesday afternoon, the weather was clear and mild. It was Michael's last day off during the Easter break, and he had met up with Paul for a game of pitch and putt at a park near where Michael lived. They'd arranged the game the previous Thursday. Paul had mentioned that he was quite a keen golfer, but since Michael hadn't played much more than on that pitch and putt course, they decided to play there.

Michael carried a golf bag containing a few select irons and a putter over his shoulder and wore a blue, long-sleeved shirt with light grey trousers and black shoes. When he met up with Paul, he was surprised to see that Sarah was also there, still wearing a blouse from work, but this time with light-grey trousers and white trainers. Paul, who had his own bag and golfing trolley, was wearing a white T-shirt and blue jeans with white golfing shoes. He said, "Hi, Michael. Sarah seemed quite keen to come along with us, so I thought I'd give her the chance. I hope you don't mind, mate. She's good company and hasn't played much either, so I thought it'd be fair to bring her along."

Michael squirmed a little bit but had to accept it, remembering that he had wondered occasionally whether she might drop in again two days ago during his Easter day meal with his parents and James, similar to how she'd come on Christmas day. He said a little reluctantly, "That's OK. The more the merrier."

She smiled and said, "Thanks. I've been looking forward to playing again, because I haven't played since last summer."

Paul said, "Oh, I play all the year round on and off to keep my hand in. It's very easy to go downhill in this game if you don't keep practicing."

Michael smiled and said, "Well then, I think if you've been playing that much and with all those irons, you must be in good practice. Surely Sarah and I deserve some sort of a start."

Paul said, "You don't need to ask, mate. I play on a handicap of twenty, so I'll give you eight based on the Aussie rules, and I'll give Sarah sixteen strokes, her being a sheila. That should be bonza enough, shouldn't it?"

Sarah laughed and said, "Yes, sixteen sounds great. That's where it's an advantage to be a so-called sheila, isn't it, Michael?" She chuckled.

He answered, "Yes. You have an eight start on me too, sheila. Excuse the pun." He laughed and then continued, "But I don't think that's fair because I haven't played much either. It'll be all right between us and Paul, but you and I should be on level terms."

Paul said, "Don't be a wus. All gents should automatically be eight strokes behind a lady if they don't have a particular registered handicap."

Michael said, "Fine, but for me, I'm basing it on level terms."

Sarah said, "I don't mind. We'll look at it from all the points of view when we're finished, hey Paul?" She smiled.

Paul said, "Yes, OK. I know you'll enjoy all that extra number crunching, Sarah, but I'll look at it the way it should be!" He laughed. They went into the clubhouse to pay. Sarah paid a deposit to hire an iron and a putter, as well as a few balls and some tees. She chose a left-handed five iron and the standard two-sided putter. Michael was surprised that she'd chosen the left-handed iron, and Paul said, "I guessed you were ambidextrous, love, but a five iron—you'll be way over-hitting that ball on a diddy course such as this. I would use at the most a seven here to give yourself a chance with some of the shorter chipping shots."

Sarah said, "Well, I'm just making sure that I can give myself the chance to hit the ball the full distance."

Paul huffed and said, "Well, it's your choice. Five irons are no good for getting out of the rough or out of bunkers, and you being a leftie and all that, you'll be no good with borrowing my irons. I just thought I'd put that to you."

Sarah said, "Fine, thanks. I'll take the seven iron then." She handed her five iron back to the attendant, who said, "That's good advice. The seven will cover you for nearly all the required shots on a course like this." He handed her a seven and smiled.

The threesome went on to start at the first hole. Paul smiled and said, "Since you're a sheila ... Oh, excuse me. Just kidding, Sarah. You can start." He laughed.

She said, "Rightly so. Girls should have at least some privileges."

Paul said, "Well, some people still believe that the word *golf* means 'gentleman only, ladies forbidden'. I don't know why ladies would want to play a gentleman's game!" He restrained a smile.

Sarah said, "Well, I've watched some ladies in tournaments. They can play as well as any gentleman." She shook her head and smiled. Paul didn't react to her comment. Sarah then placed her tee in the ground, put the ball on the tee, and hit the ball fairly well through the air. It landed just before the green.

Paul said, "That was a good first shot. I can tell you've played before." He looked a bit bewildered. He then took his shot and landed it in the middle of the green. He said, "I didn't expect a bonza one like that immediately. It's been two weeks since I'd last played." He smiled.

Michael said, "Good shot! But you have the benefit of using your own irons."

Paul said, "Fair dinkum, mate, but it's much easier than some of those three-par holes, where you sometimes need a three iron. I did this with a nine."

Sarah laughed and said, "Show off! You should be ahead of us by a lot more than a stroke a hole by the way you're talking, and especially with all those irons.

You didn't really need all those on such a diddy course as this."

He said, "I do. Whatever course I play, I always take these with me." He chuckled.

Sarah huffed and said, "Oh, whatever."

Michael took his shot with his seven iron. He topped it slightly, pushing his tee into the ground, and the ball trickled along the fairway, finishing only half way towards the green.

Sarah said, "That's a surprise. I thought you'd do better."

Michael said, "It's all this banter between you two that's put me off."

Paul smiled and said, "I shouldn't have let that put you off, mate. Anyway, from where you've finished, you only need a relatively short pitch to land that on the green. Here, try my nine iron."

Sarah said, "Oy, you needn't lend him yours as well. He's already got an unfair advantage by having his own."

Paul, "Well from your first shot, you seemed to be looking good enough."

She pouted and said, "Hey, you now. That could be beginner's luck for all you know."

Paul said, "I doubt it. You can't kid a kidder. Anyway, Michael, try it out." Paul loaned Michael his nine.

Michael said, "Thanks," but Sarah looked a little disgusted. He took the shot and it went through the air and landed just before the green and rolled onto the edge of it.

Paul said, "Wow! That was a fairly good shot for you!" Michael saw Sarah laugh as she looked at him.

Michael said, "Thanks, I get your drift."

Paul said, "I'm serious. You played that OK. You can tell now how much better it could be with a few more irons. That'll bring you further on in the game, sport."

Michael understood the greater choice of irons that he could play with.

Sarah said, "Good shot, Michael, and I only have this single one I can play with." She walked to where her ball was.

Paul quietly said to Michael, "I think it was an act that she put on when she first hired that five iron. I know her. She can bluff quite a lot and has had me fooled occasionally. I'm sure she's naturally left handed. I've seen her using the computer sometimes. What I don't understand is why she would want to bother pretending because left handedness is a natural thing."

Michael thought, *Perhaps she is reverse, but she can't be because Susan's gone back, if she was ever here in the first place. I thought all that ridiculous stuff I imagined was all over now. Come on, Michael, she's nothing like what I'd be like. She's big and feisty, and she's got red hair and deep brown eyes. She can't be.* He said, "Well, I've heard cases where some parents try to push left handers into using their right hands. Maybe that's something to do with it."

As they approached the green, Paul said, "You could be right."

Sarah said, "Come on, I've been waiting here. What have you two been bickering about?" She smiled.

Michael wanted to pull her leg a bit like Paul did, so he answered, "Well, we're talking all about you, Sarah, aren't we Paul?"

Paul laughed and replied, "Yes. Sometimes us lads like to chat, especially about a sheila."

Sarah said, "Ooh. One of you is bad enough, but two! Michael, you'd better be careful at the things he says. He'll corrupt your mind."

Michael said, "Not me. I've heard it all before."

Paul said, "Bonza one, mate. Now, Sarah, it'll be your shot next since you're the furthest from the green. Remember, you have to bend over slightly in your case, so you can keep your eye on the ball."

Michael, getting his drift, smiled.

She said, "OK." Then she looked at Michael and said, "And what's that supposed to mean?"

Paul answered, "You wouldn't want to know."

She huffed as she took her shot, just scuffing the ball onto the green. She said, "Now look what you've made me do."

Paul said, "Soz rock." She looked a little hard at him whilst sighing and then smiled. She then looked at her ball with quite a lot of concentration and sized up the long putt. She took her shot, and when the ball went in, she did a little jump for joy, saying, "Well look at that. I'm down for three after all that."

Paul didn't look too amused, but he said, "Bonza one, Sarah. That was a very good putt. Well done."

Michael was surprised about that too and thought, *Maybe she was putting on a show regarding that five iron after all. She obviously wanted to give us a false sense of security by bluffing.* He said, "Yes, good shot, Sarah."

She said, "Thanks. This game could be promising after all." She smiled at both of them.

Paul then took two putts for a three, and Michael concentrated hard and ended putting for a four.

When they got to the second tee, Paul said, "It'll be you to play first Sarah, since we both got a three."

She quickly said, "OK. It's a much longer hole, but I should still make it with this."

Paul said, "Unfortunately, it's the only one you've got. Up until now, you seemed to do most things with your right hand. Wouldn't you like to try with my five iron, if you're unsure?"

She answered, "There's no point. I've tried playing golf right handed before, and it doesn't seem to work for me."

He said, "Fair enough. Obviously, if you want to play more golf, I should think about buying a range of irons sort of similar to what Michael's got. If you take it up fully, it'll be best to go for a full set."

She said, "I'll think about that because certain holes can be too long for a seven."

He said, "Well, a seven should cover the distance of all these holes. With quite a lot of practice, you'll know that." He smiled.

Sarah said, "OK, OK. I know you know the game quite well." She then took her shot. It went into the air and landed just short of the green.

Paul said, "I think I'll use a seven too." He landed his near the centre of the green. Michael picked out his five iron and hit the ball, which finished ten yards beyond the green. He then took his second shot because he was furthest away. That one finished on the green but was still quite a long way from the hole. Sarah's second shot was similar, and then Paul took two shots to putt his for a three. Sarah and Michael each took two putts to finish for four.

After the next five holes, they compared their running totals. Paul was in the lead after the seventh hole with twenty-one, Sarah had twenty-six, and Michael was third with twenty-seven. Paul said to Michael, "She's got a bonza score, mate, considering she's a stroke ahead of you and using only one iron."

Michael, who felt bad enough about trailing in last place and behind a girl, didn't really need to be reminded of that. He said, "Well, I've just been unlucky on the third when my putt hit that part of the pot sticking out of the ground and on the last hole when it bounced badly through a divot scrape."

Paul said, "Well I've had some close ones too, where I could've done better. I nearly had a two on the fourth hole and should have got three on the fifth. I fluffed that easy putt."

Sarah said, "And my game hasn't been great either. I nearly had a four on the third hole, when my ball happened to bounce off the pin."

Paul said, "Well, since you and I've just had a three, I'll let you start."

She said, "OK." She placed her tee in the ground and put the ball on it. She took her shot, slicing it to the left, where it landed in a bunker. She said, "Oh no! I've got to take that with a seven iron."

Michael said, "Well, it can be done. You just have to stand off it a little and make your iron almost flat with the ground, a bit like a sand wedge."

Paul said, "Yes. That's the only way you can avoid it hitting the lip with that seven you've got, when you try to hit it out." He took his shot, and it finished just short of the green as he mumbled something to himself. Michael felt better that they both hadn't had good first shots, and he relaxed a bit more. He used his seven iron to tee off, and his ball landed just before the green and then rolled on.

Sarah sighed and disappointedly said, "Well, I may as well go and play mine first then. It's the furthest away." She walked ahead of them with her head down.

Paul said, "She's got a lot on to recover from that, because she still has some distance to cover." As they walked towards the bunker where her ball was, Michael felt better because he could now regain some strokes against her to probably finish second and not last.

Sarah took several practice strokes beside the bunker before trying her second shot. She then slowly and nervously got into the bunker and a took a shot that just threw up some sand that blew back in her face. She spat it out and said, "Oh, sugar, this is horrible. The wind's just blown everything into my face."

Paul said, "OK. Just take it easy now and keep your eye on the ball."

She said, "Easier said than done now!" She took another hard swipe at it, pushing the ball nearer the lip. She then threw her iron down in disgust. When she bent down to pick it up she said, "Really, this is impossible now." She looked flustered. She then paused and played the ball just to get it out on her fourth stroke. "Well at least I've gone for damage limitation after all that," she said.

Michael, feeling for her, said, "You did the right thing. I couldn't have got that out any other way, by how close it was to that lip."

She said, "Thanks for that. It was just a case of having to make the best recovery." He noticed that she was red in the face, and her bra and blouse were totally uneven and all over the place.

As Sarah walked the thirty yards from there to where her ball had finished up, Paul tapped Michael on the shoulder. When Michael looked round, he saw tears of laughter in Paul's eyes. Paul could only whisper, as he was laughing so much. "Wow! Have you noticed her?" He went into another fit of giggles again. "She's wearing nothing more than a padded bra!" He broke down again laughing. He said, "I thought it was too good to be true, her having tits as big as that. By! It certainly had to be something like this because, realistically, if those were real, she'd never be able to stand up properly by being so thin. She'd topple over! They had to be fake or super fake." He laughed heavily again.

Michael looked at Sarah in the distance, and he could see she was quickly adjusting herself. As she looked back at them, Paul turned away from her and said, "Let's just pretend we haven't noticed and hope she hasn't seen my reaction. I very much doubt it though. I've made it too obvious that I know something because she's too close."

Sarah shouted, "I've taken my fifth shot, and it's on the green. Are you two goons going to take yours?"

They looked and saw her ball near to the hole. Paul was still turned away from her whilst he was laughing, so Michael said, "We'll be over in a moment. I've just seen two blue … birds fly over."

That sending Paul into further hysterics. He said, "Why the fuck did you come out with that one? I'll never be able to stop laughing now. I've almost had an accident."

Michael was laughing and said, "I just couldn't resist it. It just popped into my head." Michael composed himself and walked towards where his ball was on the green, joining Sarah there. He said, "You'll have to excuse us. Paul and I have just had a few laughs about a bunker scene in a film we saw. It was the one where Norman Wisdom was trying to get a ball out of a bunker in a film called *The Early Bird*. It was about when he was a milkman called Pitkin."

Sarah laughed and said, "Yes, I know the film. He did much worse than I did. He actually emptied the bunker into a pile of sand by the side of it. I enjoyed that film."

Paul joined them and said, "Yes, we were talking about that. That was a bonza movie." He glimpsed at her and started laughing again. Then he said, "Yes, just thinking about it creases me up."

Sarah said, "Yes, I thought it was very funny too." She then smiled and infectiously laughed with him. Michael then did the same to help continue their pretence.

Paul said, "Well, we'll stop thinking about bunkers now so we can continue the game. I'd like to get a four if I can manage it. You may as well play yours out, Sarah, since you're so close." She took her shot and putted it for a six as Paul laughed again. He then quickly forced himself to get serious and chipped his ball onto the green. He took two putting strokes for a four. Michael took two putts to finish on a three.

On the next hole, which was the ninth, Paul hit a bad shot off the tee because he was laughing again.

Sarah said, "Why are you still laughing? Surely you've got over that film by now."

Paul answered, "Somehow I just can't. I keep imagining seeing you there, doing that."

She said, "Well, it shouldn't be that amusing. But then again, it could be, the more you think about it." She smiled and said, "Now, Paul, we've got a game to play." This made him chuckle.

They continued, and each got a four on that hole. They added up their scores for the first nine holes, and Paul said, "Well, I've done this first half in twenty-nine. How have you two done?" Sarah said, "I've got thirty-six, and it's far better than I'd expected, considering that six I got after landing in that bunker."

Michael said, "Yes, but you recovered very well to keep it at that." He remembered that, in all that mayhem over Paul's laughter about Sarah in that bunker, he had never seen her fifth shot that got her so close to the hole.

Paul smiled and said, "That's very good considering that one." He just chuckled a little.

Sarah noticed him and smiled, and then Michael said, "Well, I finished with a thirty-four, which is far better than I expected. That puts me at sixty-eight, which is the rate of a fourteen handicap."

Paul laughed and said, "I'm therefore going at the rate of fifty-eight, then, which puts me at four here. I didn't expect that, but nearly all these are easy three par holes."

After the next hole, which was the first of two longer ones, Michael got a five and the other two got four. On the eleventh, when Michael took his shot with a five iron because it was the longest hole, he landed in a bunker to the right of the green. Sarah said, "Now it's your turn to try and get out. You should make it, by how you said you could use a seven iron,"

Michael was not feeling too confident about trying that type of shot. The other two were both near the green, and Michael said, "I'll let you two play your shots first." He wanted to give himself time to think about his bunker shot.

They played both their balls onto the green, and Paul said, "Now you can do your stuff, Michael. You can borrow my sand wedge if you like."

Michael answered, "No, it's all right. I'll be curious and try out my idea with the seven iron." He took a few practice shots near to where his ball was, and then he tilted his iron slightly, standing off from the ball. He took the shot rather too hard, causing it to land on the far side of the green, where it rolled off. When he took his third shot, it finished a fair distance from the pin.

Paul said, "You may as well play it out now." Michael putted it in two for a five. The other two took two putts, each for fours.

Sarah said, "You played that bunker shot quite well and with a cool head. If only I'd kept my head when I played mine." She looked annoyed as she walked ahead of them.

Paul whispered to Michael, "I don't think her annoyance was all due to those wasted shots in the bunker. I think she was mainly annoyed because she made a mess of her padded boobs." He chuckled.

Michael said, "I think your right. She may not realize, though, that we noticed, but then again, you were laughing way too much. I think she knows we know, by the way she called us goons!"

Paul said, "I agree, but let's pretend we don't know. We could have some more fun with her."

They played the next lot of holes, scoring threes and fours, except for Sarah who got a five on the thirteenth because she landed in some rough grass in a wood. After the eighteenth hole, they totalled up all their scores, and Paul said, "Well, I got a total of sixty-two for the round. That puts me on eight handicap. How did you two do?"

Sarah looked at Michael evasively, so he answered. "My score is seventy, which I suppose puts me at sixteen then."

Paul said, "Well done, considering you haven't got a handicap. You both played equally well."

Paul then looked at Sarah, who responded, "Well I was only stroke behind you, Michael, and considering my problem in that bunker, I think I've recovered fairly well. I got seventy-one."

Paul said, "That was good, considering, but you still have the booby." He laughed at his comment.

Sarah walked up to Paul and slapped him gently out of fun, saying, "Yes. I think I at least deserve a bar of chocolate for trying."

Paul said, "Fair do's. I think you do." He undid the zip of his golf bag and handed her a Snickers bar that appeared to be a little crushed.

She said, "Eww. That looks to have been there for months."

He smiled and said, "Fair dinkum, love. It's all I've got and better than nothing. Oh, if you don't want it, then, I'll have it now."

She said, "No, it's OK. I'll have it at least, please."

He laughed and passed it to her, saying, "There you are, then. It's like all sheilas—they always have to change their minds."

Michael smiled at her and said, "Yes, it can be a woman's privilege."

She said, "Hey, you, I *am* here you know." She laughed and took a bite of the Snickers bar, which she'd transferred to her right hand.

Paul said, "You can stop pretending, you know. Why not use your left hand like you want to?"

She answered, "It's just habit, I suppose. I was brought up to be a right hander. I tried to do it, but for me it just hasn't worked." She looked at Michael, paused, and then said, "Oh, yes. I've just remembered that we haven't accounted for our net handicaps!" She looked at her score and said, "Yes, I thought so. I wasn't entitled to this bar because, by the handicap rules, I have actually won this round. Because I went round in seventy-one, I'm seventeen over par, which gives me the net score of nineteen, based on my handicap of thirty-six." She laughed and did a little jig.

Paul smiled reluctantly and said, "Yes, I thought you'd find some way of winning, Sarah." He sighed and then said, "Yes. Looking at my score and Michael's, we've unfortunately come in joint second because, after working it out, I figure my net score is twelve just the same as his, so at least nobody's come last. Can you give us the rest of that bar to share now, since you're not entitled to it?"

Michael squirmed and said, "Err, no thanks. It's OK. You may as well finish it off now since you've started it." He forced a laugh.

Sarah laughed and said, "Oh, Michael, there's no need to be like that. I'm not carrying any sort of disease, you know." She pouted and then looked disgusted at him. She then smiled and said, "Besides, I think I'm entitled to it now, but as the winning prize."

Paul said, "Well, as a gentleman, I'll also say you can finish it off now." He smiled at her.

She chuckled and said, "Thanks. That's very good of you."

Paul said, "If I'd kept my mouth shut about these handicap differences, I'd have still won fair and square today."

Michael smiled slightly and said, "And I would have come second rather than joint last, so it hasn't benefited me either."

Sarah laughed and said, "Well, thanks. It was a great surprise to find out that I technically won after working it all out."

Paul said, "Yes, technically, but I still like to consider the actual scores."

Paul smiled at Michael, who said, "Well, if we play again, we'll have to set Sarah's handicap at seventeen— where she'd finished today—to make it fair for all of us.

I don't mind mine being at sixteen, just on here of course because there's only one in it between us."

Paul said, "Fair dinkum, mate. That'll make it more interesting, and I'll play harder next time, knowing that." He smiled.

Sarah then said, "Why did you have to go and say that just now, Michael?" She slapped him gently on the shoulder and said, "He won't be giving us any leeway now."

Paul said, "No, I certainly won't, and I'm glad he mentioned it because it gives me something to play for next time." He laughed and then said to Michael, "Well, it's been an enjoyable game. Sarah and I are going for a drink and a bite to eat in a bit. I wonder if you'd like to join us."

Michael thought and answered, "Well, I'd like to, but I'd best get on my way because I have a few things to do before tea. I'll see you both tomorrow probably." He felt that he wanted some time to himself to think about things. Additionally, he felt that he should leave them together now since they could be an item.

Paul said, "OK then, mate. We'll see you later."

Sarah looked a little concerned at Michael and said, "Yes. I'll probably see you tomorrow too, Michael."

He said, "Yes, see you." He went to his car and put his clubs in the boot. He then waved to them both and drove home.

17

APRIL FOOL'S DAY

First thing at work the next day, Michael overheard Sarah talking on the telephone to a supplier. He noticed that, when she spoke slowly several times, she sounded just like Sophie. After the phone call, she and Melanie left the office as they would normally do on a Monday morning to go and visit certain suppliers. Their visits were especially important as this was the first day back after the long Easter break.

As they left the office, Michael went to the window. He saw Sarah's reasonably new Ford Mondeo parked, and he noted down its registration number. He watched as they arrived at the car. When Sarah looked up towards his window, he quickly moved away from it and sat down in his office chair, feeling annoyed that he may have been spotted. He continued processing the backlog of invoices that he had just started.

Later that day after work, Michael drove to Jack's

fish and chips shop hoping that he might bump into Sophie. He wanted to see her car and see if it was the same one as Sarah's. He went in to buy some fish and chips, and Jack said, "Hi, Michael, how are you? Is it the usual with the curry?"

Michael answered, "Thanks. I'm fine, and yes, please, I'll have that I think." He looked round to see if Sophie might arrive.

Jack said, "I don't know if she'll be coming in today. She's mainly been coming in on Fridays recently."

Michael said, "OK. Thanks." He felt a little embarrassed that Jack knew that he seemed interested in her. He handed Jack a ten-pound note, and Jack went to the till to get his change.

As Jack handed Michael his change, he said, "Yes. Sophie's a lovely lass and easy to talk to. I'm surprised that I've never seen her with a lad. She's nearly always by herself." Michael thought about that. Jack then whistled to himself until the fish and chips were ready. He scooped them up and wrapped them up, passing them to Michael. He then prepared Michael's curry and handed him that, saying, "I hope you enjoy. See you later, Michael."

Michael said, "Yes, thanks. I'll see you soon." When he left the shop, he looked around to see if Sophie might turn up, but she didn't. He drove home and put a DVD on to watch whilst eating his fish and chips.

Two days later after work, Michael decided to go to Jack's fish and chips shop again to hopefully spot Sophie and take some fish and chips home for his evening meal.

He'd purposely parked on the street he had seen Sophie walk to the previous time so he could see her car.

Jack said to Michael as he handed him his food, "Oh, Sophie's here, Michael!" He smiled and said to Sophie, "Oh, hi, Sophie. How are you? Michael was here the other day and seemed to be looking out for you!"

Michael cringed at Jack being so open about Michael's intent. Michael then saw that Sophie was wearing a white T-shirt with tight blue jeans and white trainers. He said, "Well, I was here then and just wondered if I might see you."

She smiled and said, "Thanks. It's nice to see you again, Michael. How are you?" She turned to Jack. "And how are you, Jack?"

Jack smiled and replied, "Oh, I'm fine, and I hope you are."

She replied, "I am now that I've met up with you two." She smiled.

Michael said, "Thanks ..." He then became a little tongue tied.

Jack said to Sophie, "Do you want what you usually have?"

"I think I'll just have cod and chips with a curry, please."

Michael said, "I'll treat you if you like."

She smiled and said, "OK. Thanks."

Michael then wondered why he had just blurted that out. He thought, *I must not get carried away here. I only want to see if she drives Sarah's Ford Mondeo, thereby proving that Sophie is Sarah.*

As Michael paid Jack for her portion, Jack said,

"Well, you've landed on your feet, Sophie. That's a kind gesture, Michael."

Michael responded, "Thanks."

Jack wrapped up her portion and said, "I hope you both enjoy. See you again."

Michael said, "Thanks."

Sophie said, "We'll see you again."

As they left the shop, Sophie asked, "Anyway. How have you been recently?"

Michael answered, "I've been OK. It's been a busy week even though it's only been three days. It's all the catching up, due to the backlog after the Easter break."

She said, "Yes, tell me about it. I've had very much the same."

He asked, "Have you been OK with it?"

She answered, "Well, on and off I suppose." As he walked with her up the street towards his car, she asked, "Aren't you going the wrong way?"

He answered, "No. I'm just parked up here on the right." He knew that he had parked on the left-hand side.

She smiled and said, "Well, mine's just there. It's that five-year-old Toyota Aygo on the left."

He thought, *Well, that's knocked that notion on the head. She isn't Sarah after all.* He said, "Well, mine is just two cars past that." He realized how silly he sounded, after saying that he had been parked on the right-hand side. He said, "Well I know I get carried away sometimes on April Fool's Day."

She chuckled and said, "You're not the only one. My being left handed always gets me going with the jokes, but I'm not half left, I'm all right." She laughed.

He said, "And I feel half baked!"

She said, "Steady on, mate. Don't go too far!"

She reminded Michael of Paul. He thought about that and said, "Don't go all Aussie on me. I played a game of golf on Tuesday with an Aussie mate and his girlfriend from work. He whooped us both. He was a darned professional on scratch. It wasn't fair because he wouldn't even allow us a handicap. When I worked it out at the end on the handicap basis, I had beaten him by seven strokes, based on my standard twenty-eight handicap. Sarah, though, who is his fancy piece, got nowhere near because she finished well over a hundred for the round. These Aussies—they can be way too competitive you know." He watched for her reaction.

She stared ahead, looking rather breathless. Then she looked wide eyed at him and said, "Was that so? Them Aussies, I don't know."

He smiled and said, "Just kidding—April fool! It was nothing like that. We had a fun game and it was only pitch and putt. Sarah played quite well, even though she had a problem getting out of a bunker. She finished at seventy-one, I got seventy, and Paul got sixty-two. We worked out that Sarah got the best net score though."

She said, "Sounds good. What do you think of her?" She looked at him and smiled.

He thought for a bit and answered, "Well, she's a nice girl, but she's a work colleague. She's very well organized at her job in purchasing and runs things very well."

Sophie said, "Sounds like you work for a good firm, and it seems that what I do is similar to the type of work that she does in the firm you work for. Anyway, I must get going. Our fish and chips will be getting cold if we stay here much longer." She smiled at him.

He then said, "If you like, you could follow me back to my place and we could eat together."

She looked at him, paused, and then said, "OK. That'll be nice."

He smiled and said, "Thanks. I'm glad you're coming." He told her his address, just in case she couldn't follow him all the way there. They got into their cars and drove to his flat. He felt apprehensive again about making a good impression. He drove into the car park at his flat, and she followed him in. When they got out of their cars, he said, "I'm pleased that you managed to keep up. You never know if you're going to get separated at a traffic light or something when you're following someone."

She said, "Yes, I agree. It wasn't far anyway."

He keyed in the password at the front door. As they walked to his flat, he said, "You'll have to excuse the slight mess in there. I wasn't planning to have any visitors."

He opened the door, and she said, "You're OK."

When they went in, he saw her looking keenly around. He asked, "Do you want anything to drink, like a cup of tea?"

She answered, "Yes, please. Tea would be nice."

He went into the kitchen and put on the kettle. Then he served up their fish and chips on plates. There was a bit of an uncomfortable silence during which he could hear her breathing lightly. She then said, "It's a nice place you've got here. It's a similar flat to mine. I'll probably be moving out of mine shortly. I still haven't got a permanent place yet."

He said, "Well, I hope you find something. It'd be nice to know where you stand." He laid out the knives and forks on the table, setting hers the opposite way round—her fork on the right and knife on the left. He then poured the hot water into the pot and brought the tea to the table. He saw her start to eat with her knife and fork the wrong way round for about ten seconds. She then looked at him and then quickly switched them round, saying, "April fool! I've fooled you on that one. By the way, you shouldn't play these jokes after midday." She smiled slightly.

He smiled and said, "Yes I know, but I sometimes just get carried away. Anyway, I see that you're enjoying it."

She smiled and said, "Yes, that and the fish and chips."

There was a pause and then he asked, "What sort of games do you like? Do you like Monopoly? Chess? Computer games?"

She answered, "I've played all those now and again. I like some computer games, but I prefer board games such as Monopoly and chess because they're more traditional."

He felt the same and said, "We could perhaps play a game of chess after this if you like."

She said, "OK. I'd like that. I won't be able to stay late, of course, because I have to take Fido for a walk last thing, as well as feed him."

He said, "That's OK. I understand. Do you want a little music on whilst we continue eating?"

She answered, "OK. Do you have any Coldplay or anything?"

He smiled and thought about saying, "Of course I do," but refrained from that and answered, "Yes, I can put some of that on. I can play the latest album if you like."

She said, "OK. Thanks. That'll be nice." After the music was playing, she said, "I've got all their albums. Have you?"

He replied, "Yes, I have." He thought about how similar their tastes were. He said, "My favourite is *X and Y*. There are some terrific tracks on that."

She paused and said, "Yes, that's one of my favourites, and I like this one."

He then asked her, "Do you want anything for afters?" He suddenly thought about what Paul's reaction might be to a question like that in front of such a stunning girl as Sophie.

She immediately restrained a giggle and said, "Yes, I wouldn't mind. I could have an orange juice."

He answered, "I'm afraid I don't have any of that. I drink cranberry and, occasionally, grapefruit juice." He thought again about the possibility of somebody who is laterally inverted tasting a lemony flavour when they drank orange juice.

She said, "OK. Never mind. I could maybe have cranberry juice I suppose."

He said, "OK then. I think I'll have some of that too."

She said, "Thanks." When they had both finished, he carried their plates into the kitchen and poured a glass of cranberry juice for each of them. He gave her hers, and she thanked him. He went to his bedroom to fetch his chess set. Back in the lounge, he purposely set it up incorrectly, having the black square on the bottom right, as it would appear in a mirror. She looked at it and then smiled and said, "You're being an April fool again. The bottom right square should always be white, or else you'll have the white pieces being effectively like the blacks."

He thought, *Well, I haven't got her on that one. If she is laterally inverted, then she's being smart right now and is on the ball.* He said, "Oh, silly me. I'm still going on with these jokes." They smiled at each other.

She said, "Never mind, Michael. We're getting there." She chuckled, sounding a lot like Sarah did when she tended to come out on top.

He then reset the board properly and said, "Well, OK. The most important part is what happens in the game."

She responded, "You're telling me. Thanks for that."

He thought, "What a smart Alec." He said, "Well, since you're a sheila ... Excuse me, I mean Sophie, I'll let you play white and start." He chuckled.

She responded, "Now now, Michael, how male of you. Thanks."

He said, "That's OK. I know now that you have the upper hand by starting, so if you beat me, that'll be why."

She said, "Smart Alec. But if I beat you convincingly, that won't be the reason!"

He said, "Fair enough. We'll see." He thought about her using the words "Smart Alec," just after he had thought that of her.

She moved her king's pawn two squares forward. He smiled and moved his by two. She moved her white bishop out. Michael knew that she was attempting Scholar's Mate. He knocked out that possibility by moving his white knight to two squares in front of his black bishop. She sighed slightly and likewise moved her opposing knight. She said, "Well, it was worth a try. I've had Scholar's Mate a few times before."

He said, "Me too. It's fun when you manage it, but I've never done it to the same person twice."

She laughed and said, "Me neither. I always have to play it the long way round now, and the games can be so lengthy."

He said, "Yes. Same with some of mine too." They both moved their pieces fairly quickly over the next few moves into the middle of the board. They later swapped a knight and a bishop each, and then Michael was pleased to swap queens when hers got near to putting him in checkmate a couple of times. He then castled to get his king safer, and she castled a few moves later. A short time after that, he tried his best to exchange his remaining black bishop for her knight. He knew that, if he could, his knight would be more effective than her remaining white bishop because a knight can occupy any square, whereas a bishop can only keep to its own coloured square. He had played tactically like that before, knowing that once his opponent had one bishop against his one knight, he could relax by keeping his king and any unguarded pawns safely on the alternate squares from his opposition's bishop, making it effectively redundant. She kept her knight safely out of his way, though, and that annoyed him until he was pleased to finally swap them because she was able to use hers too well for his liking. He thought, *Wow, she plays a tight game with that thing, just like I do.* They were then left with two opposite-coloured bishops, a few pawns, and two rooks.

He worked on positioning one of his rooks to get a possible checkmate on her king at the back row, hoping she wouldn't move one of her pawns forward that was near to it. If she did, the king would be able to escape from check, making it abortive. When he'd finally moved one his rooks to a position where he could do that, her rook was still on the back row. He then moved his other rook in front of it to give it away, hoping that she'd immediately take it, leaving her back row open to checkmate. He could see that she was thinking about taking his rook, but she paused and looked at him, shaking her head slightly. She then moved a pawn forward in front of her king instead. He thought, *That's that opportunity gone.* He took her rook, and she took his with another pawn. He then put her in check with his remaining rook, a move that would originally have been checkmate if that pawn hadn't been moved.

She moved her king to where that pawn originally was and said, "Good try, Michael. You nearly had me there."

He said, "Yes. I've always beaten the computer at a certain level of play by offering it a piece so it moves something out of the way to allow me checkmate."

She said, "Yes. I've used that same tactic too."

He looked at the board, wondering if she might have something similar to that in mind. He moved one of his pawns in front of his king just for safety so he wouldn't have to continue watching for that possibility against him.

He worked on moving his pawns forward for a possible queen using his king, rook, and bishop where he could, seeing that her pawns were slightly further ahead than his. She continued to use her rook very well to help advance her pawns forward, making him decide to finally swap rooks. They then swapped a lot of their pawns and finally got one each to the back row to form a queen.

The game went on for some time. Michael was being very careful and hoping that she'd make a mistake, but she didn't. She huffed and took his queen when he took hers, leaving it at a draw with just a king and an alternate bishop each. She said, "The game was getting nowhere. I'm quite happy for a draw."

He felt relieved that he hadn't made a mistake and said, "Yes. It couldn't have been much closer. It was a good game, and I enjoyed it. Would you like to play a few computer games?"

She answered, "Yes. That will be OK, but not for too long. I must get back because of my dog."

He said, "OK then. Have you got any favourites?"

She answered, "I quite like a few. I'll see what you've got."

He put on his PS4 and said, "It's funny—I came by some software last November that was called Dimensional Observer. I had it only until about the middle of January, when it suddenly expired. Have you come across anything like that?"

She answered, "I think I've heard of it. I'm sure I saw it advertised once, but it didn't really register with me. There are always new games continually coming out. Anyway, what was that particular game?"

He didn't want to go into too much detail about it at the moment, in case she thought he was obsessed by it to the point of being insane. He answered, "Well, it wasn't a game as such. It had quite a lot of variations, the main one being that I was led to believe that I could talk with other forms of myself from parallel universes. The software must have come from someone who hacked into my computer and used my exact image and voice to mess me around. Some people are always trying out some silly things."

She responded, "Yes, there are some funny people around who can try all different kinds of things to get into your system. What happened when it expired then?"

He chuckled and answered, "Well, it was quite amusing really. It flickered off and then came on again for a short time, and then it went completely. It reminded me of that scene in the film called, *War Games*. Matthew Broderick played the part of a computer hacker. When he switched off his own computer after playing a game, the central computer system suddenly went off at the headquarters."

She laughed and said, "Yes, I remember that film. It sounds as if your program went the same way."

He laughed and said, "Yes. It must have been only temporary, unless they took it away because they couldn't get any joy out of trying to hack into my system, or something like that." He thought like before, that it might have gone because Susan had returned to her own universe somehow before that.

Sophie smiled and said, "Yes, probably."

He gave her the choice of games, and they played

two different ones that they both liked, each winning one of them.

Finally, she felt it was time to leave. She said, "Well, thanks for inviting me. I've really enjoyed it. I'd best get going now."

He said, "Well, next Friday evening I'm going to Paul's birthday party—you know, he's the Australian I told you about from work. I wonder if you'd like to come along." He wanted to prove it if she was, in fact, Sarah. He thought that, if she wasn't, it would be interesting for them to meet anyway.

She smiled and answered, "Well, I could try. I may not come for long, but where will you be?" He mentioned the name of the pub and the time he would be there which was to be around nine o'clock.

She said, "OK, but no promises. I may come."

He smiled and said, "Fine. I hope you can make it. Anyway, I've enjoyed our visit. I'll see you?"

She came close to him and kissed him on the cheek, and he felt that feeling of warmth again. He hugged her, and they kissed each other on the lips. He suddenly felt a fantastic and lovely feeling. She pulled him close, and he felt her. A lovely tingling sensation ran throughout his body, and he felt that they were connected somehow and were floating on air, and that they were one. He became quite aroused, and they kept it going for a few minutes longer until she stepped back and said, "I'd best be going."

He noticed that she was glowing and all excited. He felt the same and wanted more. She said, a little breathlessly, "That was lovely, but we'd better take it easy … Ooh!" She bent over slightly and then said, "I'll see you soon, Michael."

He saw that she was having difficulty knowing what to do with herself whilst she was straightening herself out. He said, "Yes, I'll be greatly looking forward to that. That was lovely, and I'd love to see you again." He thought that he wanted to be with her so much that making a good impression with her didn't matter any longer. As she made her way out of his flat a little awkwardly, he said, "You're welcome to come anytime. I'll be at my parents' tomorrow, but you can come on Sunday if you like."

She paused, then smiled and said, "I don't know if I can, but I may pop down one evening next week."

He said, "OK. I'll give you my number in case you want to ring me." He didn't want to be overly pushy and gave her the choice.

He wrote it down and gave it to her, and she said, "Thanks. I'll see you sometime, Michael."

He said, "Yes. See you, Sophie." They waved to each other as she left.

18

PAUL'S BIRTHDAY
PARTY AT THE PUB

The following Tuesday at lunchtime, Michael walked into town for his lunch. He hadn't heard anything from Sophie since last Friday, and whilst he was walking, he saw Melanie. She said, "Oh, hi! How are you, Michael?"

"I'm fine except for this cold I've got. How are you?"

"I'm OK, but it looks as though Sarah has a worse cold than you because she's off again today. She still seems to be susceptible to a lot that's going round."

"Yes." He thought that she should have built up a stronger resistance by now so she could avoid more colds and viruses. He then said, "I've been wondering about that joke you made about SVM. My first thought was that it is the mirror image of MVS."

She smiled and said, "Oh that one. It was just my

idea, after I'd seen a reverse £10 note in one of Sarah's drawers. It was obviously something she'd got from a trick shop. It looked well used, though, but anything can be done to make something look scraggy and old,"

Michael remembered that he'd seen that note in Melanie's drawer. He laughed and decided to say, "Yes, I've seen all sorts of funny things sold in joke shops. They always keep bringing some new things out, and that was an unusual one she played."

"Yes. She's done some other unusual things too."

They walked into a café, and as they queued up, he asked, "What other things have you seen her do then?"

She smiled and answered in a whisper, "Well, just recently when I walked into her office, I saw her jotting some things down with her left hand on a pad. When I looked closer, she was writing from right to left, and I noticed it was mirror writing. I asked her why she was writing like that, and she told me she was only doodling. It was funny, though, because after that, she wrote properly with her right hand, but nowhere near as quickly. Also, occasionally when she's driving, she sometimes put her foot on the accelerator instead of the brake, and we've had some near misses. She's also braked occasionally at times when she should have used the accelerator. I know it's easy to do that sometimes with an automatic, when you're used to a clutch being there, which was what she said about it. It has been amusing, though—sometimes." She chuckled.

It was then their turn to be served, and they both ordered teas and some sandwiches. When they sat down to eat, he thought for a moment and said, "Well, she was probably doing it for a lark. I don't know, but she's left handed anyway, so that explains it." He wanted to protect Sarah in case she might be from a mirror universe. He then said, "Well, Paul hasn't quite got over her wearing a padded bra. Oh, excuse me for bringing it up." He quickly wanted to change the subject.

She laughed and said, "Yes, it's just like him to continue the joke. Poor old Sarah, though, having to take the brunt of his humour, but at least she shows herself properly now. In fact, I don't know why she ever wanted to look like that in the first place. It wasn't really in her character, and she left herself open to ridicule, especially from someone like Paul. She's taken it brilliantly though."

He smiled and said, "I know she has, and she's been very broad shouldered about it, excuse the joke. It's not something I could have done."

Melanie laughed loudly and said, "Well, I hope not. I hope you're not going funny on me, Michael?"

He laughed and answered, "Well, that's something I'll never do or even contemplate." He thought that Sarah now looked far more attractive and proportionate since she'd stopped using her padding, although she still had a bra size slightly bigger than Melanie's and Sophie's.

She said, "Oh, well, it's good to have a laugh about things."

He smiled and said, "Yes. Are you coming to Paul's party on Friday?"

She answered, "Yes. He and Sarah have both invited me. I hope she's got over her cold by then. The problem with getting them at this time of year when the weather is warmer is that they can be harder to shift."

He said, "Yes. Mine started yesterday, but I've taken plenty of decongestants to help me. If it doesn't get much worse than this, I should be OK."

She then finished her snack and said, "It'd probably be best if we made our way back I think."

"I'm almost finished." He drank up his tea and they left.

"Well, it'll be a busy afternoon having to fill in for Sarah. She'll of course ring me just after two, when we start work again."

"Well, I suppose a lot more falls on your shoulders due to her absence."

"You're telling me. We'll keep in touch on skype a few times before the afternoon's out so she can be in contact with me and some of our suppliers to make some decisions. It's good hey, when she can do a certain amount from home?"

"Yes. Computers are good in that way, if you can't always make it to the office. A lot of commuters work on trains and busses, and by the time they arrive at their offices, a lot of the work has been done."

She smiled and said, "Yes, it's great when you can work to a certain extent on flexible hours. Anyway, at least I'm not on my own. I do make some of the more definite decisions myself, and that's why we work well together. We discuss things too." As they arrived back at the office and she went to start work for the afternoon, she said, "Anyway, nice chatting, Michael. I'll see you."

"Yes. See you later, Melanie." And then he went into his office.

A few days later, on Friday evening, Michael still

hadn't heard anything from Sophie, and he wondered if she had lost interest in him. He thought, *What did I do wrong? I'm sure I left her on good terms. Oh, it would be best if I just went back to just giving a good impression.* He felt dejected. He arrived for Paul's party just before a quarter to nine. There he met Paul with his friend, who was called Gary. They were drinking near the bar. Paul wore a white T-shirt and black jeans with brown trainers, and Gary was similarly dressed, except he wore a black leather jacket. It was very crowded and noisy there as it usually was, besides being extremely warm and humid. Paul said, "Hi, sport. You'd better go and get yourself a drink before it gets too crowded. It's already filled up in here." He smiled.

Michael said, "Yes, I'm just on my way. Oh, by the way, happy birthday, Paul. I'll see you shortly."

Gary, who was very tall and plump, said, "Yes, you best make your way, or you'll never make it back here in the next half hour."

Paul said, "Right on, Gary." He turned to Michael and smiled, saying, "Oh, thanks, and thanks for the card earlier. I'll see you in a bit, hopefully."

Michael forced a smile knowing that he'd have to wait a long while again, as he usually had done before, standing behind a load of big lads. Though, now, some of the women there were big too. He felt out of his depth and therefore a little out of his comfort zone, just as he did a lot of the time when he'd been in the pubs on busy weekend nights. One of the girls in front of him, who was well built and very busty and stood about five foot eleven, looked back at him a few times and giggled.

She was very pretty and mature looking, in her middle forties with dark-brown hair. She wore a frilly white sleeveless blouse with tight black slacks. He could smell the drink on her breath as she said to him, "Are you having a good night, darling?"

He suddenly felt even hotter as he blushed. He felt that he had to say something quickly, which caused him to say the first thing that came into his head which was, "Yes, a bonza one, thanks." He felt rather foolish, then, knowing that he'd opened himself up to a possible trap.

She laughed loudly and said, "I didn't think you were the type to come from down under."

He thought and then forced a laugh, saying, "Well, I'm not actually. That chap there works at the same firm I work for, and he's from Sidney." He pointed Paul out to her.

She giggled and said, "Well, what do you know? I bet he'll have some stories to tell."

Michael caught a hint of her perfume. He said, "Yes, and some really believable ones. Anyway, are you enjoying yourself? Are you from around here?" He tried to change the subject and show an interest in her before the conversation could give the wrong vibrations and become more uncomfortable for him.

She said, "Yes, I am. I come here every week with those two girls who are in front of me." She pointed them out. One of them was a tall and fairly thin blonde girl who wore a tight pink top with tight shiny pink Lycra leggings. The other girl was shorter in height and quite plump with reddish hair that was clearly dyed, and she wore a white T-shirt with tight leather trousers. She had a large tattoo on each arm.

The one with the reddish hair turned to the girl with whom he was speaking and said, "Hey, Tracey. I see you're getting to know the young talent here!" She smiled and then chuckled, which made Michael blush slightly even though her comment also made him feel good.

Tracey said, "Yes, Karen. I'm just getting to know him." Karen then asked him his name.

He answered, "Oh, I'm Michael. I've come to Paul's birthday party. We're all meeting here to start off with. There are only three of us here so far. Anyway, it's nice to meet you two."

Karen smiled and said, "Likewise. I'm in here virtually every night, and I like to have a few drinks before moving on later. I suppose that's what you and your group will be doing later."

He said, "Yes, we're planning to do that. I'm only just starting on the drinks right now—or whenever I get served!" He wondered how much longer it would take.

Tracey and her two friends were the next to be served, and Karen said, "We'd best order now. Are you wanting your usual Pernod and vodka, Tracey?"

She answered, "Yes, please."

Just then, Michael felt a tap on his right shoulder. He looked round and saw Sophie behind him. He noticed she had pushed in slightly to get close to him. She wore smart blue jeans with a tight-fitting blue short-sleeved blouse and white trainers. She shouted, "Hi, Michael! I'm here! I'll wait for you nearby until after you're served."

He shouted, "I'm glad you've come! Nice to see you. I'll get you a drink when I'm served. What would you like?"

She shouted, "Just a pint of shandy, please." She then quickly left.

Tracey then said, "Well, I see you have a girlfriend. She looks nice."

He said, "Yes. She's OK. I haven't known her for too long."

Tracey said, "Well, if things don't go right with her, you know where I'll be." She smiled broadly.

"Yes. Thanks. I'll bear that in mind." He smiled with satisfaction.

"Yes. Hopefully I'll see you around." And then she joined her friends as she collected her drink.

Michael was then served and ordered a pint of bitter as well as the shandy for Sophie. He went to join Sophie, who was just behind him, and he noticed that Melanie was queuing up for a drink not far from where they were. Melanie was wearing her white blouse from work with tight black Lycra leggings under a blue jeans skirt with white trainers. He said to Sophie, "Here's your pint. Are you OK?" He wondered why he hadn't seen her since last Friday evening, but he didn't want to make too much of it.

She answered, "I'm OK, except I've had a bit of a cold. It hasn't been bad enough, though, to keep me off work, but I thought I'd just rest when I could over the last few days." He saw Melanie looking at her whilst she was talking. Sophie then asked, "I'm curious. Who were those girls you were talking to?"

He answered, "Oh, they were just two who got

chatting with me whilst I was queuing up for my drink. It's the first time I've ever seen them."

She smiled and said, "OK."

He then thought about Melanie being there and pointed her out to Sophie and said, "Oh, I'd better introduce you. This lady who is queuing near to us is Melanie. She works in the same firm I do, and she has come to Paul's birthday party." He then saw Tracey and her two friends looking in his direction from a few tables away. They were laughing a little, as though they might be talking about him.

Sophie looked around at Melanie and said, "OK then." They went to where Melanie was, and Michael said, "Hi, Melanie. How are you?"

She smiled and answered, "I'm OK, thanks. Are you all right?"

He said, "Yes, thanks. I'm fine. My cold's a lot better. Anyway, this is Sophie. I thought I'd invite her to come."

Sophie said, "Hi. Nice to meet you, Melanie."

As they looked at each other, Melanie said, "Yes, I'm pleased to meet you."

They shook hands, and then Sophie said, "Well, it's nice to meet some of Michael's colleagues from work. He's told me a little about Paul."

Melanie chuckled and said, "Yes, he's quite a lad. I think you'll find him quite entertaining."

Michael said, "Well, we may as well go over and join him."

Melanie said, "Well, I'll stay here until I get served. Then I'll join you. See you in a bit."

"OK, see you soon."

Sophie and Michael walked over to where Paul was. Paul spotted them and smiled and said, "Oh, hi. Who is this nice girl that you have with you, Michael?"

Sophie looked at the floor seeming to be momentarily bashful, and then smiled and answered, "Oh, I'm Sophie. I've come along with Michael."

Paul responded and said, "Oh, pleased to meet you, Sophie. It's good to see you." He shook her hand and said, "I'm Paul—the birthday boy, but it's not exactly bonza being a year older. It's all right, though, because I feel no different." He smiled.

She said, "Well, happy birthday, Paul. I hope you're enjoying it."

He smiled and said, "Yes, it's a bonza one, especially with all these girls around. I hope Sarah comes later and you get to meet her. She's been off all week because of a bad cold, but she may come."

Sophie said, "Well, I hope she's better. I'm just getting over a mild one myself. They can be difficult to shake off during warmer weather."

He said, "Yes, it often happens like that. Sarah was telling me a bit about hers."

Gary then said, "Hi, Sophie. I'm Gary, and I've known Paul since we were at school."

As they shook hands, she said, "Pleased to meet you. Do you work at the same firm?"

He answered, "No, I'm a motor mechanic. You wouldn't see me in a tie. I like being a grease monkey and getting my hands dirty."

Sophie laughed and checked her hands.

He laughed loudly and said, "You don't need to do that. I did scrub up before turning up here."

Paul responded with a belly laugh and said, "Yes, better than usual for this evening."

Gary said, "Yes, definitely, when I'm going to meet some lovely women." He looked at Sophie and smiled.

She giggled and said, "Thanks."

Gary paused and said, "You're welcome."

Michael realized he had some competition and thought, *Well, she's made herself look too attractive by the way she's dressed. Perhaps she'll be interested in Gary. She never did get back in touch with me.*

Melanie then came with her drink, and Paul said, "Oh, hi, Melanie. I'm pleased you've come. Thanks for the card."

She said, "Thanks, and happy birthday, Paul. Did you like it?"

"Yes, it was a bonza one. It was OK!"

Gary then asked Sophie, "Where do you work then?"

She paused and answered, "Well, I work at another firm similar to the one where Paul and Michael work. We sell goods online as well."

Gary said, "Good. Like Paul tells me, most internet retailers are doing quite well now." Whilst Michael saw that Sophie was held in conversation by Gary, he fetched his camera phone out of his pocket and took the opportunity to cheekily take a few quick photographs of her hands and arms. He wanted to look later for any distinguishing features, and he hoped that no one—including her—would notice. He'd prepared himself to do this after noticing on and off recently that such redeeming features of her hands could perhaps be the mirror image of his own. He then quickly put the camera phone back into his trouser pocket, hoping that the five snaps he'd just taken would be good enough to prove anything. He then quickly glanced at each person wondering if he or she had noticed what he'd just done. No one seemed to have done, as they were all laughing about what Gary and Paul were saying to Sophie. Michael hadn't heard a word of it because he'd been concentrating on taking the photographs.

Paul said, "Well, Michael, what do you think of that?"

Michael, not having any clue about what Paul was referring to, said the first thing that came into his head, which was, "Oh, it was a bonza one, Paul." He hoped it would sound like a witty remark that would impress the Australian.

Paul said, "What? Oh, I think he's with it." They all laughed, making Michael wonder what he'd missed.

Melanie leaned in to speak close to his ear, seemingly because of the loud music. She said, "It's all right, Michael. I saw what you were doing. Cleverly done."

He thought, *Oh, goodness me. She saw me take those snapshots, or was she referring to my bluff about me hearing what Gary and Paul had just said.*

Paul said, "Oh, well, I think I'll order one last one here before we move on to the nightclub."

Gary said, "Yes. Now's the time because the queue isn't that long." They both headed to the bar.

Sophie said, "He certainly is a card. He comes out with some very funny stuff when he's drunk."

Melanie said, "Yes. I heard that one before when he

took Sarah and me out for a snack one lunchtime into town. By! The Aussies really love to take the pee out of women by referring to them as sheilas. That big plump woman, though, didn't stand for it, as you'd heard just now."

Sophie said, "True, but I think she was a bloke."

Melanie said, "Well, good guess."

Sophie said, "She had to be a bloke by the way he told the story."

As Melanie quickly looked at Michael, he thought, *Perhaps Sophie is Sarah, but then again maybe not, according to the way Sophie's talked tonight. It could be no more than a coincidence that she just sussed out Paul's story. They could still be different and two separate ones, even though Susan—or Claire as she called herself—had gone back. I don't know.* He said, "Well, that looks so." He was still trying to bluff that he knew what they were talking about.

Then Melanie asked, "Are you coming along with us to the nightclub, Sophie?"

She answered, "Well, I'm not feeling that great. My cold seems a bit worse, and besides, I have a dog to get back to and feed. I wasn't planning on staying long anyway."

Melanie said, "Oh, well, it's been nice meeting you. You have had a bit of a time out." She smiled.

Sophie said, "Yes, it has done me some good. I'll leave when you move on to the nightclub."

Melanie said, "You may even see Sarah yet."

Sophie said, "Yes, quite possibly." She looked towards the door.

Paul and Gary then returned after having downed the first halves of their pints. Paul said, "It'd be bonza if

Sarah showed up now. I wonder if she'll be wearing her full package for this evening." He smiled.

Michael saw Sophie's lip curl up slightly, and then she laughed with the rest of them.

Melanie giggled and said, "I doubt it. She's not that type of girl, but I do wonder why she went to such lengths in the first place."

She looked at Sophie who said, "Yes, it was a bit excessive, if I'm imagining correctly what you're saying." She smiled.

Paul laughed in his fairly drunk state and said, "I'm sure you've got the gist. It was as though she wore two very large inflatable barrage balloons. If they were filled with helium, she'd have certainly taken off at a very high speed because they were each three times her body size. She way overdid it, and she looked even more fantastic than a super-embellished cartoon character."

Gary did a belly laugh and said, "That's even greater than some of the women I can imagine. Talking about cartoon characters, if there was a helium leak and she breathed some in, she'd have sounded just like Donald Duck!"

Paul laughed and, in his more drunken state, he said, "Yes, and she could have done with a fuck, even a flying one." Gary, and even Michael, then burst out into laughter.

Sophie said, "OK, lads, I think we get the picture. Melanie is here you know."

Paul said, "What of it? She's beginning to sound just like Sarah now, but Sarah is still quite sizeable." He laughed.

Melanie said, "Don't worry about me. I am broad-minded, you know."

Michael said, "Yes, you are, Melanie, but Sophie and Sarah are nothing like each other. Sarah is a blue stocking and dedicated to her work. Sophie is a nice girl and easy to get on with." He wondered why he'd suddenly said all that.

He looked at Sophie who seemed to be cringing slightly. But she also seemed to enjoy what he'd just said, as she smiled at him and said, "Thanks, Michael."

Paul said, "Well, Sarah is just like that when you get to know her properly. There is a similarity."

Sophie said, "I don't know how. I'm just happy to work to get by and enjoy myself."

Paul said, "Oh, never mind. I'll just drink up, and we'll head for the nightclub. Sarah knows more or less when I'm going there anyway, if she decides to come." He glanced at Gary and then at Sophie. He and Gary drank up, and Paul said, "We'll get going, Gary, but I must get to the dunny first. We'll see you all at the nightclub."

Gary said, "I'll move straight onto it then, Paul."

Paul said, "OK. I'll see you all there then."

Sophie said, "Well, I can't really make it. Anyway, it was nice meeting you both. I'll maybe see you around."

Paul said, "Oh, it was bonza meeting you. I was hoping you might come and perhaps meet Sarah if she turns up. Anyway, I'll see you sometime probably." He smiled and went to the toilet.

Gary said, "Nice seeing you." He left to head straight to the nightclub.

Melanie said, "Well, I'm ready to go when you are, Michael. It's been nice seeing you too, Sophie."

Sophie said, "Thanks. I've enjoyed this evening."

Michael said, "Yes, I'm glad you came. You're welcome to ring me sometime, Sophie." He didn't really want to push it by suggesting that he would ring her.

She responded, "OK, Michael, I think I will. See you soon, and maybe see you sometime, Melanie."

Melanie said, "Yes, see you around." Sophie waved to them both and left. Melanie said, "Well, she is similar to Sarah. I can see why you photographed her."

He said, "Well, I see what you mean, but I thought I'd just take some snaps to remember the evening." Then he said, to change the subject, "Anyway, we may as well leave and join Paul now."

She looked a little sombre and said, "OK, Michael." They drank up and then left to go to the nightclub, which was only a few doors away.

19

PAUL'S BIRTHDAY PARTY
AT THE NIGHTCLUB

When they arrived at the nightclub, Michael said, "I'll pay for both of us."

Melanie said, "OK, and thanks, but I'll buy you a drink later." She smiled.

"OK, thanks." They went in and immediately joined Paul and Gary on the dance floor.

Paul said, "I see Sophie's gone. Anyway, thanks for coming," He laughed and said, "You'd better watch yourselves. I'm about to try "Staying Alive" again. You know …" And he started doing his John Travolta–style of dancing. Gary joined him and did the same.

Melanie giggled and tapped Michael on the arm, saying, "Neither of them is doing it exactly right, but it's fun watching them!" They left the floor to watch.

"Yes, and look how quickly they've just cleared

the dance floor. Just about everybody here now is a spectator!" He laughed.

"Well, at least they're enjoying themselves."

"And so is everybody else who's watching them." He noticed Julie, the girl he'd seen before with Paul. She went over and joined in to get into the spirit of it. Now that there were three of them dancing, they completely took over the dance floor, but it was quite a sight because of the way they moved around. Both Melanie and Michael watched until, finally, Sarah turned up. She tapped Michael on the shoulder making him jump a little.

Sarah said, "Hi, Michael. I see you're enjoying the exhibition put on by Paul. He always likes doing this." She smiled at Michael and then laughed. He noticed that she was wearing her long-sleeved white blouse from work with blue trousers and black shoes.

He said, "Oh, hi, Sarah. I was only half expecting you to come. How are you? Oh, I hope that isn't a silly question after the cold you've had." He felt that Sarah could quite possibly put on a stroppy act because she was a blue stocking.

She answered, "Well, thanks for asking. It has been a bad one, but I think I'm getting over it now. I've taken a lot of decongestants so I could come here."

He responded, "Good. I'm glad you've come. They've been here for a while, and Melanie and I haven't been here all that long."

Melanie said, "Hi, Sarah. I'm glad you came in the end. I see you're a lot better."

Sarah said, "Thanks. It's good to get out after being in more or less all week. Are you two OK?"

Melanie said, "Yes, and I'm enjoying the night out."

Michael said, "Yes, I'm OK, and my cold hasn't got any worse."

Sarah then said, "Good. I'll just go for a drink, and I'll join you both in a bit."

Melanie said, "OK then." As Sarah went for her drink, Melanie said, "She seems OK."

He said, "Yes. Shall we go for a dance? It looks as though most of the others have gone back to the dance floor." He saw that Paul had just left the floor to see Sarah.

Melanie answered, "OK then." And they both went for a dance. She offered to link hands to dance with him, and when he held both her hands, he felt that same lovely feeling that he'd had before. They danced for a while and chatted about the music that was playing until Sarah came back. Melanie then went to dance next to her, and Michael sneaked some random camera shots of them, making sure that he wasn't too obvious this time as he took them.

After over half an hour of dancing, Michael went to the toilet and then for another drink. As he waited in the queue, Paul came up and said, "Well, I can't get it out of my mind. That Sophie we met sounds so much like Sarah."

"I'm aware of that. I've heard many people, though, who sound the same and are totally different." Michael played down their similarity to protect their identity in case they may both be a laterally inverted version of him.

"I take your point, but there might be a long-distance link, even though they're slightly different."

"Well, it's possible. Who knows? Anyway, I'll buy you your next pint. Would you like a Fosters again?"

"Oh, yes, please, mate. It's the only Aussie froth around here, as usual." He laughed.

"OK, then. I think I'll have the same myself now." He smiled when he was about to be served. He ordered the beers and paid for them.

Paul said, "Bonza one, mate. Get that down you. There's nothing more refreshing—except for a 4X, though, of course." He chuckled.

Michael said, "Right on!" He tried to make the remark in Aussie style.

Paul laughed and said, "Bonza one, mate. Right on!" Michael then collected the drinks and passed Paul his. Paul said, "Thanks, bonza mate. That looks as amber as usual. Get this down me, and I'll be ready for more." They then went to join Gary, who was talking with Sarah and Melanie about things that had happened at his garage. Paul said, "Oh, I've heard that one before about that smartly dressed posh sheila whose skirt was all covered in oil."

Gary said, "Yes, she was in a right mood and wanted me to use something quickly to clean off the stains. When I told her we weren't a dry cleaners, she went into a right bloody barney with me over it. As I said, Sarah, I tried to advise her to go to a professional cleaner, but she wanted me to do something about it very quickly because she had some sort of important meeting shortly after that."

Michael said, "Well. Couldn't she have just gone to

a nearby store or something and bought a new skirt and sorted the other out later?"

Gary answered, "Well that was no good because my garage was too far from the shops for the time she had, so I offered her my jeans, which was all I had on under my overalls. I took them off privately in my office, of course. I didn't want to show such a pristine girl all of my blubber and everything." He laughed. They all burst out laughing, and he then continued saying, "Well, I would actually love to have taken them off in front of her because she was so beautiful, but anyway … when I'd dressed again and threw them too her, she looked absolutely disgusted and said, with her deep green eyes sparkling, 'You're not seriously thinking I'll put these things on are you? They're bloody wet through with your perspiration, besides being bloody smelly and too fucking large, especially when I'm wearing nothing under here! I'll just look like a right fucking pillock and tossing idiot, turning up in these to see that bloody mayor. He can be a dickhead sometimes about what a person wears.'"

The girls said, "Eww!"

Gary continued: "I just suddenly couldn't bloody believe the words that I was hearing from such a pristine but bitchy woman, who was so great looking. She was speaking with such style whilst her tits were wobbling around in her way-undersized blouse without a bra." He laughed and then said, "Deep down, she was actually rougher than me by the way she talked! Talk about putting on airs and graces for the mayor! She was a right one!" They all laughed.

Sarah said, "By! It certainly takes all sorts to make a world. I can just imagine such snobby people, and it's so funny when they actually show their true selves."

Michael looked at her and thought, *Yes, you could be one. You put on quite an act.* He then saw both Sarah and Melanie look at him.

Paul laughed and said, "Yes, and if the jeans happened to be skin tight, I wonder what she'd have said to that, imagining that Gary had just jerked off in them!"

Sarah cringed and said, "Eww, your mind, Paul. That's disgusting."

Gary said, "Well, if she knew that, she may have wanted to try them out. You know some women ..."

Melanie said, "Eww ... that's even more disgusting!"

Paul said, "Well, it's got my imagination going."

Sarah smiled whilst saying, "Well. I somehow knew that it would have that type of effect on you, Paul."

He said, "Too right."

And then Sarah said, "Oh, I've had enough of this. I'm going for another dance." She got up, appearing to be disgusted, and walked off briskly to the dance floor.

Paul laughed and said, "I really love how she reacts to some of the things I say. She's great fun."

Gary said, "Me too. That was a very good wind-up story."

Melanie said, "Yes, a real lads' story."

Paul continued, saying, "And a bonza one, love, especially in front of Sarah. Anyway, I'm ready for another dance, but I have to go to the dunny again." He laughed as he walked off.

Melanie shook her head and smiled, saying, "Oh, Paul."

Michael smiled and said, "Yes … I think I'll go for a dance now."

Melanie said, "I'm going for another drink. Would you like one, Michael?"

He thought and answered, "Yes, please, but you don't need to."

She said, "Well, I made a promise. I'll get you a pint of lager if you like."

He said, "OK, then, and thanks. That'll be fine."

She went for the drinks, and he walked to the dance floor. A few moments later, whilst he was dancing, Sarah came up to him, and they talked about some of their favourite music. She linked hands with him, and he immediately felt the same sensation he'd felt with Sophie. They continued for several minutes until Michael remembered that she was Paul's girl, at which point he broke away. He thought, *How disgusting of me to intercept Paul's girlfriend at his birthday do!* He then danced apart from her.

Paul, who was nearby on the dance floor, came up to him and said, "Don't worry, mate, we're not that close. We're only just work colleagues and good friends."

Michael responded, "OK. She only means that to me as well."

Paul said, "Oh, go on with you. I can tell that she means more than that to you, and so does Sophie. They are two of a kind—know what I mean, sport?" He patted Michael on the back.

"I think so. There must be some distant connection between them."

"Well, I'll let you figure it out."

Michael smiled and continued dancing for a little longer until he remembered the drink that Melanie had bought him a few moments ago. He looked around and saw her sitting by herself with her drink in her hand and his on the table, so he went to join her. He said, "Thanks for the drink. You'll have to excuse me for getting a bit engrossed in the dancing."

"Oh, you're all right. That's what we're here for anyway." She smiled.

"Yes, I suppose that's what this is all about." He asked, "Anyway, I'm curious. When is your birthday? And when is Sarah's?" He suddenly got nervous about appearing too nosey. He clarified his curiosity by saying, "Oh, don't get me wrong. I'm only asking because I was wondering if you might have some sort of a party like this one." He tried to cover up really why he was asking.

She paused and answered, "Well, there's no need to worry. My birthday is on the tenth of September, and as far as I know, Sarah's is on the eleventh of April. That makes me wonder why she hasn't organized a party, because hers is this coming Monday. She told me before Christmas when her birthday was. I'm a little surprised you don't know birthdays by now, seeing as you do all the salaries." He knew that the birthdays were on the PAYE records, but he wanted to hear if she'd say anything different.

"Oh, well, I probably did know, but I'd forgotten. You'll have to excuse me on that. I don't remember everything." He felt then that he was playing a bit of a Columbo.

"When is yours, then? Just curious."

"Oh, mine is on the eleventh of October. It's well past now, and I was thirty then."

"Well, surely you celebrated such a milestone."

"I did a little. We just had a family get-together and everything."

"Well, OK. That's fine. Shall we go for another dance?"

He drank up some of his lager and said, "OK, then." And they both went to dance and have the occasional chat between tracks about the music that was playing. Sarah came over to talk with Melanie, and they danced next to each other whilst chatting. Michael was too far away from them to hear anything because of the loud music.

A little later, Melanie came up to him and said, "I must be heading off now because I don't want to get home too late. If you ever want to talk, you know where I am."

She held his hand for a short time, and he said, "Thanks. I'll bear it in mind."

She said, "Well, I'll see you Michael."

He said, "Yes. OK. See you, Melanie." She smiled at him and then waved to him as she left. He danced a while longer until Paul left the floor and joined Gary, who was talking to Sarah and Julie. Michael finished his drink, and afterwards, he went to Paul and said, "I think I'll get going now. I've enjoyed your party."

Paul said, "Well, thanks for coming. I'll see you next week."

Michael said, "Yes, I'll see you." And he shouted to Sarah and Gary, saying, "I'll see you soon!"

Gary said, "Yes! See you again sometime."

Sarah said, "I'll see you next week." Michael then waved to them and left to walk home whilst thinking about the evening.

20

FLUSHING HER OUT

During the middle of the night, when Michael had been asleep for about two hours, he heard somebody shout his name from outside his flat. This woke him up, and he went to his lounge window and saw that it was the same girl who'd called herself Claire. He recognized her semi-grey hair and her likeness to himself. She smiled and waved to him, and then she slowly walked away.

He quickly put on his dressing gown and slippers and went to look outside the flat. He felt apprehensive in case she might come back, but there was nobody around. He began to feel chilly, so he went back into his flat.

Since he was now wide awake, he decided to check to see if the DO program might be back on his computer since she'd somehow come back again, or another one had. He found it was still not there, and since he was still fairly excited about seeing her, he looked at the photographs that he'd taken the previous evening. He compared Sophie's with Sarah's, and he could see that the characteristics of their hands were exactly the same. He then compared them in a mirror to his own, and they were exactly the same as his. He sat down, gradually absorbing his findings. Then he compared his own hands with some of the pictures of Melanie's hands. They were very similar, but not identical like the other two were to each other. He thought, *Well, Sophie and Sarah are the same person, which is the lateral inversion of me, unless they are each from a different universe. Sarah's surname, "Morrison," makes sense too. It is easily thought of when I think of mine. Melanie could be the same person as me from another, similar universe, with the slight difference probably being due to possible randomness.* He went back to bed to think about it in a more certain way, though compared to some of his previous nights, and he thought, *Their hair is easily changeable, and so are their eyes, especially if they wear coloured contact lenses.*

The following afternoon, Michael decided to check out Sarah's house, knowing her address from her PAYE records. He knew that she could be there if she wasn't Sophie, aware that Sophie generally visited Maureen on Saturday afternoons. He rang the doorbell a few times to appear like a usual visitor, hoping strongly that she wouldn't be there because he certainly didn't want her to know what he was doing there. He took a deep breath and looked through one of her front windows. The room he saw appeared to be her lounge, and he saw a large mirror on the wall. He also saw the back of a large picture frame that was leaning against another of the walls. He walked round to the back of the house, hoping that she didn't have any CCTV of any kind. There he noticed an empty dog dish outside the back door. He looked through two of her back windows and didn't see much other than two small bedrooms. Afterwards, he decided to walk back to his car and wait to see if she would turn up as Sophie or Sarah. After an hour had gone by, he thought about his next ploy, so he decided to leave rather than to wait a while longer. After another five minutes, however, just as he was about to switch on his ignition, he saw Sarah arrive in her Ford Mondeo, which was her car he recognized from work. Because that didn't prove anything, he decided to drive home.

As he drove, he thought about a letter he would write. On the way, he bought a chicken takeaway meal, and when he got home, he enjoyed it whilst watching some television and having a drink. Later that evening, he checked his computer again to see if he'd possibly got the DO program back. He thought it might return because Claire seemed to be back. But there was still nothing.

Michael then prepared himself to write the two identical letters from the so-called Claire, the first one to be sent to Sarah as Miss S. Morrison at her address, and the other one to Sophie as Ms S. Kaye at Maureen's address.

He wrote each letter using a reasonably sharp biro on the top piece of paper. He placed a second sheet of paper and a piece of carbon paper under the top paper in order to create a laterally-inverted image of his message. The letter read:

Dear ...,

I have been observing you for some time now, and I have something very interesting to talk to you about. I think I am the same as you but from another mirror-image alternate universe, which is why I'm writing this in a recognizable hand. Please can we meet at MVS, or SVM as it reads here, at around three o'clock next Sunday afternoon?

Regards,
Claire Morrow

He then went for a walk and posted both for collection on the following Monday, knowing that Sarah should receive hers on Tuesday sometime, and Sophie should see hers the next Saturday, when she met up with Maureen, all being well. He hoped his plan would prove whether they were the same or different.

The following Wednesday morning, when Michael arrived at work, he saw Sarah talking to Paul, who said, "Hi, Michael. Last Friday was a good night, wasn't it?"

Michael noticed Sarah looking at him with a concentrated look on her face, and he replied, "Yes, it was. I enjoyed Gary's story too. That was a real bonza one!" He smiled.

Sarah said, "Ooh you! You're sounding a lot like Paul now."

Paul said, "Too right! It's time to live and enjoy yourself more, Michael. Be a bit more laid back."

Michael responded, "Yes, that's a nice thought, although it's not the easiest thing to do with work and everything sometimes."

Paul said, "Well, just relax more, and things won't be half as intense."

Sarah said, "Yes. I should try that myself too. Anyway, I'd best get on. I will feel better about things when I've got them done."

Paul said, "Right on. See you both later." And he went to his office.

Sarah said to Michael, "I'd best get on too. See you around, and don't work too hard. Don't overdo things." She looked straight at him and smiled.

He said, "Yes. See you. And, no, I won't."

She smiled and said, "OK." And she nipped quickly into her office.

Michael then went into his desk and started his work. After a short time, just before nine o'clock, he heard Melanie arrive to join Sarah in her office. He heard Sarah briefing Melanie about their work schedule.

The following Sunday afternoon, just after three o'clock, Michael went into MVS, curious to see who had arrived. He saw Sophie browsing around by herself. She suddenly looked behind her straight at him. She appeared to be surprised to see him, and she walked up to him. She was wearing a long-sleeved white blouse just like the ones Sarah wore at work, and she wore smart blue trousers and black shoes. She said, "Hi, Michael. I didn't expect you here today. I'd have thought you would have wanted to do all your shopping on a Saturday."

He said, "Oh, I just thought I'd come around town

for a bit and have a look. I happened to be in the area. Anyway, have you come here for anything special?"

She quietly answered, "Well, not really. I got a strange letter from somebody who wanted to possibly meet me here. It was unusually written in backwards writing, as a joke I suppose. And when I happened to look at it in a mirror, I could read it properly. It was a bit whacky, really. Why would somebody called Claire want to do that?" She looked searchingly at Michael.

He paused and said, "Well, there are some funny people about. Talking about mirror writing, I once saw a trick ten-pound note like that in one of Melanie's office drawers. She's one of the girls you met at Paul's birthday party over a week ago."

She smiled and said, "Yes, I remember her."

He looked over her shoulder towards the entrance of the store, wondering whether Sarah had arrived or if she would arrive at any moment. He said, "Melanie and Sarah are both unusual. Sarah, for instance, pretended that she was a right hander. I don't know why because she was so naturally left handed—like you. I mean, why did she bother pretending when she must have known that she'd have to use left-handed irons when playing golf? It had to come up sometime, especially when Paul had noticed she was handier with her left at times. You, surprisingly, are so similar to her—excuse me for saying so. Yet, you are far easier to talk to and more understanding." He wondered why he had suddenly just said that last bit to her. Indeed, he felt quite relaxed.

She smiled and blushed a little and said, "Thanks for the compliment. That's very nice of you." Then she straightened herself up and said, looking a little serious, "Anyway, I'm not really looking for anything right now, unless you're looking for something definite to buy."

He said, "No, not really. I only came to look around for a bit."

She said, "Well if you like, we could perhaps go for a tea or something."

He looked at his watch, noticing that it was nearly twenty past three, knowing inevitably that Sarah wouldn't be coming now. He said, "OK then. That'd be nice."

She smiled, and they walked towards a café nearby. She said, in a more relaxed manner, "Well, I'm glad I came when you happened to be here. I wonder if this girl who called herself Claire actually went there but then decided not to meet me. She didn't give me any idea about what she looked like, so I've no idea whether she was there or not." She smiled and quickly looked around and said, "Oh, there are a couple of young-looking girls behind us, but I don't think she'll be either of them because they're too pretty." Michael looked behind him at the two very pretty blonde girls. He noticed Sophie scowl at him a little. She said, "Well, they're not that pretty."

He said, "Well, they are ... Oh, excuse me."

She said, "Oh, I am here you know." She was still looking a little disgusted, and then she continued to say, "Anyway, if anything, by the sound of her letter, she'll be on her own and unusually shabby looking I should think, wearing a long, oversized raincoat like an eccentric train spotter with large goggles for glasses." She laughed.

Michael said, "Yes. Funnily enough, that's the way

I picture her too, because of the way you described her unusual letter. I think from what I heard once, some people such as Samuel Pepys in the seventeenth century used that type of writing as a code, which was only deciphered when somebody happened to see it in a mirror. I don't know why anybody would want to use that nowadays, though." He smiled.

"Well you know some people. They do lark about."

Just then, they then arrived at the café and Michael said, "I'll buy the drinks. Would you still like a tea?"

She answered, "Yes, please, but I'll buy them since you've already treated me to fish and chips and the shandy you bought me at Paul's birthday do. Is there anything else you'd like as well as a cup of tea?"

"No, thanks. Just a cup of tea will be all right."

She smiled and said, "OK then." And she went to buy them while he found somewhere to sit down.

When she joined him, he smiled and said, "Well, thanks for the tea."

"Thanks. That's OK. I didn't get that letter until yesterday when I went to see Maureen."

"How is she? Is she OK?"

"Yes, she's fine. We went for a walk with my dog yesterday afternoon because it was such a nice day."

"Yes, it was quite a warm day yesterday. Anyway, have you found somewhere permanent to stay at yet?"

"Well, not as such. There are a few places I'm looking at, and I am undecided yet."

"I think you'll find something shortly."

She smiled and said. "Well I hope so. Anyway, how's work and everything these days?"

"Yes, it's fine and going quite smoothly. It's a pity you missed Sarah at Paul's do. She came about half an hour after you left. It was quite a laugh when Gary told us one of his stories to wind her up, as well as Melanie. He has quite an active imagination when he gets going. It certainly got Sarah going all gooey around the edges. She got the giggles and blushed all over because of the way he told his story. Melanie, for once, was the serious one and tried to calm her down. It wasn't at all like Sarah to react as she did. I think she really is taken aback by Paul. I could tell by the way she flirted with him later." He really put it on, and he laughed.

Sophie paused and then said, "Well, from what you'd said about Sarah before, I'm surprised she reacted like that. She must really fancy Paul all of a sudden. I don't know … some people can really be turned on by the sudden flow of love."

"Yes. Goodness knows what they got up to after I left. The way Paul talks sometimes, I should think he thought it was hello Australia again."

She cringed slightly and said, "Well, maybe things aren't quite what they seem there. They may have actually been putting on a show for all of you." She smiled and laughed.

"Quite possibly, but for me it looked like the real thing. Paul is very precocious that way."

"Well, you never know. We can only speculate."

"There's more to Sarah than meets the eye. I now think she's much deeper than ever. I wonder what other things she gets up to in her spare time. Anyway, I'm sure she's happy now." He paused and then said, "Anyway, are things going all right with you?"

"I can't complain. At least things seem to be getting sorted for me on the home front, and now it's spring, there's more of a choice what to do." She finished her tea.

He drank up and, because he felt he might have overdone it slightly regarding what he'd said about Sarah and Paul—in fact, he might have made a fool of himself—he felt all tensed up and wanted to part with her now and cut his losses before her impression of him could really deteriorate. He said, "Anyway, it's been nice chatting. I'd best get going." But then he thought, *Oh, come on, Michael. You've come all this way on trying to find out all about her and must now go through with it!* So he took a deep breath and said, "Oh. We could walk out together if you like, but I must pay a call first. I won't be too long." He saw her smile.

"OK, I'd like that."

"Thanks." As he walked towards the toilet he thought, *Come on, get a grip. You can do this!* He fetched out two miniature bottles of whiskey to continue his drinking, after the several cans of beer that he'd had at home earlier that day. He purposely swilled some of the liquor around his mouth so the smell of it would be on his breath, only swallowing enough of it to give himself a little more Dutch courage, knowing that too much could impair his judgement. He then tried to relax and compose himself, and when he walked out to meet her, he noticed that she smelled it.

She paused and said, "I'd half thought you'd been

drinking before. I could give you a lift home if you like. You can't drive in that state."

"Well, thanks. OK then." As they walked to where she'd left her car, he thought, *My ploy has worked. I can now see how she drives.* And he said, "Yes. I haven't come in my car today because I felt like having a bit of a drink. Sometimes I let my hair down on Sundays, so to speak." He felt more at ease now as he continued his ruse.

"Well, you—I'd have never thought you would take such a leaf out of Paul's book." She laughed.

"Sometimes, I just have to let off steam. It does relieve some stress and everything."

"We all have our breaking points, I suppose, But I thought you were always level headed."

He enjoyed the compliment, laughed, and said, "Well, I try to be, but it's just so nice to relax and feel good sometimes."

As they arrived at her car, she smiled and said, "Me too. Anyway, here we are." It was her Toyota Aygo, and they both got in.

"Thanks for this. It's nice and comfortable in here." He looked around and saw nothing unusual. She paused and then started the ignition with her left hand. He noticed that she was concentrating a little. He could tell by the way she moved her right foot between the accelerator and brake pedal—the only ones because the car was an automatic. He said, "Well, Sarah drives an automatic like you." He thought, *Now's the time.*

She slowly said, "Yes. Paul told me that, and he told me a lot about her." She looked at him in a way that showed him she might know what he was up to.

He thought, *I must be subtler. I have to bear in mind that she must have been ahead of me on this, especially if she's actually travelled from another dimension. If she's me, she would have thought it through like me, but in much more detail before now.* He said, "Yes, he seems fond of her. Anyway, I'll guide you to where I live. It will be the next right here."

"OK ... You mean left, don't you? You can only go left here."

"All right. Oh, I mean left. Excuse me. It's so funny when this happens." He laughed, noticing that she was a little jerky with the brake as they slowed down for the passing traffic at the junction outside the car park.

"Please, Michael. I have some difficulty with my left and right occasionally because my parents tried to make me right handed. Please don't mess around with me when I'm driving. It could be fatal."

"OK. I do apologise. It's just that I can't get used to you driving on the right-hand side in this left-hand drive car of yours. I'll be extra careful with you because of that, Sarah."

"Please do ... what do you mean, Sarah?"

He thought for a bit and said, "Oh, I mean Sophie. It's just that Melanie at work has told me that she and Sarah have had similar scrapes whenever Sarah's been driving." He saw her scowl and then continued to say, "That's just reminded me of what she told me about you and Sarah. She said you are quite similar, with the left- and right-handed thing and everything."

"Well, I keep hearing about that. It's mere coincidence and means nothing." She appeared a little flustered.

She turned left when the road was clear, and he said, "It will be the next right at this roundabout."

"It's OK, you know. I do know where you live, and it's left by the way. I think you've had too much to drink."

"Yes, probably. It's just that I'm looking through your ring mirror and seeing it as right because of that."

She laughed and said, "Yes, I can see that. What's up with you today?" She quickly looked round at him.

"Oh nothing, Susan. It's just me."

"Oh, nobody's called me … What are you talking about?" She accidently braked slightly, causing the driver in the car behind them to use his horn. She then huffed and quickly accelerated and said, "Please, Michael, don't do that." Then she paused and said, "There's something I would like to say to you, but you need to say something to me first before I do."

"What's that then?"

"You'll have to figure it out yourself, and you'll never know unless you say it." She looked seriously at him with slightly tearful eyes.

He nervously said, "OK. Between you and me only, I would never ever mention your predicament to anybody else, not even my parents or my brother, James, or Michael as he may be in your universe. I know you're definitely Sarah and possibly even the lady who called herself Claire, who is really Susan. I think you called her that for a lark. If not, then there are at least two of you who've somehow come here from two slightly similar reverse universes. You're safe with me regarding doctors, nurses, and any other authorities because I've put myself in your predicament many a time, knowing that they're the last people you'd want to tangle with."

She laughed tearfully and said, "Well, it's taken all this time, and it's great. What a load of baloney and rubbish that sounds, though—mirror universes and everything." She paused and then parked the car in a nearby layby, turning off the ignition. She took off her platinum blonde wig, showing all of Sarah's red hair underneath it and said, "Yes, I am Sarah. You've got that part right, and I showed myself as Sophie, knowing you'd accepted me as her rather than Sarah, and I know why because I feel wary about bosses and hierarchy like you do. And wait a moment ..." She then slowly took out her deep-blue-coloured contact lenses. "And this is what my eyes naturally look like."

He looked into them. Then, feeling a lovely floating sensation, he said, "Yes, they are like mine in a mirror."

She looked emotionally tearful. She paused and then said, "Yes. All you've just said is right, and there is only one of me ... as far as I know anyway." She cringed slightly and looked outside her car window, saying, "Well, so far there is."

"Well, I've seen no others as far as I know, either."

She paused and said, "Whenever I've thought about it, I have decided it can be the only way because only two universes can happen to touch each other at a particular time and place."

"I've thought about that, and I did set you up with those two letters to—how shall I put it crudely—to flush you out."

She laughed and said, "Well, I know you must have done, and you didn't have to tell me."

He smiled and said, "I thought I would, and it's worked."

She perked up and said, "Yes, I know, and I'm glad because I've longed for this moment for ages now. I've played all these characters and have shouted to you from outside your flat and spoken to you on New Year's Eve, calling myself Claire for some reason then, probably as a lark due to the amount of drink I'd had." She smiled at him and continued saying, "As you thought, along with the other Michael, and heard from my parents, my name is Susan, and that photograph you saw at my parent's house was of me as a kid. When you saw me on New Year's Eve, I'd got myself drunk and really wanted to tell you then, and nearly did, but just couldn't when it came to it because I wasn't ready then. From the start, I had to take things gradually with you because you would have used similar words on me that I just said to you a moment ago, had I not. That's why I gave you the DO program— to ease you in about my situation and give you some ideas of other universes, as well as to limit you to the one that I came from. Besides, I felt I needed to see what you'd do or say when you were using the program. I didn't feel happy about doing that to you, but I felt I needed to safeguard myself, considering all of my differences to everybody here. And I'm sure you would have done the same if you could, if you were in my shoes."

He noticed her cringe again. He did the same himself as he thought about whether she had seen him on a few occasions watching the Susan from another parallel universe.

She said, "I'd shouted at you, to put you off seeing any more of my alternative self when you had looked on your PC. Yes, I'd seen what you were watching at that time. I don't know. I just happened to have staked you out on that night after Boxing Day."

"W … well. I only saw what I saw." He shook his head.

"Yes, I know. I haven't been much better myself at times." She shrugged her shoulders and smiled.

He thought, *What's good for the goose! She had every right too, I suppose.* He wondered about how much more she might have seen regarding some of his alternative selves, but said, "Oh, you're okay." They both smiled.

He then wondered for a split second about how she'd come by such a program and how she'd given it to him, but then he decided to bypass any further points right now to put her mind at ease, so he said, "Generally in your predicament, I'd have done the same if I was in your shoes. I've thought all about that and talked it out with the other Michaels, which you must have heard. You're safe with me, Susan. Also, I've protected you at times by purposely playing down the similarities between Sarah and Sophie whenever Paul and Melanie got talking about it."

She smiled tearfully with relief and said, "Thanks." Then she gave him a kiss and a hug as much as she could in her car. He felt that lovely feeling again, and she said, "Oh, did you feel that again?"

He answered, "Yes. There must be an affinity between us."

"Yes, definitely. We are the same person in effect, and that's why you're the only one I've ever wanted to confide in. I couldn't know anybody else's thoughts the way I know yours."

"Yes. Well, I have been aware of the fact that you often seemed to be a step ahead of me on things, and I wouldn't be surprised that you'd purposely taken the program away from me, possibly because maybe I was getting too warm about things when I was talking with the Michaels."

"Well, I did cheekily take it away from you after you whispered to yourself out loud about thinking I'd gone back. I contacted my parents then through the same reverse DO program that you had. I hope you don't mind, but I thought then that it was a convenient point to make you believe it was all over because I really needed the rest." She smiled.

"Oh, you're all right. I know the feeling. I felt that I was beginning to get into too much of a routine by talking to myself continually, excuse the pun." He chuckled and then said, "It was getting a little weird for me, and in a way, I was relieved, especially for you, by thinking you'd returned."

She smiled and said, "Thanks. I would have liked to, but I can't see how I can now because it was purely by random that I arrived here."

21

SUSAN'S STORY:
THE FIRST DAY

Michael asked, "How did you actually manage to come from your universe into this one, then?"

Susan smiled, saying, "Well, that was something else. I went for a walk in the woods near my flat on the last Monday night that January. It was the same flat that you're living in now, of course, which John Mitchell seems to occupy now. You know ..." She laughed.

Michael said, "Yes, of course. I know why you're laughing. You saw the same thing I did, of course, when he went to the toilet."

She laughed and said, "Yes, too true. I'm thinking that, if I did get back, I wouldn't want to occupy that flat again."

He laughed and said, "Yes. I wouldn't advise you to either."

"Yes. Anyway, back to point when I had come here—I went for a stroll through the woods to sort of relax myself and wind down after doing some overtime work processing invoices on the computer. You see, I was doing the same type of work you do still, but for another retail company. Anyway, it was about mid evening, when it was a cold and frosty but clear night. I saw a more-or-less first-quarter moon setting on the horizon as I took the gentle walk through the woods. I was quite relaxed when I noticed the trees ahead of me change slightly in appearance. The light of the moon wasn't in front of me any longer, and as I continued walking, I felt a momentary split second of weightlessness during which I suddenly felt a little faint and giddy. I kept moving ahead feeling that things were slightly different, not being able to figure out exactly why. I continued walking until, surprisingly, I arrived at the same place I'd started from, at the flats. I then recognized some of the parked cars in the road, but when I looked at the writing on the registration plates, it was rather unusual and reminded me firstly of some of the writing you see in Russia. I then realized, when I concentrated on reading it properly, that the writing was back to front. I thought, *What the heck has happened here?* in not so many words. Then I thought that I had actually fainted back there, and all this was a dream. Then I pinched myself, and I realized that it probably wasn't a dream. That rather freaked me out."

"Wow, you must have been shocked!"

She looked serious and said, "Yes, that's an understatement. I then looked behind me at the moon, which originally had been in front of me when I'd started walking. It now looked like a last-quarter moon, with the light half of the moon to the left. So that was a mirror image also. I looked at the flats, and they were unusually different in that same way. I then felt that I could be in an alien world for some reason, and then I immediately thought of that film *Journey to the Far Side of the Sun*. It was eerie. Then I looked in my purse, wondering if all my credit cards and money would be laterally inverted too. I thought that if they were like the rest of the world around me, then it would be a dream. Low and behold, when I checked them, they were the right way round. I then thought that I was in a right fix. To the people here, if there were any, my stuff would look screwy, and they would wonder what I was up to. I then thought, *Keep cool and don't, for heaven's sake, stand out. I could be the alien here, and I must keep a low profile.* I then saw two of the kids I know reasonably well and who usually acknowledge me. When they looked at me, they didn't say anything. They just continued playing football in the car park. I noticed that they tackled each other using their left feet, and I saw that the writing on their football shirts was the wrong way round too. That told me that this could be real, which gave me a deeper feeling of dread."

"Well, I've seen them play, and they are right footed."

Susan responded and smiled, "Yes, to you maybe, but you're left handed to me."

He thought about it and said, "Of course. It's like a double negative cancelling itself out."

"Yes, exactly. And that's how it is between me and everybody else here. You see me as a leftie, but I'm right handed really. Anyway, I walked to my—or your—flat building, noticing that everything was all the opposite way round. Then I got a sudden notion into my head to rush back to the point where I thought I'd crossed over here, hoping to maybe return, but when I got back there, there was no sign of anything unusual like I'd seen there before. I kept walking backwards and forwards over that area where I remembered it had happened, hoping beyond anything to get back, but it was to no avail. I just couldn't get back, and that was when the fear really deepened." She paused.

He said seriously, "I can quite imagine that."

"Yes, and that wasn't the half of it. I then realized that I was totally isolated here on my own, with no useable money, documentation, or credit cards. All I could think was, *What now?* I was nowhere, with nothing, and I had nobody normal to speak to. I felt that I was alone in an alien world—and I was the alien! This made me decide to hide and sleep rough for the night, giving me time to think about my situation." She looked seriously hard at him with wide eyes.

"What did you do then, Susan?"

"Well, I quickly hid among some dense evergreen bushes, where I had a long, hard think whilst feeling my heart beating fast. Then I realized that, to anyone I would meet, my heart would be on my right hand side. That's when my fear set in about doctors or any authorities who might find I'm different. That reminded me of the original Planet of the Apes series in which Taylor's astronaut friend was dissected for research because he could talk. That wasn't real, of course, but I believed that something similar could happen to me. I would at the very least be locked away somewhere like a prisoner, and what sort of a life would I have after that? It was a horrible thought, and I just stayed where I was. After thinking for a while about what people could possibly find on me, I checked all my clothes for any writing. Fortunately, I had a pair of scissors in my handbag, and I cut all the labels off my clothes. And, by gum, it was freezing cold in those woods! I then made sure that all the bits of label that I'd cut off were in my handbag so nobody would see anything lying around there like that, which could attract attention. I then rubbed myself briskly to get warm and settled down and continued thinking about what I should do. Finally, I felt tired. I covered myself as much as I could in my long raincoat, which, fortunately, I was wearing. I awoke sometime in the middle of the night because a dog was barking in the distance. I momentarily thought that everything was still a bad dream, but then I realized I was in the same place. My nose was running profusely. I seemed to be getting a cold, and I thought, *Oh no, that too. I'm most likely going to be prone to any virus that's going around in this strange world. This isn't good, because if I get seriously ill, a doctor will be required. I can't let that happen.* I then decided to eat every biscuit and sweet I had in my handbag, knowing that it's best to feed a cold to get better. I then wondered about whether I could spread any diseases to anybody else here. That worried me for a bit until I found that people recovered as they usually did with colds and viruses. It took longer for me though usually." She smiled and then said, "Yes, the transition and some of the stress that's followed probably caused my hair to be greyer in places compared to what it was. The red I've got now has got me by."

"Yes, it suits you." He smiled.

"Thanks." And she patted him on his shoulder.

"I've thought about all those possibilities myself. And that's just reminded me that we both got colds after we kissed."

She laughed and said, "Yes, that's why you got one. You probably caught some of my laterally inverted germs, as I did from you."

"I did think that. You pretended well with that between Sarah and Sophie."

She smiled and said, "Thanks. Anyway, the next day after that very cold and sleepless night, my cold was much worse, but in a way it did me a favour because it gave me some time to rest, think, and collect my thoughts together, after my mind had been in so much turmoil."

"What did you do the next day then?"

"Well, I was in a very sweaty and delirious state due to my terrible cold, and I even had a thumping headache, probably brought on by thinking about everything as well as the stress and trauma of it all. Since I was so thirsty and needed a wash after that night, I went to a nearby dyke and swallowed a few gulps of water. It was so cold, and when I rubbed some over my face, even with my bunged up nose, I could smell how awful it was. I quickly stopped and spat out as much as I could, especially realizing how muddy it felt on my face. Goodness knows why I did something as silly as that. I knew that that ditch water was absolutely filthy, and I must have been really delirious to do such a thing. I walked to a local store that I knew had toilets. I hoped it was still there!"

He frowned and said, "I hope you were all right after drinking that amount of awful water."

She smiled. "Well, I think so. I couldn't feel much worse than I was anyway. I did have a stomach upset afterwards, but I think that that was more due to the cold. Anyway, I found this store by thinking in reverse, and when I was nearly there after having just left the woods, there were too many people around who saw me. Two lads who were there started on at me because of how muddy my face looked."

"Oh dear. What happened then?"

"Well, you know what lads can be like when they get carried away, especially when they see a rare sight like me looking as I did." She laughed and continued, "Yes. The cheekier-looking, taller lad said, 'What have you been up to? Why have you put all that on your face for? Is it one of those beauty mud packs or have you been mud wrestling? The way you look, I think it's that!' He cheekily chuckled whilst I noticed his school uniform with the emblem on his right and the diagonal stripes on his tie running downwards from left to right as they would look in a mirror. The other lad laughed and then smiled straight at me, saying, 'Well, I think she looks lovely like that. She's rather fetching and has turned me on.' I replied, 'Yes, whatever. I did happen to just slip and fall into a muddy ditch back there, and I'll soon be OK when I get cleaned up.' I felt afterwards that I could have been a little bit more witty, but I just felt too tired and ill then. I could have easily shouted back at them 'Oh, whatever turns you on' but then that may have been a bit too much, especially when I'd seen an elderly couple watching us from nearby."

"Yes, I can see that. You never know what those lads could have said after that. It sounds to me that they may have liked what they saw." He smiled at her.

She blushed a little and said, "Oh please, Michael, don't get like Paul. I actually thought that myself when I looked back over that situation, and it wasn't greatly appealing. But then again, it's nice to be noticed, but it didn't feel exactly great at that moment."

"Yes, that's understandable."

She then looked at him resolutely out of the corner of her eye and continued saying, "Anyway, after I walked away from those two kids, the elderly couple came to me, and the man asked me if I was OK. I said, 'Thanks for asking. I'm all right I think, except for all this on me." And the gentleman said, 'I hope so.' I said, 'Thanks.' Then I walked into the store, noticing a few prying eyes on me as I went into the toilets. Yes, I certainly needed to go there first. I went to the sink to try to turn the right-hand tap on anticlockwise for cold water, but I realized that it had to be turned on clockwise for me here. After that, I just drank the water that gradually became warm, but which still tasted lovely because I was so parched. I then took a look in the mirror and noticed how filthy I actually looked. I saw that everything looked usual there, even the writing on the door behind me. I then thought that my image in the mirror was how other people actually saw me here. I touched the mirror with the hope that I might be able to get back through it, but that wasn't to be. I then looked behind me to see what I saw, getting that eerie feeling once again of being in this reverse world."

The thought of it made Michael's hair stand on end again.

Susan continued, "After that, I just washed myself as much as I could do in a public place and then stupidly got carried away and walked the long distance from there to my parents' house. Because I so wanted to share my situation with somebody, I overlooked the possible consequences of doing that for now. I was still very much in a bad state and couldn't, of course, go there on the bus because I didn't have any proper money with me. Even though I wasn't well, I still had a slight holiday feeling of being in Europe when I saw all the cars driving on the right-hand side besides the unfamiliarity of where I was, though it wasn't nice when I came back to my senses because, again, I felt all alone and isolated because I felt I shouldn't share any of my experiences or my thoughts with anyone."

"Oh, I can quite imagine that." He paused and felt bad for the situation she was in. He then said, "My mother told me about meeting somebody she said was in a poor state just after you left her house as Sarah last Boxing Day."

"Yes, that was me, and I felt literally very sweaty after that long walk, and still dirty, of course, because I hadn't been able to wash so well at those toilets. I was still very ill as well as unkempt. You'd have called me Stinky Sue if you didn't know me. I hadn't used the deodorant I fortunately had with me. It was a good job it wasn't summer, or else I'd have attracted all the flies from half a mile around I should think!" They both laughed. She then said, "Anyway, I had all I could do to hold myself together when I arrived at my reverse parents' house. I knocked on the door, and when my 'like mother' answered, I had the greatest urge to tell her everything about who I was because of that terrible lonely feeling. I'm just pleased that I kept my cool and didn't say too much to her then, other than to ask her where the library was. I just wanted to see what she was like here, or else I could have easily invited the wrong attention. I'd have been locked away as a looney, I should think, and all the doctors would be looking at me for research. That would have most certainly been it." She looked at her hands on the steering wheel, seriously reflecting over what might have happened.

"How did you find her then?"

She answered, "The same as always, except her eyes looked slightly different—they looked as they did when I viewed her in a mirror." She became a little emotional for a bit.

"OK, I understand. It must have been hard to hold yourself back then."

She perked up and said, "Yes. I just sort of stared at her for a bit until she told me where the library was, and then I quickly walked away before allowing myself to actually tell her who I was. She shouted back at me, 'Are you sure you're all right?' I waved back to her and continued to walk away, whilst breaking down." She became tearful and then said, "Seeing her then was enough to tell me where I was. At least I knew then of my situation and could take it from there."

"What did you do after that, then?"

"Well, the only thought in my mind then was to get some shelter. I went to the Salvation Army soup kitchens, being very careful from then on what I would say to anybody. That's when I first met Maureen, who was absolutely great with me. When I arrived, I felt very hungry and ill. I must have been on my last legs because I actually fainted. When she brought me round, presumably a bit later, she gave me something to eat and then some medication to help my cold. I was pleased it was tomato soup because I could use the spoon in my right hand. She commented on me being left handed then, which made me think even more of the problem I'd have using a knife and fork properly." She smiled and then said, "Yes, you caught me out with that for a few seconds when I think you purposely put my cutlery the wrong way round with that April fool's joke."

He laughed and said, "I know. I did similar things a few more times too."

"Yes. You had all but sussed me out then." She frowned at him and then smiled and continued, "Things tasted differently to me, too, from that first time, which was no surprise considering that my molecules are the opposite way round; excuse me for how that sounds." They laughed, and she continued, saying, "The medicinal lemon drink that she gave me after the meal tasted more like orange, just as you said it would when you talked to one of the Michaels. It was so bizarre, and that tomato soup I had before that tasted a little funny too. Virtually everything here is unusual, but I'm used to it—well more or less—by now." She smiled and then laughed and said, "That actually makes me think about food now. I'm feeling quite hungry. Shall we go and have something?"

"Yes, that would be quite nice. Shall we go for a Chinese takeaway and take it back to my house?"

She smiled and said, "OK, and I'll be buying since you bought me those fish and chips."

"It's OK. I'll go halves with you since you're driving."

She started the car and said, "Fine, thanks." Then she smiled cheekily, saying, "Did you pretend to drink too much so you could see my driving?"

He laughed and said, "Yes, I purposely drank a bit because that was part of my way of bringing you out, after what I'd heard Melanie say about your driving."

She drove off and said, "Well, you, you cheeky thing. You've really had all this thought out, haven't you? I knew it would be only so long before you'd catch up with me."

"Yes. Considering everything, I had to think of something elaborate." He laughed.

"Well, I'm still pleased." As she drove towards a Chinese takeaway, she said, "Well, to continue with what happened … Maureen helped me from then on. She was very concerned about me later that evening because that's when I had a real stomach upset, excuse me for bringing this up before tonight's meal—not literally of course." They both laughed. She then continued saying. "At that time, besides wondering about that bad water that I'd drunk from the dyke, I also thought about whether my system would reject any reverse food or drink I might consume. I was also worried about the effects of any foreign germs I could get, or again, as I said before, any germs I could pass on. That reminded me of the end of that H. G. Wells novel, *War of the Worlds*. All these things came to me as I was in my delirious state. Maureen took me back to her house later that evening so she could watch over me and see that I didn't get any worse. I told her to be careful not to catch what I had, and she said, 'I should be all right. I've had the flu jab because I have to help out different people here.' She was great with me." Susan shed a tear again and said, "Later that night, I had a thorough shower, and she washed my clothes, which were just plain trousers and a blouse. To her, I knew it would have appeared to be buttoned like a shirt. I told her it was all I could wear when coming here, and I was pleased there wasn't a top pocket, or else she'd have seen it as being on my right hand side. She loaned me some spare clothes after my shower, which of course took a bit of getting used to. After that, I just went to bed and fell asleep."

22

SUSAN'S FIRST WEEK AT MAUREEN'S

Susan and Michael arrived at the Chinese takeaway and paid half each for their meal. When she started to drive to his flat, she said, "Thanks for this. It's great for me to share some of the things I've been through with you now. I mean, look at my dashboard. To me it looks like I'm doing maximum speed when we're actually standing still. When I had first hired an older car here which had a horizontal petrol gauge, it was confusing then. I'd nearly been caught out because it looked as though it had been reading full when, in fact, the tank had almost been empty. Now you know more or less what it was like for me here from the start."

"Yes, I can quite imagine that." He thought for a moment and asked, "What sort of program was DO then?"

"Well, it sort of works in a similar way to the way

Skype works. The program somehow scans various universes that are parallel to our own so we can see them. It has to do with advanced digital technology, I suppose, by scanning with the use of subatomic particles or perhaps other things, such as dark matter, that physicists say wanders through our matter as we know it. Maybe that's how it moves through different parallel universes ... Excuse me for sounding like a Trekkie—beam me up, Scottie!" She laughed.

"I can follow what you're saying, and it does sound logical, Spock—excuse me saying."

They both laughed and she then said, "Well, I'm not so sure, but the technology from the universe I came from must have discovered some way of doing this before yours because I've seen nothing of it here yet. It was only made available from where I come from, and it was developed just before I arrived here, so that makes me wonder whether it's actually been discovered here yet. That's why I've been very careful about how I've used it here so far."

"Wow! I can understand that. It's been good that you can use it to contact your parents and keep in touch with them."

"Yes. I managed to contact them for the first time just before New Year's Eve, after trying a lot before that. You heard them talking about a time when I'd next get in touch with them."

"How did you give me the program then?"

"Well, I'd downloaded it onto your PC one lunchtime after you'd gone out. When I saw you using it for a bit, I later limited your Inverse choice to my universe only so you could clearly see where I'd come from, that being the main reason I gave it to you in the first place."

"I'd thought as much because of the way you sent me that tempting message to try it out. You have done well in keeping two or more steps ahead of me each time."

"Yes, I did that because I wanted to know how much you believed it and everything."

"Thinking about it logically, I would have probably done the same thing if I'd had your resources." He then asked, "I'm just wondering whether those profits you made on the stock market may have been made because the universe you came from is ahead of this one, especially as we don't have the DO program yet."

"Well, I got quite a bit of it that way. I used some of that knowledge to my advantage, but I didn't get it all right. Nothing's exactly the same. It's like some of the races and sporting events you compared between the two Michaels—random and unpredictable. Anyway, if I hadn't, I wouldn't be where I am now because I had to start from nothing. It's helped provide me with a car and my own rented home, which I only just managed to have since last October, and of course this Aygo." She smiled.

When they arrived at his flat, they carried their meals inside. As Michael served the meal on plates, not wanting to be too direct, he asked, "Is there anything you miss from where you come from?"

She forced a rather coy smile, saying, "Well, yes. I miss my family, and I had a few friends. I knew quite a few lads there, but there was nobody special. I enjoyed playing golf occasionally, and I liked board games and cards."

He thought, *Yes, I like those too*. He said, "Well, we seem to have the same interests, and we've played some of those already. I did enjoy you coming round on Christmas Day. Had you planned that?"

"Yes, actually. I so wanted to see you all over Christmas that I had to do something that seemed really authentic, so I slashed those two tyres and then spread some broken glass around so people would assume the glass damaged the tyres. My hitting the curb to avoid the glass seemed a more feasible story, as to why they were a write-off. I smashed up half a dozen beakers to get the glass." She smiled.

"You're mad, you. You could have done something less expensive and that wouldn't have put you to so much trouble."

"Well, it was absolutely worth it all because I had to make it really believable. It meant that I could at least stay a day longer with you, and I could get to know you all better. I imagine that you might have done something similar, too, if you'd been me."

"Yes, quite possibly, especially after the loneliness you've experienced."

"I wanted so much to see you all on Christmas Day, especially since I was all by myself. I missed the Christmas spirit with my family, so I took the chance. I hope I hadn't spoilt it for you."

Before they sat down for their meal, he put the kettle on for a pot of tea. He said, "Well I was shocked at first because of who you were from work, but shortly after that I really enjoyed it, even though I felt at times that

I had to be careful with a work colleague higher up than me."

"Yes. Knowing that I've had that same feeling myself, I felt guilty about putting you on edge for some of the time over those two holiday days, and that's the reason I posed as Sophie shortly after that—so you'd be more relaxed, and I'd get to know you better."

"Thanks. You played her a lot more coolly than you played Sarah, and you were convincing, although your voices were the same, though there are a lot of girls who sound similar but are much different." He smiled, and then they both laughed. He then went to prepare the tea. When he came back into his living room, he saw her eating some of the chips with the knife and fork the wrong way round.

She laughed and said, "Yes. I'm showing you now that I can really relax and eat in the normal way that I'm used to. It's nice to feel momentarily like being back, even though these surroundings in this flat are still the wrong way round."

"Yes, why not? Just let your hair down. It's about time that you did things that are more natural to you. I'd like to see how you do things in your own way and even see how you write. It would give me a greater sense of what you have been through."

She smiled at him and then paused and whispered, "Thanks. I feel OK about that, provided we're just by ourselves and keep it quiet between the two of us."

"I understand. Oh, I've just remembered the time on that Christmas night when I heard somebody shout outside at me 'Happy Christmas!' I thought that was perhaps Susan or Claire, as she'd called herself later. It couldn't have been her, though, because you'd just come into my room to tell me that you'd heard the same thing."

She paused and then smiled, saying, "Well, that was another of my tricks. I wanted to make you think that there could be a few more of us here from a reverse world because I felt that that could give me more cover. Excuse me for that."

"Well, it had me and the Michaels guessing. It even had me wondering for a short time whether we might be overtaken by ourselves from reverse universes. Boy, there was a lot of scope then for imagining anything of a sci-fi nature. Anyway, how did you manage to do that sound effect?"

"It was quite straight forward. I used a mini MP3 player that I'd left in your parents' front garden under some bushes just before I rang your doorbell when I arrived at your house. Later that night, I just activated the player by remote control to play something I'd previously recorded, and that's what you'd heard."

"Well done. You've covered yourself well."

"I'd had plenty of time to think about things, and I wanted to do them very carefully, knowing that I'd rather gone too far at times by getting carried away. I suppose that's because I've been on my own too long in this situation."

"You're all right. I've overdone things, too, myself sometimes because I have an over-active imagination."

"Yes, our thinking is the same. Like you said to the Michaels occasionally, and must have thought of a lot at times, I have been ahead of you, especially because I'm in this situation fully and before you even knew of it. By the way, I went outside in the early hours of that Boxing Day morning to pick up the MP3 player when all of you were asleep. I could tell by the way that all of you were snoring, even you Michael." She laughed.

"Well you, you cheeky thing. I actually heard you, too, when I got up briefly around seven o'clock that morning."

She laughed and said, "Yes, probably, with that extra grey hair of mine perhaps. Anyway, continuing with what happened during that first night I slept at Maureen's … I woke up in the middle of that night feeling very sickly. As soon as I got up, that was it! It went all over the bed and down the front of me. I was then terrified about whether I could digest the reverse food from here. I knew that if I couldn't, I would never survive. I hoped above hope that I could get back, and if I couldn't, all I hoped for then was that the sickness had been caused by that dirty water or the virus I'd had, and not by my system rejecting the food. I then looked at the clock again, hoping that things would be back to normal, but they weren't. The digits were still in reverse. I actually felt better then after having been sick, but I felt weak, and I somehow just managed to clean things up. Whilst doing so, I was at least pleased to still have a blocked nose or else the smell of that could have made me sick again. Excuse me for saying that whilst you're still eating."

Michael had a disgusted look on his face after having just dropped a piece of chicken onto his plate. He said, "Great, thanks. I'd almost eaten that, and you could have waited a little longer before telling me those things so graphically."

She laughed and then said seriously, "Oh, excuse me. I was just focussing on the enormity of what I was going through then. I know that I shouldn't have explained that part right now."

"OK. I'll finish my meal now I know that part's finished." He laughed.

She laughed and said, "Well put. Anyway, after I'd sorted that out the best way I could then, I quickly fell asleep until Maureen came in later to see how I was. When she saw that I had only had part of the bedclothes and was wearing the blouse that she'd leant me, she asked me what had happened. When I told her that I'd been sick, she said I should have woken her, so I said, 'I didn't want to disturb you, and I was OK with clearing it up.' She told me to keep resting, and she came back a few minutes later with two blankets, which kept me warm. I fell asleep again until she woke me to tell me she was leaving to prepare breakfast at the kitchens and that she'd be back in the early evening after serving the last meal there. I had the house to myself, and she trusted me. For that first day, I just rested. I was afraid of having any more food, in case I'd reject it again after being horribly sick before. I wasn't sick later, but I'd had a couple of bad dos again on the toilet."

"Please don't go into that. It isn't necessary."

She laughed, saying, "No, I wasn't intending to, but then again … Anyway, that evening, she brought some food back for me and made sure I ate it. I was concerned after that and felt a little queasy, but somehow I digested it.

I just basically slept for all of that day. The next day, which was Thursday, I didn't feel quite as bad. It was a nice sunny day, so I got up about midday after noticing that the sun moved round in the opposite direction to the left, like it does down under. It's funny how the conversation somehow gravitates to Paul again. Excuse me."

"Yes, I thought of that. I knew that that factor would remind you of him somehow."

"Yes. It's unusual for that in this country, besides driving on the right—well, for me anyway." Then she paused and said, "Yes, and that Monopoly game was funny for me at times. I don't know whether you saw me laugh at odd times as we played, but, because I saw things backwards, I did notice some amusing words. Park Lane and Bond Street are two that come to mind, especially Park Lane."

He thought and then laughed, saying, "Yes. Not the kind of thing you'd say in front of a lady."

She smiled and said, "Well, thanks for that. Anyway, after having got up at around midday and washed, I looked at the newspapers that she'd got that morning. Of course, it was easy for me to read them by holding them up to a mirror. I risked eating again, too, because it was all I felt like doing. I was so hungry, and I knew that food was the best thing for a cold."

"Were you sick again because of it?"

"No. I was OK from then on, but certain foods still made me feel queasy, and even sick occasionally back then, especially rich food with a lot of ingredients. It took me some time after that to get used to certain types of food."

"Would you like a cup of tea?"

"Yes, please. That would be nice."

He smiled and poured her a cup first. They helped each other to the sugar and milk, and then she continued saying, "Thanks. Anyway, after seeing the similarity of the news in the papers, I thought that it might be possible that I'd somehow got reversed by teleportation when I came here, and that I was the only one who'd changed due to that. When I thought about those kids not recognizing me after they'd looked at me a few times, I realized that I was in a different world, which of course I know now. Shortly after that, I looked at an atlas in a mirror to see if things were any different from the world that I knew, and they weren't."

"Well, I've thought about it, and the best conclusion that I can come to is that the big bang somehow happened in reverse in our two universes. The matter is the same except for that. I'm sure that some universes alongside ours are made up of antimatter such as positrons, which are positively charged electrons, and antiprotons, which are negatively charged protons."

"Yes, I've thought of that too. These types of matter couldn't coexist because they'd destroy each other and become energy. In fact, we found some such universes I think, but couldn't go any further into them because of such reactions. Anyway, after looking at a few more books that were the same as what I have in the world I came from, I then focussed on my predicament here. I tried writing like you do here a little that afternoon, and it came rather naturally when writing from right to left, though I had to think a bit with a's, e's, and s's and various others. It was quite slow progress." She smiled and then said, "I then thought along the same lines as you did with regard to carbon paper. That was quicker for me."

He laughed and said," Yes. I only picked up that method by accident, when I once got the carbon paper the wrong way round. It happened when I was preparing a copy of an invoice. It came out in reverse on the back of a sheet."

"Actually, I did that same thing once. It was easily done when I was working too fast!" She laughed and then smiled, saying, "Yes. That made me want to tell you even more after seeing your two letters—we think alike!"

"Well, I'm pleased you started to do things that would help you. That would've taken your mind off your cold."

"It did do for a while, and it was the first time I could see myself possibly moving forward. After that, I looked at a few more books and compared some of the history I knew. All of that looked the same—like the map book. I then watched some television, which was peculiar because it was laterally inverted, so I watched through a little pocket mirror I have. I watched a quiz program. I knew the person who was chairing it, so that was no different. That kept me occupied until Maureen arrived back in the early evening with a readymade meal for me."

"Was it anything good?"

"Yes. It was some tomato soup and bread as a starter. After she saw me eat that and noticed I was OK with it, she cooked a steak and kidney pie with some potatoes, cabbage, and gravy for both of us. I enjoyed it, even though it tasted not quite the same in certain ways, again because of the slight differences in things. After that, I felt queasy again, but it wasn't enough to make me sick. I told her that I came from the Ukraine, that being the first thing I thought of. It seemed most feasible. She asked me my name. I called myself Sarah Morrison—Morrison was the first thing to come into my head."

"But Maureen seemed to know of you as Sophie."

"I put her up to that by priming her about you. I told her that I'd done a stupid thing by telling a lad that I'd just met that my name was Sophie Kaye. I also had used that wig. She went along with it for my benefit when you met her. She doesn't know about how I'd really got here. You're the only one who knows that."

"Wow. I thought that had to be the case."

She smiled and said, "Anyway, just before the end of the evening, when Maureen thought I was getting better, she gave me some money in case I wanted to go out the next day to buy some food. The money was definitely unusual when I looked at it—possibly you felt the same when you saw that tenner."

He laughed and said, "Yes. I thought about that and wondered if it could have been from a joke shop."

"Yes, well, I was in the thick of it all, but it was a nice surprise that she trusted me enough to lend me some money. I was looking forward to shopping for some food for the first time here—until I had another bad stomach upset during that night. I then began to feel worse again with the cold, which made me wonder if I'd started rejecting the food again. The worry came back as to whether I could survive here. The next day I was laid up again as the cold thickened, and I was afraid to eat even though I'd felt hungry. I then had another bad turnout that morning and felt weak again. When Maureen got home later that evening with some more food for me, I ate it, but I was very tired. She was concerned about those stomach upsets and the fact that they had got worse, so she phoned a nurse she was friendly with. She said she would arrive in an hour."

"Oh, that would be worrying."

She responded, "Definitely— because of where I'd come from. I said to Maureen, 'You didn't have to do that. It was only a stomach upset, probably brought on because my cold is thickening.' She said, 'Well, I'm only doing it for your sake because you seemed to be getting better yesterday and are worse again today. That shouldn't be the case.' I said, 'OK. I'll have to go to the loo again.' And I pretended to go there, but I quickly put on one of her warm pullovers and my raincoat, and I left for a while. Funnily enough, when I was outside, I felt a lot better, so I went to buy some sandwiches. I felt better still after eating them. I walked the short distance into town and caught a bus. It was unusual again to get on the bus and pay the driver with that money. I looked at all the reverse writing on the advertisements in the bus. It felt weird riding on the right-hand side, with the left-hand drive. That got me to where my flat was—or yours is—here of course." She laughed.

He smiled and said, "Yes, of course. What did you do then?"

"Well, I was curious to know who might be in my

place. I wondered if, perhaps, it would be another me or someone I knew. Or maybe it would be a complete stranger. A lot went through my mind until I saw you come out to go for a walk. I felt faint at the shock of seeing the likeness—you looked like me as a man. It was weird. I wondered then if I had a sister instead of a brother, or if my father was my mother and visa versa. It certainly got me thinking all ways."

"Well, I didn't see anything of you until I met you as Sarah, or that girl similar to me walking through a shop last November after you had just started working—as Sarah—where I do."

"That's what you think. I dressed up in all sorts of clothes and make-up to start off with so I could see you from a distance and get a feel of the situation. I know it sounds weird, but I had to work out what to do besides getting started here. That night I was only just careful and quick enough to keep out of your sight after being surprised to see you for the first time."

"Well, I don't remember seeing anything back then particularly. What did you do then?"

"I followed you a short way and then turned back when I began to feel a little queasy again. It wasn't quite as bad as before, so I decided to walk back, especially because I didn't feel very weak. And I knew that I'd at least arrive back at Maureen's well after that nurse had left. Those sandwiches that I'd eaten earlier helped me feel better somehow, and I think that being back on my feet helped me too. Anyway, it was well after ten when I arrived back, and Maureen was quite cross because I'd caused her to worry. She didn't know where

I was, and she wanted to get to bed because she had to work first thing the next day. She said, 'Well, you could have stayed. I only wanted her to see you in case there was something seriously wrong. After all, you've been feeling sickly, and you've been having those stomach upsets. You never know these days what different flu germs are going around. I didn't want you to go down with pneumonia or anything like that.' I apologized after that and said, 'It's just that I'm not keen on nurses and doctors, and when I felt OK after moving around a bit, I decided to go for a walk to see if that would help me, and it did. I know that I should have at least come back to tell you.'"

As she paused, he asked, "Well, what if you ever had an accident and needed treatment?"

She responded, "It near enough happened once when I had sprained my wrist, but I got by. Anyway, back to that time after I had left Maureen's. I suggested giving her a hand the next day, if I still felt better. She agreed, and the next day, which was a Saturday, I went with her to help serve breakfast at the shelter. We got on OK after that, and I enjoyed the feeling of helping out and being part of something again." Just then, they heard someone knock on his door.

"Oh, I've just remembered—that'll be my brother. He's come to take me to the evening service."

"Oh, I'd better get going then. I do have a few things to do. We'll talk sometime later—maybe on Tuesday if we can be alone." She finished her tea and then took her things to the kitchen to be washed.

"Thanks for doing that." And he took the rest, saying,

"Yes, we'll try when we have the opportunity. Anyway, my brother will know you as Sarah from work." He hoped that would be all.

She got fidgety and opened her handbag to look for her brown-coloured contact lenses. She said in relief, "Ooh, I've found them. I'll now look fully like Sarah again." She quickly put them in.

He smiled and asked, "Are you all right now?"

"Fine. Hopefully we'll talk again on Tuesday."

Michael finally went to open the door.

James said, "Hi, Michael. I'm ready to go when you are."

"OK. Sarah—from work—has been here because she had a few things to tell me."

Susan said, "Hi, James. How are you?"

"I'm fine Sarah. Are you OK?"

She smiled and replied, "Yes. Anyway, I'd best get going. I'll see you at work, Michael."

"OK, see you soon." He wasn't able to say her name.

James said, "Nice seeing you again, Sarah. We'll all have to meet again sometime."

She froze for a moment and said, "Yes, we will sometime." She looked at Michael, who smiled at her. She then waved to them and went to her car.

James said, "I know she's a work colleague of yours, but she's a nice lass. You should get to know her better."

"Yes, it's early days yet. She could be a good friend … a bit like a sister really."

"Oh, go on. There could be more to it than that. You seemed to get on well with her when we all met at Christmas."

"Yes. I'll just wash up and we'll go." They both

waved to Susan as she drove away. As Michael began the washing up, he noticed her fingerprints on her teacup, so he put it to one side. He then washed up the rest of the things. As he and James left, Michael wondered how a girl as lovely and as great as Susan could have possibly been in his place in another universe. When he arrived home later that evening, he compared one of her fingerprints on the cup to one of his own, and it matched exactly except for a few odd warn lines, which he figured could be explained by the lateral inversion of her print on the cup, which he then washed up and put away.

23

A MEAL AT SUSAN'S

Two days later, just before nine o'clock on Tuesday morning, as Michael arrived at the office, he saw Melanie with Susan, who was still pretending to be Sarah. Melanie smiled and said, "Hi, Michael. How are you?"

"I'm fine thanks. Are you OK?"

"Yes, I'm all right."

He smiled whilst thinking back at those jokes about being half left.

"Well, anyway, it's going to be a busy morning after yesterday."

He saw Susan smile at him, and he said, "Yes, I think it will be."

Paul then arrived, jolly as usual, and said, "Hi, everybody. I can see it'll be another bonza day in the office."

Susan smiled and said, "Yes, as usual." She passed some invoices to Michael, saying, "Here are some more invoices for you to process." She winked at him and then smiled, saying, "Well, I'd better make a start. The sooner we start, the sooner we'll finish." She went into her office.

Melanie said, "OK, I'll see you all later." And she followed her co-worker into her office.

Paul smiled and said, "OK, some of us are keen! I'd best get on then."

Michael said, "OK. See you later." And he went into his office. He looked through the invoices he'd just received from her and saw a note amongst them, saying, "Michael. You're welcome to come around to my house this evening at around seven. If you do, I'll prepare you a meal. I'll hopefully see you around then, Susan."

That evening, just before seven o'clock, Michael arrived for the first time at the address that he knew to be Sarah's house from her employment records. He knocked at the door and when she—Susan—opened it and saw it was him, she hugged him immediately, and he felt that lovely sensation again. She wore her work clothes, but had removed the brown-coloured contact lenses. She said, "I'm glad you've come." She gave him a peck on the cheek. He felt that he'd love to take it much further, but she was too much like a sister for that. She backed off herself and said, "I know how you feel, and I feel the same. It isn't right though."

He shrugged and said, "I know. I've thought all about it, and it'd be too fantastic because of the way I've felt already."

She dropped her head whilst hugging herself and said

in a light high-pitched, annoyed sort of voice, "I know, but it's how it is." She then looked very disappointed.

He said, "Oh well … Oh, I've brought along a bottle of strong, sweet wine. I know you should like it because it's one of my favourites."

She smiled and laughed, saying, "Mine too. That's a lovely wine."

"Anyway, I'll give you a hand with preparing the meal."

"OK, thanks." He took his summer coat off, and they went into the kitchen to start preparing the food. She let Fido in, and he made a fuss of them both. Susan said, "I've wondered, if I'm stuck here, whether I could have children if ever I meet the right man. Personally, I don't think I could because the DNA and everything that I have, is in reverse, so nothing could form properly. If it did, it would be a still birth because of the way some of the organs could develop, such as the heart. For example, there may be two separate undeveloped hearts on each side of the foetus, so it could never function properly and would therefore abort itself."

"Yes, I've thought about that too. In addition, the two types of DNA would be different and incompatible. Nothing would come of it because of that. It would be like crossing two different species."

As she put on the potatoes and cabbage, she said, "Well, it's all speculation, and I've studied biology only up to GCSE standard."

"Me too. I concentrated only on maths, physics, and chemistry at A level."

"Those were the subjects that I took too. I then went into accountancy work. I tried it out with my father and liked it. I saw that you did the same when I found out a few things about you from work."

He smiled and said, "Yes, that would have been reasonably straight forward. Anyway, how was it with working with Maureen at the Salvation Army soup kitchens?"

She smiled and answered, "It wasn't that easy at first because I still had a cold and it wasn't the type of work that I was used to. She let me help with the washing up after we'd all had our breakfasts. I'd just had a bowl of cornflakes and baked beans on toast that morning. I could have had some bacon, eggs, and sausage, but I didn't because I didn't want to be queasy again." She laughed and then said, "Anyway, it was all go after that with the amount of washing up we had to do. I was a little worn out then and had to spend the rest of the day taking it easy, especially because I still wasn't right. The following day, I was a little better and beginning to get my sense of smell back. Some things from then on didn't quite smell the same because, again, the sensations of smell are based on chemical reactions like taste. It's not so noticeable now that I've got used to it." She smiled and continued, "I worked again that Sunday, washing up, cleaning, and doing various other small jobs. One of the lads who worked there got quite friendly, and we had a few laughs. He was quite amused at some of my habits because I'm more than just left handed. I slipped up a few times with the knife and fork and did my best to laugh it off as one of my jokes about being left handed."

As they laughed, he said, "Well, don't worry here. I'd

like to see you continue to eat as you normally do. It's quite interesting."

She said, "Yes, as you are to me." She looked at him flirtingly and said, "From then on I used a spoon as much as I could, until I'd got used to using the knife and fork as they do here. Maureen laughed about it a few times, too, and wondered out of fun whether it was an ongoing custom in the Ukraine. I soon dropped that habit because I worried about what people might think about it, especially if they thought about where I'd come from. Anyway, because I was so prone to illness at that time, I had a very bad bout of flu the next day, and I was back at Maureen's. I rested from that Monday until the following weekend. It took me until Wednesday before I could digest anything because that's what flu does to you. I was sick quite a lot and couldn't hold anything down because of the continuous stomach upsets. I used that time, though, as I had before, to practice writing, but this time, I also practiced using the knife and fork like you do. I also practiced reading backwards as well as typing on her typewriter so I would be ready to use a computer as it is here. In a way, that time I got to myself was very useful as I started to become familiar with things here. I began to look at my situation more positively and saw it as a bit of an adventure." She smiled.

"You did well to do that in the circumstances. A lot of people would have got depressed and let it get to them. You had the right attitude, thank goodness, to bounce back."

"Thanks for that. It took some doing while I was on my own, but the differences intrigued me, and I wanted to succeed here and take on the challenge. In a way, it became a bit of a vacation, and it was like being somewhere new."

He said, "Yes. I got the feeling of interest when I saw those different universes on the DO program."

She paused and then smiled, saying, "Yes, so did I. Anyway, on Sunday, when I was well enough to help out at the kitchens again, a lad called Phil tried to get to know me, which was difficult at times because I didn't want to say too much, especially in my predicament, so I wasn't really that forthcoming."

"What happened then?" He turned the heat down under the potatoes, as they were about to boil over.

"Well, he gradually drifted away. He probably thought I wasn't interested. He was OK, but I was in too much of a dilemma then. Anyway, since I was nearly better and had got over the worst of the flu, I stayed that night at their hostel and shared a dormitory with Lisa. I'd seen her only there and had never spoken to her before."

"How was she?"

"Well, she was quite rough and ready with a tattoo on each arm. She was a little taller than me and punk like with jet-black, greasy hair. All she wore after she'd taken off her shabby, long, green raincoat, was a purple, grubby-looking, thread-worn swimsuit under a brown Hessian-type miniskirt." Michael remembered meeting Lisa for the first time a while ago.

Susan continued, "She also wore dirty brown trainers, which she was quite happy to sleep in." She smiled whilst rolling her eyes and then said, "Yes ... I naturally wanted to be friendly, so I asked her how long she'd been there, and she said very curtly, 'What business is it of yours, nosey?' She looked daggers at me with her piercing green eyes. She then slumped onto her bed with her back to me, seeming to pick her nose besides doing other things." Susan gave a wry smile and continued saying, "And I said, 'Well, I was only being curious.' And she said, 'Well don't be, or else I'll turn this finger up.' We said nothing more to each other for a while."

"Ooh, I wouldn't like to think what was on that."

"Eww, Michael! Please. It doesn't bear thinking about."

He chuckled and asked, "What happened after that?"

"Well, I settled into bed myself and heard her do nothing but shuffle around in hers for the next two hours, which kept me awake. There were also a lot of other background noises in the other dormitories. People were talking and playing loud music and everything. In the early hours, she woke me up with a loud noise." Susan laughed and said, "Yes. She giggled to herself then and said, 'Oh, do excuse me. It's those fucking beans I had earlier.' Then she actually said, 'Ooh! That felt just like a tapeworm!' I could then smell her, excuse me for saying."

They both laughed, and he said, "Well, what a lass. You do get some types about."

She smiled and said, "Yes, definitely, and she had quite the attitude, too, with it. She then asked me why I was there. I felt like being as rude as she'd been with me earlier and asking, 'What business is it of yours?' but I didn't. What was the point? After all, she'd laughed herself into a better mood. I told her the same story I'd told Maureen, and she was interested then in what the Ukraine was like. I obviously had to tell her something realistic that would match up with current politics. She told me that she'd been here for over two months, doing the begging bowl thing during the day. Before that, she'd left home and became a prostitute. She'd got hooked on drugs and had only just come off them then."

"That seems to be the way of the world for a lot of people who are down and out."

Susan said, "That's what it's like with a lot of the girls around there. She became friendlier with me after that, probably a bit too much sometimes." She looked at Michael and then smiled, saying, "I only kept it on a friendly basis, and she was all right once I got to know her. Anyway, she moved to a different dorm a few days later, and I see her only occasionally now when she visits Maureen."

"What happened after that? Did you share with anybody else?"

Susan answered, "Yes, quite a few different people, all girls of course. There was always a minimum of two to a dorm." She smiled whilst he nodded with a smile, and she said, "Anyway, when I'd fully recovered a few days later after that first Sunday night with Lisa, Maureen helped me out with all the form filling so I could obtain my identity as Sarah Morrison. I applied for my NHI number, passport, and new provisional driving licence, since I hadn't existed here until now. After we had both worked at the kitchens during the day, we worked for two evenings on the forms before sending them off. I couldn't get properly started with finding work until my new papers arrived. Maureen knew all the ins and outs with that, having had taken many people in before with the same problems. You got the gist of all that, I think, when you met her before."

"Yes. She's a very knowledgeable lady. You did well to meet her for the first time."

Susan smiled and said, "Yes. I felt that the Salvation Army would be one of the best places to try first. Anyway, after we finished the forms before that weekend, I thought of my family. I wanted to choose somebody I could safely contact. And, as I've said, you were the only person who seemed suitable."

He smiled and said, "Yes." He felt that he truly knew her because he could see himself in her. The difference was that she was more worldly and experienced because she'd had to become so successful here.

Susan shared out some chicken pieces between them and added cold sausages and some bacon that she'd just cooked in the microwave. She said, "Anyway, on that Saturday, which was Valentine's Day, I received a card that I found out later from Lisa was from Phil. She said I should have at least given him a try, you know." She smiled and continued, "But I just couldn't get involved with anyone here then, just as I can't now. You know why?"

"Yes. I can just imagine you still feel that you're in a foreign world."

"Too true. I still have the same weird feelings occasionally that I don't belong here, though they are wearing off now. Anyway, that evening after finishing all the clearing up after dinner, I was allowed to borrow a spare bicycle from the Salvation Army. I cycled to your parent's house, and when I got there, I wondered why I had gone there because I just couldn't make myself go inside to see them then. I remembered when your mother had seen me on my first day. I remembered the way she'd received me before. I didn't want to worry her again or alert her in any way, so I went to your flat to see if I could see you again."

"I admit that, when she told me about you, she was concerned about what your intentions might be."

"Yes, I could see that, and that really saddened me and made me feel even more alone at that time. That contributed to my breaking down then." She shed a little tear.

"Oh, I'm sorry for bringing that up."

"Oh don't be. It was a natural reaction. You're all right, all of you." She smiled tearfully. She paused and then said, "Anyway, I saw a light on in your flat, but I didn't want to bump into you either. I cycled around for a bit after that, sometimes losing myself, especially when I inadvertently cycled on what was my left-hand side of the road. A car full of rowdy young lads tooted at me, and the driver shouted, 'Get back to Calais where you belong, you silly froggy mare!' As you can imagine, I was embarrassed a bit and quickly said, 'Ooh la-la, excusez-moi,' when he stuck up one finger outside his window." She laughed.

He chuckled and said, "Wow, I think I know who they could be. One or two lads like that, live where I live."

"Yes. He could be one of those two that I'd recognized. Anyway, after that I got to thinking about dressing up like a real tramp so I could see you without possibly alerting you in any way, because tramps do tend to loiter around a bit." She started to serve the potatoes whilst he made the gravy and then drained the cabbage. He helped her serve the meal, and they went into the lounge, which was decorated with golden-coloured wallpaper and a burgundy-and-green-patterned carpet. She had a settee along with two matching white, flowery-patterned easy chairs facing her fairly large widescreen television. She said, "Well, when I'm by myself, I close the curtains and watch TV through that big mirror there." He remembered seeing the back of it when he'd looked through her lounge window some time ago. She continued, saying, "That way I can relax and see things normally for me." She positioned the mirror so she could see the television through it from where she sat at the table.

He sat down at the table and said, "Good idea. At least you can feel you are at home again."

"Yes. It's good for me because I feel my usual self again."

They started eating as they watched the news for a bit, until he said, "You've done a lovely meal here. I like a mixed-meats type roast with vegetables and lots of gravy."

She smiled and said, "I knew you would because it's delicious for me too, except of course for some still-unfamiliar tastes, you know? Anyway, to continue what happened … The following week, after that Valentine's Day weekend, I had a chat with Lisa about begging, and she gave me some ideas about clothes." She smiled and laughed, saying, "Yes, you can guess the next bit." They both laughed as he watched her pick up her knife and fork in the wrong hands and smile at him, just as she started to eat. She then gave Fido a piece of chicken, and Michael gave him some from his plate. Fido wagged his tail. She continued, "I went to look around a few charity shops and got quite a lot of things, some very nice actually, for next to nothing. Some of the things you can buy at those shops are at real bargain prices, and some are just given away."

"I know. My parents and I have given all sorts of stuff away that we didn't want. My mother's given away some lovely dresses that she couldn't wear anymore."

She smiled and said, "Yes, we were the same. We've given some rare gifts to some of those places. Anyway, I saw you a few times over the next couple of weeks after leaving work, which gave me the idea of how I might be able to observe you better, to somehow maybe know you without you noticing me too much. On the first Monday in March, I sat in the subway where I knew you came through quite often." She looked at him directly and continued to say, "Yes. I was with Lisa then. She wanted to come with me to show me the ropes." She smiled and then said, "You saw me in a very shabby brown raincoat with too-long purple trousers tucked over my dirty black trainers. When you looked at Lisa, who was wearing similar togs to mine and a long, black, dirty-looking wig, I noticed you holding back a laugh as you walked by."

"Yes, I remember. I thought you might be sisters or something."

She laughed and said, "Or something."

He curled up laughing and said, "Well all sorts crossed my mind. You know?"

"Yes, well, it wasn't that way though. I felt embarrassed that you'd seen me then, but she wanted to help me because that was the first time I'd done any begging." She forced a smile and then said, "Well, you could have at least given us some kind of a token donation, Michael." She laughed.

He responded a little guiltily, saying, "Yes I could've, but I felt awkward seeing you two girls there, wondering what might happen."

"I know. We saw it on your face as you passed us by reluctantly, and that's what made Lisa say something after that."

"Yes. I heard her say, 'Well, Saza, that's another lad who's given us nothing,' which made me feel more uncomfortable." He remembered her deep, husky voice with a broad Yorkshire accent.

"You're forgetting that she'd also called you a stunning lad."

"I remember, but I didn't want to make too much of that." He nervously coughed and laughed.

"Well you should've." They both laughed. She then said, "But she could've left out the Saza bit. That made me sound rough, but it made me feel like quite a cool kid, the way she'd said it." She smiled at him.

He chuckled and said, "Yes, it could suit you actually, Suza. It's quite a becoming name for you."

"Oy, you! Cheeky! Stop that!" She laughed.

"Why? You look so lovely when you screw up your face like that."

"Oh, please." She shrugged and then pulled a face, saying, "Anyway, we both had quite a laugh after that about certain other people who passed by. It was interesting to see their reactions whilst we were down there. One middle-aged man smiled at us and gave us a couple of quid, saying, 'You deserve that for the risk you're both taking in this secluded place. I'd be careful if I were you in case more than two lads come and try to take advantage.' Lisa said in her butch way, 'Well if they dare to try something on with me, they'll get three times as much back and more. They'll be walking awkwardly for the next couple of weeks!' She can be quite a rum lass when she wants to be." Susan laughed and then said, "And she put that more bluntly than I've just said. Put it this way, there were quite a few Fs and Bs as she'd said it, and the man was so amused, he gave her another pound afterwards. You'd have thought it was a swear box she had!" She chuckled.

Michael smiled and said, "It could've been because he was worried, perhaps, about being mugged by her."

She laughed and said, "Probably so, but she wouldn't do that."

"Well, I wouldn't be too sure. She approached me a month or so later whilst I walked through town to an ATM, asking me for fifty pence. She said she was short for getting home. She sparkled her eyes at me." He thought back to seeing her beautiful, emerald-green Irish eyes, and her very curvy thin figure in that old-looking, thread-worn purple swimsuit under her tight, raggedy blue jeans trousers and jacket. He continuing to say, "And she jiggled her body a little to persuade me. I actually gave her something then, feeling foolish for doing so." He remembered her pulling him directly to her and then giving him a wet kiss on the lips followed by her tongue, which had given him a tingly feeling, arousing him as he smelled a hint of her deodorant. He said, "She then said, 'Thanks … I'll see you around, Bud.' As she walked away, she turned back and asked me my name. I told her my first name, and she said, 'Oh, I'm Lisa. I'll see you, Michael.' And she walked off." He remembered the broad smile on her face.

"Well, she seemed to like you then. I've seen how she flirts with people she likes sometimes." Susan blushed a little and then said, "Anyway, I saw you around a few more times after that, but I didn't want to show myself again to you for a while. I finally got my NHI number in the middle of April, and then I began to look for work. I landed the stacking job by the beginning of May, and that's when Maureen took me in as a lodger.

Michael said, "That reminds me. Is your birthday on the eleventh of April?"

She smiled and answered, "Not really. It's actually the same as yours—the eleventh of October. And if you look at my fingerprints, you'll see that they are the exact mirror image of yours. I did a check based on how my brother Michael did them, who in your case is James." They both laughed. She continued, "Anyway, I had enjoyed working in the soup kitchens up until then and had been doing a bit of everything there, including serving and preparing some of the food. I continued, though, to work some of my spare time at the kitchens, and Maureen took account of that as part of my boarding costs." She smiled and said, "Yes, I enjoyed staying with her then for the company."

"Well, you've done OK then."

"Yes. I was only really just getting onto my feet, and that's when I'd started studying some share price movements over the previous few months. That gave me the confidence of what to invest in, especially when I compared the information to what had happened where I came from. Not everything happened in exactly the same way, even though the place I came from seemed to be ahead of what is happening here with regard to the discoveries of these alternative universes. I've actually noticed that, in certain cases, things here are ahead of where they are where I come from. I learned this after I was able to contact my parents. Nothing is obvious, however, and that's why I've taken some losses at times when the timing was just not what I expected. It wasn't great starting in May, either, you know?"

"Yes, I've been caught a few times buying in May because too many people heed that saying 'sell in May and go away'. It's not always the case, though, if you're selective in what you buy."

"Fortunately, most of my decisions worked out well. It was messy, though, when some of the bigger losses compromised my gains in the beginning. Fortunately, by July, I'd overcome a lot of those and could afford some things like extra clothes, furniture, and driving lessons. I needed to learn to drive an automatic so I could finally have my own transport, which I need in my current job. My provisional licence arrived only shortly after I'd got my NHI number. In order to buy shares, I had to have a fixed abode, which was Maureen's house."

"Well, you did right by making it easier for yourself by choosing to learn on an automatic."

"Definitely. It would have taken me much longer to pass a manual test here, and it was bad enough having to take the driver's test all over again. I even had to take the automatic test three times before I passed it last October. When I think about learning on a standard transmission, I realize it would have taken me forever because of all the gear changes, which would have been the opposite way round from what I was used to." She laughed and then sighed. She then said, "I first took the test in the middle of June and made a right mess of it by driving on the wrong side and then indicating the opposite way round, after having mistakenly put on the windscreen wipers! I was so used to doing things the other way round. It was sort of like what happened on Sunday, too, when a couple of times I pressed the brake instead of the accelerator. At times I nearly strained the starter motor by turning the key the wrong way to switch the engine off, which, by the way, didn't happen in the test." She looked at him and laughed.

He smiled and said, "Yes. It is definitely a topsy-turvy world for you, isn't it?"

"Yes, absolutely! And still is. On my second test, though, I braked so hard that somebody ploughed into the back of me. The examiner had had enough at that point and was pleased that the damage was too bad to continue the test." She laughed loudly and said, "I certainly didn't get away with it then—not the way I avoided it with you two days ago."

"What did the examiner do then?"

"He was certainly sweating a lot more than he would normally do on a warm August day. He rang one of his fellow instructors to help him tow his car in for repairs, and he suggested that I not take another test for six months. He also said I should warn him when I drive next, especially if I'm one car in front of him! He did have a sense of humour. He wondered how the heck I could do that, after seeing how well I could normally drive. Again, I had to hold back making the excuses that came into my mind then." She then finished her meal just before he did and said, "Would you like anything more? A sweet or something?"

"No, thanks. I'm OK after that. It was a good meal." He smiled and almost said, "You're sweet enough as it is."

"OK, fine. We could have something later maybe." She took some of the things into the kitchen to wash up. She then said, "Oh, I'll show you some of the things that I've kept private when I came into this world."

As she nipped upstairs, he said, "OK." He was curious.

She came into the lounge carrying a small box. As she opened it, she said, "This contains only the stuff I saved. Looking at it still makes me feel I'm in contact with home." She gave him a little smile.

As he looked inside, he saw the labels she'd removed from her clothes as well as a few notes and coins, which all were laterally inverted. He then saw Fido's dog tag and couldn't stop himself from saying, "Ooh, that's Odif's."

She said, "Oh, Michael, he doesn't smell, you know."

Michael responded, "Oh, do excuse me. I do know now." They both laughed.

He then picked out a credit card, and she said, "You can see it properly in the mirror."

He said, "OK." He stood and held it to the mirror Susan used to watch television. He saw her name on it and noticed that the expiry date was September of the current year. He said, "This is no different to the ones that we have here."

She smiled and said, "Yes, that was a good job. It was hard enough with everything else as it is."

He smiled and said, "I can fully understand that." He laughed. He then took some of the other things from the dinner table to the kitchen, so they could be washed up.

"Thanks. I'll just wash these and let them drain." She began to rinse them under the warm tap.

24

SUSAN AND THE
DO PROGRAM

Susan said, "I've been thinking that it's time I show you some of my findings on the DO program, but I think we have to just keep it between the two of us."

"Yes, of course," said Michael. "I've never told anybody anything of my findings on the program you gave me, especially when nobody seemed to be aware of anything like that here."

"Well, I've seen many other variations of myself here, and for each one, things could have worked out differently. For instance, in one, I saw myself telling you everything on New Year's Eve, as I almost did in that drunk moment."

As she looked intriguingly at him, he said, "Well things would probably have continued from then as they may do now. What you saw then could be an indication of how things could continue from now."

"Yes, exactly. It's given me an idea of what could easily happen next. The one big thing is that I remain here in all of them, and I continue to contact my parents using this program." She paused and then said, "Come on. I'll show you a few recent things I've seen on my computer." She logged-in on her laptop and plugged in a memory stick. She said, "Events could move on from here as they did after New Year's Eve when my alternative talked to you then as I've done now. I'm sure, now, that you could be aware of Melanie in a certain number of ways because of the way I've seen you together at times."

"Yes, certain things have struck me, though it could only be coincidence."

"Well, you'll know. She's greatly similar to me and to you."

"I've thought of that. Has she come from an alternative universe like yours, but from one exactly like here?"

"No. She's from here and is special to you. You're lucky because it's rare that anybody finds someone directly compatible to themselves. I thought I'd let you know. I'm the only other traveller here as far as I know, except for Fido here." She patted him and continued saying, "He somehow wanted me to be his master, and all I could think of when I saw his dog tag in the usual writing for me, was that he took to me as a friend because he came from a reverse universe like mine."

"Well, I saw a reverse newspaper article in your world at John Mitchell's flat. It was about a dog that had disappeared. I wondered if that may be Fido."

"I saw that, too, on my recordings, but he came to me last June. I was walking home one evening after helping out at the kitchens, and he came up to me, sniffing me. After I made a quick fuss of him, I walked on, and he just followed me and whined when I tried to ignore him. That's when I saw his dog tag and realized he was lost just as I'd been. I cut the tag off because I knew that, in his predicament, he could become a curiosity show if I was unfair and left it on. Dogs sense things, and he knew my regularity to him. I've never been a dog person because I prefer cats like you do, but I took him in because I was relieved to have a friend from somewhere like where I'd come from, especially when he was so friendly with me. Maureen wasn't too happy about it, though, but she likes dogs and was impressed with how close Fido seemed to be to me."

"Well, it figures. He smelt me a lot at first, and that must have been because our scents are so similar."

"Yes, probably because they are actually identical, except for the hint of the reverse part of it." She smiled and then said, "Oh, here we are. You'll now see a recording of me talking with myself yesterday. Excuse me for how that sounds."

He chuckled and said, "Yes. I felt just as uncomfortable when I said that." He then focussed on the screen of her PC where he saw her, saying, "Yes, I'd been out again with Paul last night. Michael and Melanie joined us too to see a film."

Susan stopped it and said, "That shows you how things are now, after I told you everything on New Year's Eve. Just as you were with the Michaels, I

322

have been with myself. The origination date of this particular Susan was last October." She looked at him and smiled, continuing to say, "And things between us have diverged further away as times gone on. I thought I'd show you this to indicate that the things between you and your other selves were as different as they have become between me and my selves. In addition, this shows you that you're with Melanie and I'm with Paul in this version of events. Every time I see my parents again, they're always different to how they were before, so that tells me that, if ever I get back, the odds are infinitely small that I'd return to the exact same place I came from. That makes me hope that I never return now because it could never be the exact same place. If I did, I would be back to square one. I'd see my parents and everything, but there would be differences to what we'd been through. That is even more the case the further we move on, so we wouldn't know each other the same way. Because it was so remote that I would have gone in the first place, the most likely aspect would be that there would be two of us there." She looked wide eyed as she smiled, saying, "Logically, you can imagine all sorts of outcomes. It's like time travel, if that's possible. If you could go into the future and then back again, you would retrace the exact same steps down that timeline to the same present moment you had started from. It would be similar to moving back along a tree branch. If you could go back in time and then forward again, you would follow any random route moving forward from that past time. That would be like being in a parallel universe then, so whatever changes you had made after that past time, wouldn't affect the time where you had come from because that had already been set. You would instead continue along the alternative path where you are now. If, for instance, something different happened to your father and you were never born, you'd still be there but as a traveller from an alternative world, but there just wouldn't be two of you there."

He said, "It's all logical that we've come from somewhere. Another thing I've thought about is hypnotic regression. Some people who have been hypnotized have told stories from the point of view of someone else— someone from whom they may have been reincarnated. And the stories are slightly different to what supposedly really happened. This, I think, indicates that they may have been that person in an alternate world, where things occurred differently."

"Yes, I've thought about that too, and this idea of infinite possible universes explains it and tells us that we can make what we want of our lives. I'll now show you some other alternative todays, with origination dates before humans ever existed." She smiled at him, continuing to say, "Yes, here we are." The image came on the screen of her PC, and she said, "This is what I saw."

Michael saw several dinosaurs roaming through the countryside. He said, "It just reminds me of what I first saw in space when the Earth didn't exist because I hadn't selected any date of origin."

"Yes. I saw that too when I hadn't selected anything. Everything you see is completely random based on the date of origin that you use, and there are so many variations based on that."

"Have you seen yourself with any other lads? Oh, excuse me for asking." He seemed nervous over what he'd just asked.

"Oh, you're all right. I shouldn't be saying this, but one version of me I spoke to from an alternative world told me that she first met the version of you when she was in a pub. Neither you nor she knew at that moment how the two of you were related because it was only just after she'd arrived after having that bad cold. Unlike me, she hadn't thought that there could be somebody else—the alternative of her after she'd gone there from her world. We—or should I say they—after meeting up, got well and truly infatuated with each other because of those feelings we'd felt together. Excuse me for saying." They both smiled. She then continued saying, "When they found out about how they were connected, they felt awful about it because they knew, as we do, that it wasn't right, and like us now, they are just good friends."

"Wow. I don't like to say it, but it must have been terrific at the time."

She smiled in awe and said, "Michael, we shouldn't be going any deeper into this, but from what she said, no amount of words could ever describe how great she felt then. They must have known every little single detail about each other the way she described it." She paused and then laughed, saying, "Ooh, I think you've got a good idea now." She swooned a little and then straightened herself up.

He felt aroused and said, "Yes, I can." He thought about it and then the morality of it.

She then said, "There were one or two more variations

with you, too, but that was all through the strength of Melanie and you. I suppose that's what gave me the idea of leaving that ten-pound note in Melanie's drawer—to kind of take the heat off myself, knowing you thought that Melanie could have come from an inverse universe. I had put a little face powder on it, to prove if anyone had touched it. Yes, I know it was rather a silly thing to do, but I wanted to play for more time, besides making you even more aware of the inverse thing."

As she looked and smiled at him, he said, "Well, it worked for a while."

"Yes, that's all it could do. Anyway, besides you being largely with Melanie, I saw you very remotely being friends with Lisa, and there were quite a few versions of you with Julie, who works in reception."

He smiled and said, "Yes. I was interested in Julie, but there was always somebody else she was with."

She said, "Well, from what another one of my selves said, you asked her out whilst you were drunk at an office birthday party last summer. She went out with you, but it didn't last long. She always had her mind set on being with a friend of the family whom none of us had ever seen until she'd met Tony online before last year's Christmas party. I remember seeing you talk with them at the table then."

"Yes, I remember. I nearly asked her out at one particular time during Brian's birthday party at the pub. I didn't, though, because I saw Paul talking to her after only just getting another drink after queuing up for a while at the bar."

"There were two others that different versions of me

talked to me about, one of which I don't know. She was called Sarah, whom he or you had known from your college days, and they were married. You may know who she is."

"Yes, I did know a girl called Sarah then, and I was quite interested in her, but she met someone else." He remembered Dave.

"That version of me told me that was on an origination date of when we were fifteen. This other one, though, was on a date of origin just over a year ago, shortly after I arrived here, who, by the way, was Lisa. Somehow, you'd got quite friendly with her since last August and are still going together in this other alternate world. I was surprised to hear you were anywhere near her. Has anything happened between you here?"

He thought, *Well, well, well. Lusty Lisa. I've never ever thought that she was actually interested in me in that way. I thought she was only doing it out of fun.* He answered, "I've spoken to her when we happen to meet on the off chance. There was nothing more than that." He remembered her tapping him on the shoulder one late June evening last year, saying, "Hi, Michael. I'm wondering if you could give me another fifty pence. I need it to make up my bus fare to get home. I'll make it up to you now, darling, with a kiss if you like." She'd pursed her lips together and flashed those alluring Irish eyes at him. She'd worn those same scraggy jeans with a white T-shirt, showing her large, colourful, love tattoos on each fairly muscular arm, the left one saying Kevin and the one on the right being for Mick. Although he was taken aback and aroused by how she'd said it to him, he'd said, "Sorry.

I don't have any small change." He didn't want to feel like a mug again. She'd then said, "Oh, please. I do need it." He'd then quickly given her a pound coin, saying, "OK, here you are. This'll get you by." As he walked off feeling rather embarrassed, she'd tapped him on the arm, saying, "Thanks. I'll remember you." And she'd smiled at him.

Two months later, she'd come up to him wearing similar raggedy jeans and jacket over a second-hand-looking shiny pink Lycra leotard. They had chatted over a cup of tea then, which she suggested paying for. When they had talked a bit about work, he told her about a job vacancy where he worked, and she'd seemed interested. Nothing had come of anything though since then. He asked Susan, "Do you know anything more about her?"

She smiled and answered, "She's only told me as much as I've just told you now because I've only spoken to that one version of myself once. That's all you can do, because each one is different every time. It's all due to randomness. Anyway, Lisa's a nice lass when you know her well. It's not her fault that she's had a very rough upbringing. Anyway, I saw you a few times whilst I was stacking shelves over the last summer. You saw me too at times but never realized that, when you first saw me as Sarah working with you at the firm because, at the supermarket, I'd dyed my hair plain brown—you know, to cover those new grey streaks I had." She laughed and then continued saying, "And I'd worn quite large glasses and a slightly oversized uniform."

He remembered the girl who'd worn the name tag that said Sarah. He'd seen her look at him a few times whenever he was there, and once he had curiously asked her where something was. Now he was amused over what it was. And now he realized that, when she'd told him the aisle it was on, she'd sounded just like Susan sounded then. He said, "Yes. I think I do remember you there."

She smiled and said, "I saw you there regularly and was nervous when you asked me where those nuts were." She laughed and said, "I felt like I was going to go nuts at that moment because I wasn't really ready to speak to you then."

He said, "I felt that you weren't, and I put it down to … oh, excuse me." He restrained a laugh.

She giggled and said, "Well! I know what you were thinking, and it wasn't that, you … Don't get like Paul again!" She looked hard and straight at Michael and then laughed.

He laughed and said, "The thought never crossed my mind."

"Oh, it did, you know." She blushed a little and said, "Anyway, I used my plain looks then to keep from being noticed because I just wanted to do no more than get by at that time."

"That's all right. You still needed to adjust, and you have done well to have got used to everything here this quickly."

"Well, believe it or not, I'm still not used to it even now. That's why I needed you, the one person to confide in. I've had enough of being on my own on this, and talking to you in the last couple of days has helped me no end."

"Thanks. I understand, and I will help you further."

She smiled with a slight tear in her eye and said,

"Thanks." She hugged him, and he felt that nice tingly sensation again. She then calmed herself down as she straightened herself up. Then she paused and said, "Yes … I first saw Melanie last July when she started working where I was. I noticed that she was a near mirror image of me. I'd wondered myself, as you just said, if she had travelled from a universe like this one, but she wasn't the same because her birthday is different. Besides, her eyes and voice pattern are different. She worked in recordkeeping, and when I was promoted to help in accounts, I got to know her."

"How were you promoted then?"

"There was a sudden vacancy in purchasing, and because of my success in investing in shares, they gave me a try. I later moved on to the work I'm doing now. At that point, I had my car and this rented house. I had made just over seven thousand pounds on shares in addition to my savings from income. I couldn't have done that otherwise." She smiled. She then said, "I've tried other origination dates, and things have generally been the same regarding news events, except for occasional minor differences due to randomness. Certain events that were very close to being different were so occasionally like in sports."

He wondered whether the dog called Gellert from North Wales could have alternatively survived, if his master had found out beforehand, that Gellert had in fact saved his infant son from a wolf. Michael asked, "What were those then?"

"Well, in one instance, in the world that I came from, you were there instead of me. We could go on continually finding more slight alternatives. Another thing is that, if you happened to be in -1 speed universe, you'd see all negative colours and everything moving backwards. What is more, you'd hear all the sounds around you, like an echo going to the source it came from." She looked at him and smiled.

"Yes, like a reverse recording. That reminds me of other speed functions on the DO program, such as universes I've seen moving at half speed and twice the speed, forwards and backwards."

"I've seen quite a few of those. I think that, like our regular-speed ones, there are an infinite number of those moving alongside our own. It means that, if people came from a minutely faster one than this, they would come from that now, but to them it would be like stepping from somewhere in our past to now. They would think that they would have travelled to the future."

"Yes, and if it was slower, they'd think that they'd have travelled to the past."

"It all depends on relative speeds, and there are countless possibilities. You could really go on thinking all sorts here." She smiled and paused. She then said, "That reminds me—when you were at your parent's house just before Christmas looking into my particular world using the DO program, I'd been there and had been able to use the key from where I'd come from, since it was even on both sides. I couldn't do that with my flat key because that wasn't symmetrical. Don't get me wrong, if I could've, I'd have used it only to find things out about you, as I'd similarly done at work. I had also put on their broadband, so I could contact my Mum and

Dad on the DO program. Our… your Dad had left it off, as he'd said."

He remembered that, and her telling him about downloading the DO program onto his laptop at the office. He said, "Well, you told me. I fully understand that you were interested because of the circumstances and the fact you were on your own here."

"Yes, that was exactly why. When I was there, I saw you looking at the photograph of me and my brother, Michael, on your PC." She looked at Michael and then said, "For you, of course, he is James and still is a policeman from where I come from. Seeing you look at that rather gave me a jolt, and that's when you heard that sound."

"I thought it was the radiators coming on when I hadn't seen anything after I looked around a bit. Where were you?"

"I hid just behind the bed in my old bedroom, which of course for me was in reverse. Patch came in and snuggled up to me, which made me feel even more nervous. I was afraid that she'd meow or something and give me away. I only heard you come in and expected you'd find me then. If you had, you'd have seen me as Sarah but without the brown-coloured contact lenses. I would have felt forced to tell you then, and for me that was far too soon. I imagined at that point that, if I did, you wouldn't have been able to absorb it, and you would have thought me mad. You probably would've let the cat out of the bag with everybody else."

"By then, I don't think I would have. I was fairly well focussed on your predicament."

"Well, afterwards, I found that out. I spoke to a few versions of myself again. It was quite difficult then because you hadn't had the program long enough to see things as clearly as you do now. You wondered more about what my intentions were, and the odd version showed you being concerned about me possibly being an alien until you'd thought about it. You were OK once you had some time to absorb it."

He smiled and said, "Well at least it worked out. Were there any differences that followed that, when you'd compared it to what happened after New Year's Eve?"

She smiled and answered, "Things were about the same, when you'd still got together with Melanie, but there were a few versions still showing you with Lisa—" She stopped in midsentence and said, "Yes, things still seem to have moved on a similar course, a few of weeks earlier then."

He wondered what she might have said, thinking that there was, perhaps, a bit more about Lisa after the last time they'd met just over a month ago. He'd remembered late that evening when he'd gone for a walk from his flat and saw her sleeping rough in the woods not far away. She'd looked to be in quite a state with a sweaty and muddy face, and when she'd seen him, she'd smiled and flashed him by, quickly opening and then closing her shabby, long, green raincoat. He could then see that all she was wearing underneath was her now-grubby shiny pink leotard, which really did reveal her full figure, taking his breath away and making him feel rather flustered. She'd said, "Hi, handsome. Have you got a light?" He'd walked over to her feeling a little nervous, but aroused, and said, "Oh, hi, Lisa. Unfortunately, I don't smoke. Why are you here? I thought you might at least be staying somewhere in this day and age." She'd said, "Well, I had a bloody tiff with some girl because her boyfriend was talking to me. We were both thrown out after I had a tantrum with her. She said terrible things to me. It didn't help that I was drunk. That's why I fucking lost it."

Michael had seen an empty bottle of vodka on the ground next to her. He'd said, "Oh dear. Perhaps some other place might take you in." She'd said, "I don't think so somehow, looking like this." She blew her runny nose noisily into the tail of her raincoat, saying, "Oh, do excuse me. That's another reason. Anyway, it won't matter to the coat because it's that green colour anyway." She'd laughed and then said, "Perhaps you could take me in, Michael?" She'd flashed her eyes at him, which made him think, at that time, that she was either taking the mick or trying something on. He hadn't dared do that anyway, wondering what he could be letting himself in for because she could try anything like stealing, maybe crying rape, or even giving him an STD. So he'd said, "I'm sorry, I haven't the room, but the Salvation Army should take you in. There's a lady called Maureen there who could help you." Lisa responded angrily by saying, "Oh, her! She bloody won't because it's Maz, the mad cow, who threw us out!" She then immediately calmed down and smiled, saying, "She's friends with Saz, you know, the girl you once saw me with in the subway. You just remind me of her. It's funny how some girls, you know, look like a lad you see." She'd flickered her eyes at him. At that time, that reminded him of the girl he'd seen who looked similar to himself; she'd called herself Claire then. He'd never associated Sarah as the girl she'd referred to at that time because he'd thought then that Sarah had naturally red hair and brown eyes. He'd thought for a bit and said, "Well, there are plenty of other places you could try." He'd started to walk away and then stopped, as he'd heard Lisa say, "Well, I don't really blame you, Michael. In fact, I've got your name tattooed on my right arm here." She took her coat off, giving him a full-frontal view of her body, whilst saying with a flirtatious smile, "This name can be for you. If you don't like the name Mick, I can have it extended to read Michael or Mike, whatever you like." He'd become aroused even more. She'd looked at him and said, "Wow, Michael! You're as hard as Mick ever was. Come on, give me a go. You'll love it!" He'd nervously said, "No, it's OK. I'm seeing another girl." He'd thought of Sophie. The situation had become too much for him. Lisa had said, "OK, but you'll never know what you're missing." She'd given him an alluring smile and then continued to say, "I'll see you around possibly, and you'll maybe think differently then." He'd waved to her and walked away. That had almost given him second thoughts at that moment, and he wondered now whether there were any versions back then in which he had actually turned back. He asked, "Does Lisa still stay at the Salvation Army dorms sometimes?"

"Occasionally still, when she doesn't have a tantrum. She's thrown a few of them at times, and her Irish temper hasn't helped." He was pleased to know about that now, considering what she might be like with him if they ever got involved. Susan smiled and then continued saying, "Anyway, a couple of weeks ago she found herself a job stacking shelves." She mentioned the name of the store on the other side of town. She continued, "It sounds as if she could be following in my footsteps from now on." She laughed.

"Just when I heard your parents talking on my PC about soon chatting with you whilst I was at my parents' house, I saw you as Sophie walk past with Fido."

She paused and said, "Yes. I had listened to that live then and wanted to show myself as her, since I happened to be there at that time, hoping you'd happen to see me. I wanted to put you off the scent. It was just a coincidence that that happened then. Also, it was Fido who you had previously seen running towards me outside your flat, when you had compared what was happening there to my inverse program. I wanted you to see the contrast between the two. Fido would always stay near to me."

"Well, I saw Fido go towards you here then. I didn't see him there, and I couldn't see whether you were there because of my small PC screen. Anyway, looking back to when I'd seen you as Sophie walking Fido outside my parent's house, I'd have liked to have seen you then, but my parents had just arrived, and I was helping them unpack some of their Christmas shopping. I really liked you as Sophie then."

She smiled and said, "Thanks for that. Yes, I really enjoyed playing her because I got to know you better, and that was lovely."

"Well, you were great as her. I think it's time for me

to leave now because it's getting late." He felt a little tired and looked at his watch, whilst saying, "I'll see you tomorrow."

"OK. I've enjoyed this evening very much, and it's been great to tell you the main things so far that have come to mind. There's lots more that I can show you, and I'll even give you the download to the DO program whenever you like." She smiled.

He thought for a moment and said, "Thanks for that. I'll think about it." He knew that he would need to do plenty of that before wanting to use it again.

She smiled and said, "OK. Thanks for coming." She gave him a kiss on the cheek, causing him to feel that lovely sensation again.

He kissed her too and said, "Thanks. I'll see you tomorrow, Susan—or Sarah." He smiled.

She laughed and said, "Yes. See you, Michael." He walked to his car. They waved to each other as he left to drive back to his flat.

Lightning Source UK Ltd.
Milton Keynes UK
UKHW041040060219
336838UK00001B/4/P